MAN WITH THE GOLDEN FALCONS

MAN WITH THE GOLDEN FALCONS

BOOK 4 OF THE GEMS SPY SERIES

Doug Solter

To my father, his hard work has allowed me the opportunity to become reborn.

MAN WITH THE GOLDEN FALCONS

CHAPTER 1

Emma Rothchild peered through the high-powered binoculars at four armed terrorists guarding the entrance to a small Namibian village with circular huts and thatched roofs. Three out of the four wore some sort of headscarf while the fourth terrorist wore a Yankees baseball cap. Emma didn't care much for the hat. Not that she didn't love the Yankees, because she was still a New York City girl at heart. However, that Yankees cap didn't belong on the head of some dirt-bag who kidnapped young women and assaulted them because they had the nerve to want an education.

"May I see?" Miyuki's sweet voice asked.

Miyuki Kaiko wore sunglasses as her straight dark hair flapped in the desert wind. Her normally pink-tinted skin had a slight orange burn. The rubber wheels of the Yamaha motorcycle she sat on were half buried in the hot sand.

Emma gave her friend the binoculars, then checked her own face in the dune buggy's side mirror. Her creamy white skin was baked orange as well. Even with a gallon of sunblock, the desert sun was still brutal on a girl's skin. At least her blond hair didn't look too bad, although it was probably dry as heck now.

"If you can distract them, I should be able to race inside for a little mischief," Miyuki said with a hopeful grin.

Emma shook off her personal appearance and studied her target instead. The terrorist-held village was tucked under a high cliff that overlooked the South Atlantic Ocean. Any ships passing by would easily miss the village. Something the terrorists had obviously thought of when they took over the village and ran off all the people. Emma noted a barbed-wire fence that protected the perimeter of the village.

"I wish there were a ramp on the outside so I could jump the fence like Evel Knievel!" Miyuki said.

"Who?"

"Evel Knievel! He jumped all kinds of things with his motorbike. One time, he jumped over a row of thirty school busses."

"Why did he do that?"

"Because it's fun!"

Emma ignored her friend's enthusiasm and listened to the nerves poking at her stomach. Personally, she wasn't looking forward to this part of the operation. Driving a dune buggy in the desert wasn't a problem—there were fewer things to hit out here as opposed to a city street—no, the problem was the creating-a-diversion part. If Emma didn't get close enough to the terrorists, then her diversion wouldn't work, and her friends would be trapped inside that village forever. And getting close meant Emma would be close enough to get shot.

But those men wouldn't shoot a pretty blonde girl in a dune buggy, would they? Not if she acted friendly. Emma found that most guys would loosen up when she smiled at them.

"Are you ready?" Miyuki asked.

Emma took in a deep breath. She reached for the sand goggles hanging around her neck and placed them over her eyes. "No, but let's do it anyway."

"Okey dokey. I'll wait for you." Miyuki jumped on the starter and the Yamaha roared to life. She put on her helmet and slipped on a face mask with a pipe attached to a slim oxygen tank on the bike.

Emma started the dune buggy and put it in gear. Lately, Nadia had been teaching Emma how to drive a stick, and so far Emma had the basics down. Well, kinda. At least she didn't stall the car most of the time by letting the clutch out too early. Emma concentrated as she eased her foot off the clutch and squeezed the gas pedal. The engine revved and the transmission engaged… throwing the buggy backward.

"Damn it."

Emma hit the brakes. Wrong gear.

Miyuki watched her through those scary-looking black goggles, probably wondering why Emma couldn't get her crap together.

"I got it. Don't worry," Emma said as she found first gear and the dune buggy went forward through the sand.

As she cleared the second dune, Emma knew the terrorists at the front gate had now spotted her. She was committed. Emma put her foot to the floor and let the buggy bounce along the sand like a happy dog playing in the snow. When Emma was about five hundred feet away, she turned the wheel and did a few donuts, kicking up sand and letting the wind carry it into the air. She then eased her dune buggy back on course towards the checkpoint.

Emma noticed the men gripping their weapons as they spread out into defensive positions.

At two hundred yards, she waved at them and smiled.

They aimed their weapons at her.

Her heart beat faster than the dune buggy's pistons. This was a terrible idea. Olivia's grand plan was about to get her shot. But the actress inside Emma was still in character. She was portraying a fun-loving girl out for a joyride, and that girl wanted the whole world to have fun too. Her character would say, *What terrorist camp?* That girl only saw some local people standing around a fence, and she wanted to brighten their day.

Emma yanked the wheel hard to the left and did a few more donuts, causing the sand to kick up and surround her dune buggy before she braked to a stop. She allowed the sand in the air to clear before she climbed out of her buggy.

The men had their weapons drawn, but Emma could read their faces from here. They weren't sure what they were looking at.

Emma slipped off her goggles and waved at them again. "Hi! I didn't mean to disrupt your large family get-together. I'm only passing through. I'm sure having fun in your desert. My family and I are from Texas—the Lone Star State. Y'all have a lovely country. It's so sandy."

Emma felt her character would be from Texas. Maybe her daddy had hit it big in oil and gas a long time ago and invested it in real estate. Anyway, Emma went with that and her thick Texas accent.

The three men with head scarfs all checked with the man in the Yankees hat. That man lowered his rifle.

"You're American?" he asked in decent English.

"Well, I'm a Texan. But basically, yeah." Emma rubbed the sand off her legs and readjusted her tank top. The other men were shouldering their weapons. A few cracked some grins. Yes, they were all getting a better look at her. So far they didn't look too

3

alarmed. "Do you mind if I play around in your large sandbox out here? If I'm disrupting anything, you just let me know, and I'll go elsewhere."

The man with the Yankees cap walked toward the buggy. "Come here."

Emma played stupid. "What's that, sugar?"

"Come. Let us speak with you." The man with the Yankees hat was getting closer. His eyes wandered down her legs and stayed a little too long on her tank top.

A shiver went down Emma's spine. Her body was telling her to run. Her eyes were noticing a pistol strapped to the man's side as well as the rifle hung over his shoulder. If she let him, he would grab her and drag her into the compound to do God knows what

Emma swallowed her fear. She needed to act. "My daddy warned me about talking to strange men in the middle of the desert."

The man in the hat gestured for her to approach him.

Emma backed away. "It's nice for y'all to invite me to lunch, but I have other places to visit, so I'll just be on my way." Emma hopped back into the dune buggy. As her hands touched the steering wheel—the muzzle of a pistol pressed against her cheek.

The man with Yankees cap was not smiling now. "You...come with us."

Emma knew she would mess this all up. Now these men would kidnap her too.

Olivia would be pissed.

A motor revved in the distance.

The man took his attention off Emma as he glanced over at the dunes.

Emma seized the opportunity. She slapped his arm to the side and fell back on the passenger seat while twisting her body towards the threat. Then she used both legs to drill the man in the face with her sneakers.

Emma jumped on the clutch, shoved the stick into first, and feathered the gas pedal, coaxing the dune buggy forward. As the men were breaking out their rifles again, Emma spun the dune buggy in circles, kicking up the sand around her to obscure their vision. She then pointed the dune buggy away from them as she felt around in the back seat and took out a gas mask.

She slipped it over her mouth, turned on the oxygen, then

pointed the dune buggy towards the checkpoint. The men were struggling to see through the sand, but they fired anyway. Emma's windshield exploded.

Emma ducked down and turned the wheel hard to the right, making more circles in the sand. But this time she clicked a switch on the buggy's dashboard, which unleashed a plume of gas that blew out of a third tailpipe. The wind carried this gas toward the checkpoint, making the men cough and cover their mouths.

Wearing a gas mask over her face, Miyuki raced her motorcycle towards the checkpoint. All four guards were passed out. Miyuki stopped her bike to pull open the large wooden gate.

Emma put the dune buggy in gear and gunned it through the front gate while Miyuki followed her inside the camp.

CHAPTER 2

Two hours ago, Olivia Spencer had been kidnapped by a group of terrorists who had stormed into a local Namibian school. Thanks to intelligence gathered by the Authority, the principal of the school had been warned of the pending attack and briefed his teachers and staff not to resist. The principal had even asked the school's security officers not to show up that day, fearing their presence would trigger the terrorists into using their weapons.

So far it was all going to plan.

After driving the girls across a desert, the truck entered a small Namibian village with circular huts, thatched roofs, and a large barbed-wire perimeter fence. Riding in the open-air truck, Olivia didn't see anyone who looked like a local villager, which meant the terrorists had since driven them all away. Those armed men were everywhere, walking between the huts, carrying rifles and grenades strapped to their backs.

Nadia Sharif sat next to Olivia. Both girls were dressed up in Namibian school uniforms, which blended in with the thirty other kidnapped girls stuffed in the back of the truck. It also helped that Nadia and Olivia were both blessed with darker shades of skin. Plus Olivia could speak Swahili well, while Nadia was fluent in Arabic.

Most of the kidnapped girls were between the ages of twelve to eighteen years old. Their families had sent them to the school for an education, and these armed men didn't approve of their Western education, so they kidnapped them. The attacks had started in Nigeria months ago and this particular terrorist group had migrated their way south, building bases along the way to spread their kidnapping operations to other African countries. Olivia told Nadia over three hundred girls were being held prisoner somewhere in Namibia.

"I think we've found it," Nadia whispered to Olivia.

"Let's hope Miyuki is following the truck, or we'll never get out of here," Olivia said.

When the truck came to a stop, armed men yelled at them in Swahili to get out. Many of the girls were crying as they were herded into one of the village's larger huts. Olivia and Nadia followed them inside and discovered almost four hundred school-girls stuffed into this hut, like tiny boxes in a warehouse. The girls appeared hungry and scared. Many of their eyes were filled with hopelessness. The new batch of girls were huddled together in a cleared-out corner of the hut.

After counting the girls again to make sure she had the correct number, Olivia observed the guards who had followed them inside the hut. Two of the four had stepped outside for a smoke. The other two were talking about football. Four guards for over four hundred girls. Very sloppy security.

"There're only two of them," Nadia whispered. "This could be our only chance."

"Not until the diversion, love. There are hundreds of men outside. We won't make it past all of them." Olivia looked down at her watch. They had been delayed because their truck overheated on the way. It couldn't be anticipated, but Olivia hoped the delay wouldn't mess up their strict time-table.

"That one is beautiful," the first guard said in Swahili.

Olivia froze as one of the guards approached, yet she soon realized the man's eyes were fixed on someone else.

Nadia stared at the ground.

The first guard lifted Nadia's chin. His hand was dry and cracked. "Look at her light brown skin. Do you think she's Libyan?"

The second guard joined him, his eyes treated Nadia like a statue. "Maybe Saudi. Very cute. She must have a rich dad from Riyadh who works in Namibia. Maybe we should issue a different ransom for her. Those Saudis have large bank accounts."

Nadia flicked her eyes over to Olivia. She didn't understand what the men were saying. But Olivia did. And she didn't like what she was hearing.

"That's a wonderful idea," the first guard said. "We should separate her from the rest. How much do you think we can get?"

The second guard knelt and examined Nadia. "I would say—half a million dollars—at least."

The first guard's eyes lit up with greed. "Keep her in your tent. We should hold on to the girl until her rich father begs us for her safe return."

The second guard made Nadia rise from the floor. "Come with me. Don't worry, you will be well treated."

Olivia's stomach sank. To pull the plan off, she would need Nadia's help. Being separated from each other would be the worst thing ever.

Nadia didn't understand the guard's words, but she was able to read her friend's eyes. Now she was worried too.

"If you're nice to me, I'll be nice to you. Come." The second guard dragged Nadia out of the hut.

Olivia coiled up like a snake. Her heart raced. Every instinct inside her body screamed for her to do something. But her brain clamped down on the anxiety. It yelled at her body. She still had a mission to complete, and causing a commotion now would jeopardize all these girls' lives.

But Nadia was in trouble. Her best friend would be hidden away somewhere in this large camp, and they might never find her again.

Olivia's paranoid mind went into conflict.

Do it. Go. There's only one guard.

But the mission…

She's your best friend. You talked her into this mission.

You owe her.

These thirty girls are counting on us…

Stop wasting time. Go! Now!

As Olivia stood up…the other two guards came in from their smoke break.

It was now one against three. The opportunity was gone.

Olivia dropped down to the ground. Despite her personal feelings, her duty was to stay with the girls until they could be rescued. Nadia would have to deal with the guard herself. But her best friend was smart and very capable. If necessary, Olivia knew Nadia could take care of herself. However, it still worried her. Hell, everything was worrying her right now.

Olivia glanced at her watch again.

Time seemed to be slowing down.

Until the clatter of gunfire floated in from the outside as men yelled an alarm. Two out of the three guards rushed out of the hut. The remaining guard kept his post, but craned his neck to peek out through the opening of the hut.

It was all the time Olivia needed.

She knelt and took out a pen hidden inside her sock. Pressing the top button, a tranquilizer dart replaced the ballpoint pen. Olivia carefully circled behind the guard and stabbed him in the neck. The guard whipped around and struck her in the face with his palm. Olivia then swung herself around and swept her leg under his, toppling him to the ground. The guard failed to get up as his eyes fluttered. The dart was now taking full effect.

Olivia grabbed the man's rifle.

The girls inside the tent were amazed at what they just saw. Their mouths hung open in astonishment.

"My name is Emerald," Olivia yelled in passable Swahili. "I was sent here to rescue all of you. Please stay here and wait. I'll be back."

Olivia slipped outside—and into chaos. Armed men were running all over the place as clouds of gas floated around the village. Olivia covered her mouth and tried to figure out where Nadia had been taken. She dove into the nearest hut. It was empty.

She searched a second hut and found no one. A third hut only contained boxes of toilet paper.

Olivia now panicked. Did they take Nadia out of the village? Was she already too late?

She stepped inside another hut and noticed Nadia's guard was tied up and unconscious on the floor.

An automatic rifle swiveled around. Its muzzle pointed right at Olivia's head.

"Oy—it's me," Olivia said.

Nadia took her finger off the trigger and lowered the weapon. She sighed. "I'm so pleased to see you."

"Any trouble?"

"Not really."

"Brilliant. Ready to get out of here, love?"

Nadia and Olivia rushed back to the main hut. They had all the girls stand up.

Olivia knelt and pulled out a tiny radio from her other school sock. It was already pre-tuned to only one frequency. "Emerald to

EVAC. Emerald to EVAC. Packages are on the move. I repeat, packages are on the move."

The radio came to life.

Roger, Emerald. ETA is ten minutes on EVAC.

"Roger. Message received. Emerald to Ruby and Black Opal. . .what's your status?"

I did four wheelies already!

Olivia recognized Miyuki's voice. She wished she were taking this more seriously. "Did you find an escape route for us? Over."

Ten-four, good buddy. Beacon is active. Take the path behind your hut. It leads to the back of the village. Safest route.

"Right—Black Opal, what's your status? Can we safely leave the hut now?"

Yeah. Most of the men are knocked out. I switched off the gas and—

Olivia heard Emma yelp as a gunshot sounded through the radio.

"Black Opal, are you okay?"

I lied. There's still a few men around. You'd better go now.

Olivia signed off and palmed the radio. "Do you have the beacon?"

Nadia checked her small watch. It looked cheap but wasn't. It did much more than tell time. "Yes, I have Ruby's beacon. Path behind the hut, correct?"

"Yes." Olivia pointed at Nadia as she addressed the girls in the hut. "Follow this girl. She'll lead you to the helicopters. We're going to get you out of here."

Through Olivia's translation, Nadia told the girls to line up single file as best they could. "If the girl in front of you falls, please help her up. Carry her if she's little," Nadia said. "We must all leave together."

Soon Nadia led the way as one by one the girls began evacuating the hut. When the last one left, Olivia followed her.

Outside, there were still sounds of gunfire echoing around the village, but things seem to be winding down. Olivia saw men lying on the ground who had been knocked out by the gas, which still lingered in the air. Nadia led the girls around to the back of the hut; then using Ruby's beacon, she followed the path that ran behind most of the village before coming to an open rear gate in the barbed-wire fence.

Miyuki was waiting for them on her motorcycle. She held out

her fist.

Nadia gave her a fist bump before taking off through the open gate. Olivia watched all four-hundred plus girls run through the gate.

"I hope we have enough helicopters for all these girls," Olivia said to Miyuki when she finally reached her. "Did Sapphire switch over her watch so she could detect the helicopter landing zone beacon?"

Miyuki shrugged. "I think so."

Olivia checked the direction Nadia was headed. Up in the clear blue sky, she could make out some large transport helicopters coming in. They were also making a lot of noise, but at least the girls were all on their way.

"We'd better get a move on ourselves. Where's—"

The dune buggy raced into view. Emma was driving way too fast.

Olivia and Miyuki exchanged looks.

Miyuki gunned her motorcycle to get out of the way while Olivia jumped to the side as Emma blew through the open gate.

"Oy—you're supposed to pick me up, you cow!" Olivia yelled, but the dune buggy was gone.

Miyuki circled back with her motorcycle. "Wasn't Emma supposed to—?"

"She forgot. Can I bum a ride, love?" Olivia climbed behind Miyuki on the motorcycle. "Please take it easy. I'm not a big fan of —"

Before she could finish, Miyuki gunned the motorcycle. Olivia felt her body fall backward as she grabbed on to Miyuki's waist right before the Yamaha popped a wheelie.

"Yahoooo!" Miyuki yelled as the motorcycle went through the gate on one tire before lowering its front tire back to earth.

"No more wheelies!" Olivia yelled.

"More wheelies? Okay!"

Miyuki gunned it again, and Olivia held on for dear life.

CHAPTER 3

Two days later, Emma woke up to a warm, wet tongue licking her cheek. Snoopy was on her bed giving her good morning doggy kisses. Emma caressed the Russell terrier's head, making his tail wag. Emma wasn't ready to get up or go to school, but she made herself roll out of bed.

As usual, she was the last one downstairs. In the kitchen, Olivia drank some coffee while Nadia had juice. Miyuki bobbed her head to Korean pop music over some tea. Emma knew this because Miyuki had the music cranked up to the point it was leaking out her ear-buds. Emma's grandmother Bernadette yawned over her herbal tea.

"Hello," Emma said.

"We have forty-five minutes until school starts," Olivia said. "We should grab our breakfast on the way."

"Oh, okay." Emma's mind was still thawing out. "Grandma, did you not make any...?"

"Got up about ten minutes ago, young one," Grandma Bernadette said. "Right now, I couldn't even burn a plate of eggs."

"Everyone woke up late," Nadia added. "Are you ready to go?"

Minutes later, Emma drove her Mercedes AMG C63 S Coupe to the nearest Heisenberg Brothers bagel shop. Since Emma didn't want food inside her car, the Gems went inside to eat. It wasn't too crowded, so it didn't take them too long to order and grab a table. Emma was the only holdout.

"No breakfast?" Miyuki asked.

"I'll make a quick stop at Kaffee Kadre," Emma said.

"You can't live only on coffee," Nadia said. "It's not good for you."

"Please share half my bagel with me," Miyuki said. "You'd like

12

it. It has salmon-flavored cream cheese."

Emma's stomach growled. She took the offering and bit into it. The salmon did taste yummy.

A wall-mounted flat-screen television presented the morning news from a cable news channel. They cut to video of a fleet of helicopters arriving at some military base.

Yesterday, South African special forces conducted a successful raid on a secret terrorist camp inside Namibia, freeing more than four hundred girls who were kidnapped and held in captivity by members of the terrorist group…

Nadia beamed at the screen. "We made the national news."

Olivia shook her head. "All they did was supply us the helicopters. We did all the work."

"Wouldn't it be awesome if we could tell people it was us," Emma said.

"Yes, but we can't," Olivia said.

"Someday I'll be interviewed for my Oscar-winning role in some critically acclaimed film, and they'll ask me if I have any great stories to share. And wouldn't it be cool if I said—yes, one time I freed four hundred women who were kidnapped," Emma said. "And another time I saved thousands of Chinese teens from killing each other in Beijing. And also my friends and I saved most of the world from a famine—"

"You can never tell anyone," Olivia said. "You swore an oath. I don't care if Mrs. B is your relative. The Authority will make her get rid of you."

Miyuki rolled her eyes. "Emma is just kidding. Jeez, Olivia. You're too serious."

Emma licked some cream cheese off her finger. "Can't a girl dream for one day?"

"What's your dream, Olivia?" Miyuki asked. "If you could be anything…what would it be?"

Olivia thought about it.

"I don't know if I have a dream."

"Whatever. Everyone has a dream," Emma said.

"Why must I have a dream? Maybe I'm still figuring my life out. I mean, what's the flipping rush?"

"The world is so competitive now. If you don't have a plan early, you might get left behind."

Miyuki made a face. "You sound like my father, Emma. His entire life was planned, and he was stressed out and unhappy. I don't want his life. My dream is to be free. To not be one of the thousands of screws holding a company together or a mother raising a future worker. I don't think my future is in Japan. It's here. In America." Miyuki paused, as if surprised by hearing her personal thoughts expressed out loud. "Olivia, you should take as long as you need. Find out what makes you happy."

"Thanks, love."

"Yeah, but seriously, don't turn into some lonely old woman who hoards thirty cats inside her apartment," Emma said.

"But I adore cats," Olivia said.

Emma cocked her head.

"I'm kidding, you cow."

Actually, Olivia did like cats.

After fitting in a drive-thru stop for coffee, Emma managed to get everyone to school before the first bell. With the skill of a professional high-school junior, Emma sucked down her double-caramel mocha iced-coffee masterpiece in record time to make her first class. The brain-freeze she suffered during Mr. Tyler's lecture was definitely worth it.

The same boring routine greeted the rest of Emma's morning. Class lectures, quizzes, tests, and unsolicited approaches by guys Emma wasn't interested in. She always tried to be firm yet kind to them because her previous reputation as West Berkeley High's untouchable ice queen had bothered her. It was a reputation she wanted to change.

Finally it was lunch, and Emma was starving. She headed for the Gems' familiar table near the corner. Her friend Kayla was already there, bouncing on top of her seat. The girl had more energy than ten power stations.

"How was your weekend?" Kayla asked. "Did you do anything fun? How's your grandmother? Oh wow, you got a huge tan. Where did you go? It must be a tanning salon because it was so cold this weekend I think you would've froze if you were outside in a bathing suit. Why didn't you text me? I'd love to go tanning with you—"

Emma touched Kayla's forearm, a gesture that usually got Kayla to stop talking.

"Can I answer a few of your questions?"

Kayla's face turned red. "Sorry, I talk too much. I know. Go ahead."

At this point, Olivia, Nadia, and Miyuki showed up at the table.

"What's up? How was your weekend?" Kayla asked them. "Wow, you all got lots of sun. Seriously, Emma, you need to tell me where—"

Emma laid her hand on top of Kayla's.

"I'm doing it again. I can't help myself."

"Doing what again?" Miyuki asked.

"Talking. I just get so excited and I talk and talk." Kayla pressed her lips together. "But I'm stopping…right…now. Okay, done."

"I was about to tell Kayla about my grandmother taking us all out to Florida this weekend to visit my aunt," Emma said.

"Which aunt was that?" Miyuki asked.

Olivia and Nadia fired off a look.

Emma gave Miyuki a long stare. "My aunt…Josephine. The one with the dune buggy."

Miyuki's eyes went wide. "Oh—that aunt. Yes, we visited with her. She's very nice."

"Wow—your aunt has a dune buggy?" Kayla asked. "My aunt only has an old Buick. Did she let you drive the dune buggy around?"

"All over the beach," Emma said.

"And she let me ride her motorcycle too," Miyuki added.

The other Gems shot her a second look.

"Wait, your aunt has a motorcycle too?" Kayla asked.

A boy with rich brown skin stopped at the table. "Whose aunt has a motorcycle?"

"Hey, Lewis—yeah, Emma's aunt in Florida does," Kayla said. "She has a dune buggy and a motorcycle."

"Nice," Lewis said. "Do you ride, Emma?"

"Oh no. I'm not much of a motorcycle fan."

"I love riding motorcycles," Miyuki said. "Especially wheelies. I'm very good at wheelies."

"She's a very talented beginner," Olivia said, giving her the shut-the-hell-up look.

Miyuki looked away.

"A girl who rides motorbikes, that's choice." Lewis took a swig of his bottle of Pepsi. "I'd love to have a bike."

"Are you too cool to sit down with us?" Emma asked.

Lewis spun a chair around and sat. "What did you do in Florida besides tearing up the beach?"

"Not much," Emma continued. "We did go to Orlando and—"

"Did you know I'm taking flying lessons?" Olivia blurted out, interrupting Emma's made-up story about going to Orlando to see the land of Disney.

"Oh yeah?" Lewis said.

"One day I'd love to fly helicopters. Do you like helicopters, Lewis?"

He shrugged.

"They're faster than motorcycles or dune buggies. And you can land them almost anywhere you want to. In fact, I think they're better than even airplanes."

Lewis sucked on his bottle of Pepsi, still acting cool and not at all that interested in helicopters.

Olivia fidgeted in her seat before pretending to look at her phone in an act of surrender.

Emma felt sorry for her. "Will you be at rehearsal?"

"Nah, rehearsal is canceled," Lewis said. "Mrs. Lynn has the flu, so without the choir, Mr. Tennant doesn't want to do the concert run through until Thursday."

"Oh, okay."

"Last Friday Mrs. Lynn barfed in the teachers' lounge. It was nasty. You could smell it down the hallway."

"Thanks for that detailed update. Maybe the choir should buy her some flowers or bring her some chicken soup."

"She needs a barf bag."

"Sometimes, Lewis, you're such a dude," Emma said.

He grinned as he stood up from the table. "Thanks, I'm gonna go spread my masculinity all over this place."

The Gems all made faces.

Lewis drank his Pepsi. "What did I say?"

No one answered.

Lewis shrugged while he eased his way across the commons area, talking with some other kids.

"Oh my God, Olivia. Would you just ask the guy out?" Emma asked. "This has gone on for way too long."

"Lewis isn't interested in me," Olivia said. "He couldn't have cared less about what I was talking about."

"So he's not interested in helicopters," Nadia said. "That doesn't mean he's not interested in you."

"Lewis is easy-going and sensitive. You have to be up front with him," Emma said. "Take charge and ask him out."

"Order him around like you do us," Miyuki said.

Olivia flipped her a puzzled look.

"You let him know up front that you're interested and want to go out with him. Don't give Lewis an excuse to bail. You have to leave him no alternative but to go out with you."

"But if the roles were reversed, wouldn't Olivia feel that Lewis was acting desperate?" Nadia asked.

"Confidence and desperation are two different things," Emma said. "Lewis responds to confidence. As long as you don't abduct him, I think you can avoid coming off as being desperate."

"Let me think about it," Olivia said.

"Do you want me to hook you two up?"

"No, I don't want you to do that. Give me some time, love. I want to think this out."

Emma felt her phone vibrate. She glanced at the screen and saw a new text. It was from Ryan Raymond. Again.

Call me. I miss your voice.

After not hearing from him for weeks, suddenly Ryan blew up her phone a week ago with texts and missed calls. Ryan was now in Montreal, Canada. and wanted Emma to come visit him, like she didn't have school or other things going on in her life. But after telling him no for the tenth time, Ryan downgraded his needs to a simple phone call.

Emma wasn't supposed to be communicating with Ryan. He was the enemy according to Mrs. B and the Authority. But Emma saw him differently. Ryan was complicated. His father went to prison for his plot to starve millions of people for money. However, Ryan's disillusionment with his father had happened even earlier, allowing him to be recruited by the criminal organization known as Venomous. But the boy Emma had met on her first mission was kind, loving, and empathetic. He'd joined Venomous more as revenge against his father rather than for the group's twisted principles. Emma knew if given the opportunity Ryan was a boy who could be saved.

She checked to see if her friends were paying attention before her thumbs typed out a response.

Call me right before bed. I'll let you know when.

Emma hit send.

"Emma?"

The woman's voice made her turn around.

It was Mrs. Bracket, the school counselor. "How are things going? It's been a while since you've been in to see me."

Emma didn't need this woman up in her personal business. "I've been totally busy lately."

Mrs. Bracket crossed her arms. "Aren't we all? I have some time after school. Let's talk about your busy life."

"I'd love to, but I have choir rehearsal after school."

"But Mrs. Lynn is sick," Kayla said.

"What?"

"Don't you remember? She has the flu, so you don't have rehearsal today."

"Oh…I totally forgot."

Emma hadn't forgotten.

Miyuki, Nadia, and Olivia were all holding back large smiles.

"Wonderful, I'll see you after school, then." Mrs. Bracket walked off quickly, giving Emma no chance to escape.

Emma closed her eyes and wondered how many years in prison she would get for running over Kayla with her car.

* * *

Emma read the medical degrees above Mrs. Brackett's head. Her office walls were still painted with dark oranges and browns. That hadn't changed since the last time she was here. On Mrs. Brackett's desk was a new box of Kleenex waiting for her next victim.

The woman walked over to her mini-fridge. "Do you want anything? I have sparkling water if you prefer that over soda."

"No, thank you," Emma said.

Mrs. Brackett took out a bottle of Diet Coke before sitting down in her office chair. She pulled out a clean glass and poured some of the liquid in.

"Why don't you drink that out of the bottle?" Emma asked.

"I find this more refreshing."

Emma let it go. She didn't actually care.

After Mrs. Brackett took a sip, she sat back in her chair. "How are things going?"

"In general? Or was there something specific?"

"We haven't talked in a while, so let's talk about new things," Mrs. Brackett said. "Your grandmother took in three foreign exchange students this year, and I was pleased to see all of you sitting together this morning. How's that dynamic working out?"

"Dynamic—?"

"How's that situation working out? Everyone getting along?"

"Yeah, I guess."

Mrs. Brackett waited for more.

When Emma didn't spill, she went on. "So Olivia is from the United Kingdom. Miyuki is from Japan, and Nadia is from—Iran?"

"Saudi Arabia," Emma corrected.

"Interesting...you must hear some fascinating stories about their cultures."

Honestly, Emma never thought of her friends like that. Once in a while, they would talk about their culture, but only how it related to things they encountered in America. Emma never considered treating her friends like travel bloggers on Utube, throwing them stacks of questions to find out more about their "strange" and "exotic" lives in another country. Emma figured that all girls—no matter where they lived—had to put up with the same kind of crap that she did but only wrapped up in a different flag.

"In the United Kingdom, they call women cows," Emma said. "Like—fat cow. Stupid cow. Kinda like that. And they drive on the other side of the road."

"How about Nadia? What has she told you about Saudi Arabia?"

"She says they have a lot of sand."

Mrs. Brackett tilted her head. She didn't like Emma's answer. "Japan is a beautiful place. What does Miyuki say about her country?"

"That the boys are a-holes. But I think she's biased because her last boyfriend really pissed her off."

Mrs. Brackett sighed. "You're not taking this seriously, Emma."

"What? I'm answering your questions."

"I want you to talk to me. Not play games," Mrs. Brackett said. "Now...how have these foreign exchange students affected your day-to-day life?"

Emma paused.

"Are you going to be honest? Or will we play another game?"

Emma didn't mind being honest, but not about everything. She couldn't tell her what the four of them actually did in their day-to-day lives. Emma switched gears and told Mrs. Brackett about how the four of them would spend time together hanging out at Kaffee Kadre. How they went to movies. How they would come to Emma's plays and choir performances. How they would hang out at school football and soccer games. It was everything she thought Mrs. Brackett wanted to hear.

"Do you ever feel lonely?" Mrs. Brackett asked.

"Not now. I did a few months ago when I first came to live with my grandmother. But not now."

"Do you think about your dad?"

"That's a stupid question. Of course I still think about my dad." Emma stopped herself. She was overreacting. "I'm sorry. I didn't mean for that to come out so—bitchy."

Mrs. Brackett grinned as she sipped her drink. "Any depression lately? Any anxiety?"

"Not really. I haven't felt that way in a long time."

"Sounds like hosting these exchange students has been good for you. Overall."

Emma thought about it. "I think so. I'm glad my grandmother allowed them to stay."

Mrs. Brackett crossed her legs. That meant she was about to change subjects again. "I was going over my notes from our last few sessions, and I realized that we haven't talked a lot about your mother."

"She died when I was young. I don't remember too much about her."

"What do you remember?"

Emma thought about it. She pressed her brain hard for anything. "I remember—images. Like, she had long blond hair and she would let me comb it for her."

"Blond hair like yours?"

"Yeah. It always felt silky to my little fingers, and it always smelled nice. I liked the scent."

"What was her name?"

"My mom? Angela," Emma said. "What I know about her

mostly comes from my dad. He dearly loved her."

"How old was your mother when she passed?"

"She was twenty-eight years old."

"She was young."

Emma nodded.

"Do you mind if I ask how she died?"

Emma swallowed. Her mother died on a mission and it tore her father apart, according to her grandmother Bernadette. He resigned from the Century Group and the Authority, then never looked back. But there's no way Emma could tell her school counselor any of this, so she switched into actress mode and summoned some tears.

"You don't have to tell me if it's too uncomfortable," Mrs. Brackett said.

Emma wiped the tears away. "She died from..." Emma stopped talking and broke down crying. She took two pieces of Kleenex from the box on the desk and blew her nose. "Sorry—I can't—my father was so sad. Even when you're a little girl, you can tell when your daddy is sad. The happiness in his eyes was gone." Emma's real life began to blend into her performance. Bringing up her father was now stoking the sadness of his death inside her as well. If she wasn't careful, the misery would take her over and Emma would have a real breakdown. She held the real sadness at bay and refused to let it percolate to the surface.

"Can I have that water you offered earlier?"

Mrs. Brackett went to her mini-fridge and took out a sparkling water can, popped the top, and gave it to her.

Emma drank it. The cold, sparkling water helped her gain back control over her emotions. A part of her was shocked at how rapidly the sadness had overwhelmed her. Emma thought she was finally getting a handle on it. Finally able to say goodbye to her dad. But this only proved her heart still wasn't healed.

And she wondered if it ever would be.

CHAPTER 4

Inside the girls' bathroom at school, Olivia stared at her image in the mirror. Her dark piercing eyes. Her thick eyebrows. Thin lips. The red bumps of acne breaking out over her otherwise smooth dark skin. She wished her lips were thicker like Emma's. But at least her hair was gorgeous. It was the one genetic trait Olivia's mother had blessed her with. Strong, healthy hair that she could braid or pull back with a hair ribbon. Most of the time she let her hair fluff out naturally after combing it. She liked how the curly strands would spread out, giving her hair all this volume. It made Olivia feel proud and closer to her mom's Jamaican heritage.

But the more important question for Olivia was…did Lewis like her hair?

When she'd mentioned helicopters yesterday, Lewis couldn't have cared less. He wasn't an aviation geek like she was. He'd only seemed interested when Miyuki talked about motorcycles.

But that was all right. Olivia could ride a motorcycle. She could do fun things like that if Lewis wanted. She wasn't boring. She enjoyed having fun too. Surely if Lewis could see that side of her, he would want to hang out with her all the time.

Hey, Lewis—I've scaled buildings. I've skydived off cliffs. I landed a huge jet full of passengers when the pilots were poisoned. I'm the leader of a team of girl spies who helped save hundreds of lives all over the world. Yeah, I'm kinda awesome so you should be begging me to be your girlfriend. Olivia knew she couldn't tell Lewis any of that.

Emma was right. She should just go up to Lewis and ask him out.

Olivia sighed. She'd once led a team of Navy SEALs into a fortified mountain. But that seemed easier to her than asking Lewis out.

How should she do it? Be sassy and direct? Be subtle and smile a lot? Kidnap him and force him to say yes?

Acting subtle and smiling a lot hadn't helped her so far. Kidnapping a boy and breaking him down using the interrogation techniques she'd learned in training seemed too over the top. Sassy and direct? That might have to do.

Olivia checked the mirror one last time before stepping out of the girls' bathroom and heading down the hallway to her next class.

As she passed one of the main doorways into the commons area, Olivia caught Lewis eying a snack machine. Olivia stopped so fast other students almost ran into her.

Side-stepping out of the flow of student traffic, Olivia headed over to the snack machine.

"Searching for a treat?" Olivia asked.

"What's up? Yeah, I'm still hungry," Lewis said.

"Cool."

Lewis kept his eyes on the chips while Olivia stood there.

"Fancy a bag of crisps or a couple of biscuits?"

Lewis shot her a confused look. "What did you ask me?"

Olivia pointed at the packaged snacks inside the machine. "Crisps or biscuits?"

"I don't see any biscuits."

Olivia realized her mistake and kicked herself. She was not using the correct American slang. No wonder the boy was confused. "Sorry, I meant potato chips or cookies."

"What do they call 'em in England again?"

Olivia went over to the machine and pressed her finger against the glass. "Those are crisps. And those are biscuits."

"Nice. Finally I can tell my mom that I learned something at school."

That made Olivia smile. She watched Lewis slip in some coins and hit one of the selection buttons.

"I'm having jalapeno cheese crisps, then." Lewis grinned as he reached down in the tray and retrieved his bag of crisps. He pulled the small bag open and threw a chip in his mouth. His eyes closed. "That's some good hot-crisp goodness right there." He tilted the open bag towards her.

Olivia took a large chip and tossed it in her mouth. It was like licking a hot grill. She ran over to a nearby water fountain and drenched her tongue. After the sting wore off, she turned around. "I've had my share of spicy food. . .but those crisps are wicked."

Lewis grinned with satisfaction. "I know, right?" He ate another one. "They taste like Satan's potato chips. I love 'em."

"So—what are you up to this weekend?" Olivia asked.

Before Lewis could answer, another boy interrupted. "Did you see the Arsenal-Liverpool game last weekend?"

Lewis brightened. "My man Brice with that header in the eighty-ninth minute…it was epic."

"And that bicycle kick Suarez made off that corner—was that not amazing?"

"I forgot about that! Liverpool was on a roll." Distracted, Lewis walked down the hall with his friend as they geeked out over the most epic soccer match ever to be played on the planet.

Olivia sighed and headed for class.

After fourth hour, Olivia followed her class towards the gymnasium for a mandatory school assembly. She had no idea what it was about, but she was sure it was more than likely a waste of time. Then Olivia changed her mind as she approached the gymnasium's entrance.

Lewis was waiting in another queue of students piling into the gymnasium. It was the perfect opportunity to talk to him again. Hopefully, they would get to sit together, and then Olivia could ask him out.

When she reached the doorway to the gymnasium, Olivia decided to drop her phone. She then 'accidentally' kicked it over towards Lewis, who picked it up.

"You sure you don't play soccer?" Lewis asked, handing it back to her.

"Can't believe I did that," Olivia said. "I'm such a twit."

"I keep running into you," Lewis said. "How do you explain that?"

"Maybe I'm stalking you," Olivia said.

You stupid cow. Did you really tell him that? Olivia asked herself.

"I wish more girls would do that," Lewis said.

They entered the gymnasium. The raised bleachers were crowded with students.

"Do what, stalk you?" Olivia asked.

"Hell yeah, cute girls following me around everywhere. Staring into my bedroom window. Leaving me love notes in my locker."

"You wouldn't find that creepy? Because a girl would be

flipping out if a bloke did that to her."

"A bloke?" he asked.

They moved farther into the gym. The queue was moving faster.

"A man," Olivia explained.

"You English talk funny."

"And you Americans butcher our lovely language," Olivia said. "But in your case, love, I'll overlook it." She flashed him a smile.

Lewis returned it.

A girl's voice then pierced through the noisy gym. "Hey, Olivia, we're over here!"

Olivia refused to look at them. Not now. She was on the edge of victory, and Emma wasn't going to ruin it.

Emma whistled. "Olivia! Olivia! Over here. We saved you a space."

Olivia still didn't turn around. It sounded like Emma was on the opposite side of the gym and miles away from where she and Lewis were being guided over to sit.

However, before they could sit down—a hand fell on her shoulder.

Olivia turned.

Nadia pointed at the stands opposite them. "We saved you a place over there with us."

"Oh—okay. Do you have enough room for Lewis?"

"Nah, don't worry about it," he said. "I was gonna sneak out in the middle of this assembly anyway. They get so boring, you know? Go sit with your friends."

"But—but I'm sure we have room. If not, you could sit on my lap."

Lewis leaned back. "Yeah, I'm not sitting on any girl's lap."

"That was stupid. I didn't mean it that way. I meant I could sit on your lap."

"Nah, you two sit together. It's not a big deal." Lewis hopped up to the top bleachers while Nadia dragged Olivia to the other side of the gym. They climbed up the stairs and scooted over with Kayla, Emma, and Miyuki.

"Didn't you hear me calling you?" Emma asked.

"The entire state of California heard you calling me," Olivia said.

"Why are you mad?"

"Did I make you mad?" Nadia asked.

"No, love, it's just—I was this close—" Olivia pinched her fingers together "—to asking Lewis out. But then you had to start yelling across the gym."

"How was I supposed to know you were hitting on a guy?" Emma asked.

"I'm sorry, Olivia," Nadia said.

"Me too. I didn't know," Emma repeated.

The assembly started. Soon some expert invited by the school began talking to the students about drugs and alcohol. Olivia closed her eyes and settled into a good forty-five-minute waste of her time.

But Olivia's phone buzzed with an incoming call. She checked the screen.

It was Mrs. B. The woman who ran the Authority's California station as well as being the Gems handler.

"Hello?"

"I apologize for bothering you at school, Emerald. But this is urgent. I need the Gems in my office right after school."

CHAPTER 5

After school, Olivia rode shotgun as Emma drove her Mercedes out of the city of Berkeley and headed north towards wine country. Emma turned into the public parking lot for the Burlington Winery. She drove past the lot and stopped the car at the employees-only gate that led into the winery's private grounds.

After the plain-clothed guard verified their identities, Emma drove through the gate and parked inside the small stand-alone garage, which closed its doors and became a giant elevator, lowering the Mercedes down to a secret underground parking lot.

Once the full-body and retinal scans were completed, Olivia led the Gems into the sprawling, open-office building, which had two levels. The second floor had offices and meeting rooms with clear glass walls while the first floor had no desks, only benches and paths that led to other areas of the underground complex. A grand circular staircase glued the two floors together.

Olivia took the path that led to the Labyrinth, a maze of dark blue walls, floors, and ceilings where the only light source was a series of white strips running along the top and bottom of each wall. It was the most ominous area of the entire complex. An area where the Authority's most sensitive secrets were hidden.

Once inside the office, Olivia sat down on one of the two white metal office chairs while Mrs. B worked behind an old steel desk that was painted pink. Her office had a vintage '60s feel to it, especially with all the Beatles, Jefferson Airplane, and other band concert posters. Emma took the other white chair as Nadia and Miyuki made themselves comfortable on the nearby couch. The thick door to the office was shut behind them, causing a sucking sound as the seals around the door frame were closed and the air inside the room was equalized.

"Thank you all for coming." Mrs. B picked up a remote to turn on a large plasma television on the wall. On the screen were two teenage girls with striking red hair. They looked like exact twins. "Your old friends the O'Malley sisters have been spotted in Amsterdam."

A cold chill bit into Olivia's spine. Venomous was bad enough. Their secret criminal organization was behind a lot of the mayhem that occurred around the world. Basically, if they weren't directly involved, then their members were most likely profiting from it. But add Bridget and Sophia to the mix and you had a real flipping problem.

"The twins have been traveling around Europe, recruiting teens to join some environmental organization called Heart the E."

The screen changed to a young man with curly blond hair smiling for the camera while planting a tree with some friends.

"Heart the E was founded by an American named Cody Walker Kurtz when he was sixteen-years-old. Now he's twenty-one and the head of a large non-profit organization." She switched back to the twins. "We know the O'Malley sisters are now members of Venomous so—"

"Excuse me, Mrs. B—," Emma interrupted, "—but I've never seen those girls before."

"Oh, I forgot about that. Do you mind filling her in, Emerald?"

Olivia nodded. "We first encountered Bridget and Sophia during a mission in New Zealand—this was before you joined us. These girls are from Ireland, and they're both mental. Bridget is the calm one. She's smart, manipulative, and ruthless. Her sister Sophia has—to put it nicely—anger management issues. She's highly emotional, violent, and vindictive. Don't let your guard down around either of them." Olivia went on to tell Emma about how the twins kidnapped her. How they fell in love with Dr. Yes, their school headmaster and the Venomous agent who masterminded a plot that the Gems broke up.

"They were wicked girls," Miyuki added.

"Whatever they're up to, it's not good," Nadia said.

Mrs. B changed the screen to a map of the world. "That's what concerns me. We've seen a large uptick of Venomous communications between their various entities all over the world. It feels like something big is about to go down, and I need every resource at my disposal to find out what's going on." Mrs. B turned her chair towards them. "Because it involves the twins, I need the Gems to investigate what they're up to."

The main office door opened, and the air was sucked back out as a large man with a deep scar running down his throat entered with a report in his hands.

"Ah, thank you, Aardvark." She took the report from him and scanned the information. "We've managed to track the O'Malleys thanks to a virus we put on their 'infected' phone. The virus sends copies of itself to each phone that it calls, giving us the phone's location and helps us identify the owner of the phone it contacted."

Mrs. B studied the list closer.

"I see the twins have been in contact with Ryan Raymond. That makes sense. Next to the twins, Ryan is one of the youngest of the Venomous operatives. All three of them could be working together."

Mrs. B continued reading.

"We've infected Ryan's phone as well. Excellent. Let's see who he's been in contact with. Two Venomous assets in Mexico we already know about—" Mrs. B's expression changed. "And a girl in Berkeley, California."

Olivia couldn't believe it. Not again.

Mrs. B's eyes addressed Emma, who shifted uncomfortably in her chair.

"Um—he only wanted to see how I was doing. Seriously, it was an innocent conversation."

"Have I not warned you time and time again about maintaining contact with that boy?"

"Ryan still could be useful for information. Remember when he helped us find Tyler Cho, that food engineer?" Emma asked. "We would never have found him without his help."

"You're letting your feelings about that boy override your judgment. I can't allow this to continue."

"Oh my God. It was a phone call. I'm not going to have babies with him."

"Watch your tone. This isn't a joke."

"I didn't say it was a joke. But I think you're overreacting."

"And you're a compromised asset. One that's useless to me and this organization."

"Wait—what does compromised mean?"

"It means none of us can trust you," Olivia said.

"I didn't tell him anything."

May I say something?

The smooth male voice belonged to Aardvark's phone communicator app.

"Yes. Of course," Mrs. B said.

Aardvark typed out his thoughts before his phone replied.

If you would permit me, ma'am, there could be an opportunity here. May I have a moment alone to discuss it?

* * *

Inside the underground cafeteria, Olivia ordered some cheese fries for everyone as they waited for Aardvark and Mrs. B. It was approaching dinner-time and they were all feeling a little hungry. Miyuki picked out a couple of fries from the cheesy pile and munched on them, causing some of the cheese to get on her chin. Nadia tapped her own chin, and Miyuki wiped off the cheese with a giggle.

Olivia dipped a fry in ketchup and popped it into her mouth. She took a quick glance at Emma before exchanging a longer, more meaningful look with Nadia. They both seemed to be on the same page. Emma had messed up once again.

Emma caught their exchange. She picked at the pile of fries with her fork but didn't eat anything.

Miyuki glanced at everyone, then ate another cheese fry.

Nadia pulled out a couple of fries and picked off the cheese to eat it separately.

"Don't everyone yell at me at once," Emma said.

Olivia had wanted some food in her stomach before she jumped all over Emma. But if Emma wanted to go there…

"You're on thin ice," she said. "If you're not careful, Mrs. B will kick you out of the Gems. She doesn't mess around."

"I still don't understand what you see in that boy," Nadia said.

"I'm not having another conversation about Ryan again. You know what I said in there was true. He's helped us in the past. There's still some good left in him," Emma said. "I can save him."

"Every girl who falls in love thinks like that," Olivia said.

"Whatever. I'm not going to argue about it. None of you understand."

"You're right. We don't."

"Ryan is a complex boy," Miyuki said. "Maybe Emma can still turn him."

"Or he'll turn Emma against us," Olivia said.

Emma looked shocked. "I would never hurt any of you."

"Consciously, maybe not," Nadia said. "But if he can get you to tell him some secrets—"

"You could put everyone in danger," Olivia added. "This is some serious crap, Emma."

"Mrs. B will be fair," Miyuki said, nodding to herself. "She will consider her options and treat you accordingly."

Emma sighed. "That's what worries me."

Aardvark came into the cafeteria. He motioned the Gems to follow him into an area with large green pods and fake full-grown trees scattered throughout. It was nicknamed the Jungle. One of the green pods was open, revealing large comfy chairs arranged in a semicircle. Mrs. B waited on one of those chairs.

All four Gems stepped inside the pod.

"My apologies, Black Opal. I won't need you for this mission after all," Mrs. B said.

Emma froze. "Why not?"

"To be perfectly honest, I'm afraid you've been compromised. You'll have to stay home for this one."

Miyuki and Nadia exchanged glances.

Olivia couldn't believe it. She was right after all. Mrs. B wasn't messing around.

Emma hesitated. The embarrassment was plastered all over the girl's face.

"Our time is short, Black Opal," Mrs. B said. "Would you please excuse us?"

Emma reluctantly stepped out of the pod.

Mrs. B tapped a panel next to her, and the pod sealed up tight before a low hum announced that the cone of silence mode was activated.

Miyuki floated a worried look over to Olivia, who smiled to reassure her that everything would be fine.

"Let me start by saying that I have the utmost confidence in the three of you to handle this new assignment." Mrs. B activated a 3-

D map of the state of Oregon. "Our goal for this new operation is intelligence. We must find out what the O'Malley twins are up to. And to do that, we'll have to approach this from a different angle. I'm sending you three to Heart the E's main base camp in Oregon where they're having their annual fall conference. Once there, you'll investigate Cody Kurtz and his organization for any links to Venomous."

"Question, why don't we go to Amsterdam and follow the twins there?"

"Because, Emerald, you've worked closely with the twins in New Zealand, and even with a good disguise, your cover could be blown. I feel this will be a safer approach. Once you've established yourselves as members enjoying the conference, I think it's only a matter of time before the twins show up in Oregon. However, by then you'll have a feel for the camp and know how to make yourselves melt into the background to observe the twins' movements," Mrs. B said. "I don't want you girls to tangle with the O'Malleys directly. We need intelligence, not a fight."

Mrs. B switched off the 3-D map. "You'll be leaving Monday morning. Tomorrow, you'll need to come back here after school so we can work on your disguises and have additional briefings for the mission. That's all."

"Pardon me, ma'am," Miyuki said. "But is Black Opal really staying home?"

"I'm afraid so. And I must insist that none of you can tell her anything about your mission. Is that understood?"

CHAPTER 6

Emma waited outside the green pod as Aardvark stood nearby. She was frustrated and kind of angry. Why didn't Mrs. B trust her? She knew Ryan more than any of them did, and because she was a teenage girl, Mrs. B instantly thought she was being manipulated and too stupid to be rational about her friendship with Ryan. But Emma knew the dangers and was willing to take that risk to save someone. Wasn't that what the Authority was all about? Saving mankind? Or in this case, one human?

Emma shook off her worries and opened up her purse. She popped open a container of mints and offered one to Aardvark.

He took the mint and typed something on his phone.

Thank you.

Aardvark placed the mint on his tongue. He grinned at the taste, but then his grin soured. Something was troubling him. He typed something else.

Do you believe in what we're doing here?

Wow. Emma couldn't believe it. Did anyone on Earth trust her anymore?

"Of course I do."

Aardvark nodded.

Good. Remember that. We might be asking a lot from you in the next couple of weeks.

He pointed at his chest.

You must be strong in here.

He pointed at his head.

And here. I believe in you and what you're capable of. If your insights are correct, then we have a great opportunity. I hope you see it that way.

"See what that way?" she asked.

The green pod opened as Olivia, Nadia, and Miyuki stepped out.

"I'd like to talk to Black Opal now," Mrs. B said. "Alone, please."

The Gems glanced at each other, then at Emma, before leaving the pod.

"Have a seat," Mrs. B said.

Emma stepped inside as the green pod closed up again. The cone of silence mode was activated.

Emma braced herself for another lecture. *Why are you still speaking with Ryan? Didn't we already tell you to stop? What is wrong with you?* Maybe this time Emma would be suspended or have to clean up the cafeteria or bathrooms at headquarters. Still, those punishments didn't feel as bad as being excluded from a mission. And she was only being excluded because Mrs. B questioned her loyalty.

That hurt.

You know what? Why should she wait for a lecture? She wasn't a traitor. She was loyal. She hadn't told Ryan anything he didn't already know. This was totally unfair, and she wasn't going to keep quiet about it.

The angry words gathered inside Emma's simmering stomach. Soon they pushed their way up her throat and hit the air.

"This is all bullshit. I'm loyal and I resent you assuming that just because I talk to Ryan that I'm—"

"We're not here to discuss that," Mrs. B said, cutting off her tirade.

Emma gathered her thoughts. "Then why did you exclude me from the mission?"

"Because you'll be on a different mission. I would say the most difficult part of the operation. You'll be our defector."

"Our what?"

"Black Opal, you'll be infiltrating Venomous by playing the role of a lifetime. You'll contact Ryan, and through him, you'll flip to their side and gather intelligence on that group's operations and what they may be planning in the short term." Mrs. B paused. "Just to be clear, I still don't trust Ryan Raymond, and neither should you. However, one thing is clear. He's desperate for your approval, and that weakness should be exploited."

"Ryan won't turn on Venomous."

"But he has strong feelings for you. So he's vulnerable."

"If Ryan finds out I'm lying to him, it will destroy any chance of him ever trusting me again."

"This is when we put down all our money on the poker table, Black Opal," Mrs. B said. "If you say you can turn him, then now is the time. I'm going to give you this one opportunity. I suggest you use it well."

Emma didn't want to do it this way. She wanted to slowly work on Ryan. To chip away at his loyalty while his feelings for her would grow stronger and stronger. Then he would be so much in love with her that one small suggestion from her would be all it would take to finally convince him. But according to Mrs. B…she had run out of time.

"Call Ryan tomorrow. Tell him how frustrated you are because I found out about you two still speaking to each other. Then fly out to Montreal. Spend time with him. Conduct a honey pot operation against him. Just like you did in your specialized training with Lioness. Do everything she taught you. Treat Ryan like you would any other asset. Make him fall in love with you, then use him for information. If you can, flip him into a longtime asset for the Authority."

Emma wondered if she was ready to carry out such a mission by herself. Could she separate her private feelings for Ryan to deceive him? It would be difficult, but this might be Emma's last opportunity to save Ryan.

Mrs. B leaned forward. "As soon as you leave this pod, we must convince everyone—including the Gems—that I'm angry with you and that you're not to be trusted anymore. Otherwise, your wavering loyalty to us won't be convincing."

"Do I have to lie to them?"

"As far as the Gems will know, you're Ryan's best friend. You must now play the role of a lifetime. A performance so good that even your best friends will be convinced that you're about to flip to the other side."

Emma didn't want to do this. It felt wrong. Deceiving her friends felt all wrong.

"What if I refuse the assignment?"

Mrs. B's positive smile curdled. Her eyes squinted. "If you refuse to participate—we will immediately detain you and your grandmother Bernadette before setting her house on fire. The investigation will determine frayed wiring as the cause. The world will mourn the death of four teenage girls and their beloved caretaker, while you and your grandmother will be secretly given new identities in some far away country to begin a brand-new life."

Mrs. B sat back in her seat. "However—knowing Bernadette as well as I do, she will refuse this arrangement and threaten to tell everyone about our organization. That would be most unfortunate. Because it would mean that…her life would be in danger."

Emma froze.

"Despite my personal feelings on the matter, my superiors will order me to carry out such a difficult task." Mrs. B paused. "However, I don't want to be put in such a difficult position, Black Opal. Please accept the mission and do your best. Prove to us that we can trust you again."

Emma lowered her head. She could feel a headache coming on.

Mrs. B waited for her answer.

Emma felt like she didn't have much of a choice.

"I'm sorry about the inflexibility of the situation. But if Venomous is conducting a large terrorist operation, your mission could save many lives."

Emma knew that Venomous did a lot of horrible things. Things she and the Gems had stopped in the past. Whatever her mission would reveal, most likely it would be something horrible that needed to be stopped. Just because she didn't like how Mrs. B wanted her to treat Ryan, it didn't mean Emma still couldn't win him over to their side. To save him from that horrible group. To give him a chance at a new purpose in his life.

But why did Mrs. B threaten her grandmother's life? Why was that even necessary? Would Mrs. B actually do that? She would be killing someone from her family just to keep a secret?

Mrs. B was hard to read. When they first met, the woman was mysterious and presented herself with a hard edge. Even when Mrs. B revealed that Emma was indeed her granddaughter, there was a wall between them. Unlike Grandma Bernadette, who took Emma in and cared for her after Emma's father died. Did Mrs. B not see her as a granddaughter? Was there no love left inside that old woman's cold and steel heart? Did being a spy drain all those feelings out of your soul?

"What's your answer?" Mrs. B asked.

Emma swallowed. Maybe she couldn't make her grandmother love her. But she could save Ryan.

"I'll do it."

Mrs. B's neutral face relaxed into a shallow smile. "You've made the right decision. Let me know when you're ready. It would look better if you were upset after I...bitched you out."

Emma nodded. She closed her eyes and dug deep inside herself. She pulled out the frustration of being told countless times to stop seeing Ryan. Emma then remembered her father's funeral, and a wave of misery hit her as she unlocked the grief and the pain. The tears came out. The sobbing bubbled up on its own. Her acting tools were still as sharp as razors.

Mrs. B popped open the pod. Miyuki, Olivia, Nadia, and Aardvark were still waiting for them.

Emma climbed out of the pod and just stumbled away from the group, like she was in a drunken stupor. So overcome with emotion that she couldn't walk straight.

Miyuki was the first one at her side, holding up Emma like the best friend ever. "What happened?"

Emma tried to speak, but the tears kept choking off her words.

"Black Opal is on probation until further notice," Mrs. B said with an edge. "You girls should be heading home. You have school tomorrow."

On their way back to the car, Emma told the Gems about how Mrs. B told her she couldn't be trusted and that she was having second thoughts about keeping Emma on the team. They might even replace her with another girl. Emma told them how she pleaded with Mrs. B to give her another chance. But the woman was angry, telling Emma she was lucky they didn't just eliminate her for being disloyal.

"Mrs. B actually said that?" Olivia asked.

She actually didn't. Emma had improvised most of the story thanks to her superior ad-lib skills. The actor inside her was loving this new role. Running with it like an Olympic athlete does a torch.

"She hates me," Emma said. "I really screwed up this time."

They reached the Mercedes.

"Maybe you shouldn't be driving right now," Nadia said.

Emma ignored her and got behind the wheel. Soon the Gems were on their way south towards the city. It was dark outside as the street-lights flashed over the hood of the Mercedes as it cruised along the highway. The clock on the dash displayed ten thirty.

"Perhaps she needs more time to think it over," Nadia said.

"Mrs. B is normally very rational."

"Yes, you keep pushing her buttons, Emma," Miyuki said. "You drive her crazy."

Emma held on tight to her emotions. The sadness. The despair. She allowed it to flow over her body.

She was still on the stage. Still giving her performance.

"I'm doomed," Emma said.

"You're not doomed," Nadia said. "Once our mission is over, we should speak to Mrs. B together. As a team."

"Why? I'm not defending what Emma did," Olivia said. "She's not supposed to flirt with the enemy."

"Ryan isn't the enemy," Emma said, her voice was loud. Emotional. It was like another girl was talking from Emma's mouth. "He's being manipulated. Brainwashed. He's in a bad situation, and I'm trying to get him out of it."

"Ryan deserves the situation he's in, love. If he wants to get out of it, he can pull himself out of it."

Emma was sick of her. Olivia never understood Ryan. Never gave him a chance. She would always be the first one to cut him down.

A new pulse of anger pressed Emma's foot on the gas pedal. The Mercedes surged forward.

"Well, you're an expert on everyone, aren't you?" Emma asked.

"I never said that," Olivia said.

"Wasn't today's school assembly interesting?" Miyuki asked, trying to change the subject.

Nadia picked up on what Miyuki was doing. "I thought it was boring. There are better presentations about drug abuse on Utube."

"Emma, do yourself a favor and dump your feelings for this guy," Olivia said. "He's not worth it, love."

"It's hard," Emma said. "When you love someone, you can't just—drop all your feelings for them."

"Do you love him?" Nadia asked.

Emma reached deep inside her heart. The actor inside her didn't have to fake this feeling.

"Yes."

"God, you're pathetic," Olivia said.

"Oh, Emma," Miyuki said.

"Why are we going so fast?" Nadia asked.

"Is someone following us?" Miyuki searched the back window

for a tail.

The Mercedes was so easy to drive that Emma sometimes forgot to pay attention. But the actor still had full control over her body, and that character she was playing felt overwhelmed with her life.

"Okay, fine, I'm pathetic," Emma said. "I'm so fucked up now that I want to give up because I'm sick of being yelled at and threatened because I care about someone. Someone who gets me. Someone who understands me. None of you understand me. But he does." Emma heard her voice crack. "I just want to save him."

Olivia leaned closer to Emma. "Maybe you should pull over and let one of us drive."

"Maybe you should shut up and stop telling me what to do." Emma stomped on the gas. It didn't take long for the Mercedes to hover above the dark pavement at over a hundred miles an hour.

Emma never liked driving this fast, but the actor inside her had shoved Emma to the side and controlled every impulse her body had.

"Stop the flipping car!" Olivia yelled.

Her character didn't stop the car. She wanted to be heard. She wanted her friends to pay attention to her grief and the sadness pouring out of her.

Miyuki popped her head in again, her voice low and soothing. "I love you, Emma. Why don't you stop the car and talk to me about what you're feeling right now."

Emma looked over.

"Please? I want to listen."

The character liked what she said. Her foot lifted off the pedal, and Emma began to take back control of her body.

Emma then realized the exit to Berkeley was coming up fast and she was in the far left lane. Emma jerked the wheel hard to the right, forcing the Mercedes to cut across four lanes of traffic. Emma managed to point the Mercedes down the exit ramp at over seventy miles an hour.

Down the ramp, there was an intersection. Across from that, a donut shop with its lights on. Someone has to start making the donuts.

Emma realized the danger and hit the brakes. The car squealed as the anti-lock brakes struggled to slow down the car. At this speed, trying to make a turn to the left or right would only flip the car over. Besides, Emma was too scared to try.

Emma gripped the wheel and braced herself.

The Mercedes plowed through the intersection, hopped over the shallow curb, and obliterated the Apple Fritters sign as the car skidded right up to the donut shop's large front window...

Where the bumper kissed the window.

Through that window, a man and a woman with brown skin glared at the Mercedes that almost took out them and their small business.

CHAPTER 7

Emma couldn't sleep. Her mind was thinking about Ryan. How she would talk to him. How she would make him fall in love with her. *Make him.* That sounded awful. Manipulating him was more like it. Tricking him into thinking they would be together forever.

But why wouldn't they be together forever? She had the same feelings for him. Would it be so bad if Ryan did fall in love with her? That love could literally save him from an evil future. A future that would ruin his good soul. Emma knew that Ryan would forgive her eventually. Surely he would see everything she did would be out of love. Saving him from a life he was tricked into. Seduced by the money and the power that Venomous offered him. Ryan was being manipulated too, wasn't he?

Yes, he was. And now Emma had a chance to save the boy she fell in love with next to a lake in Missouri.

A wet tongue reminded Emma that it was time to get up. She ran her fingers over Snoopy's back and kissed him before she got up to start her new day.

Emma came downstairs ready for school as Miyuki, Olivia, and Nadia were finishing up their breakfast.

"I can't believe I'm just now hearing about this," Grandmother Bernadette said to Olivia.

"Sorry about that. The mission came up last week. I'm sure Mrs. B sends her apologies."

Grandmother Bernadette leaned against the counter as she addressed Emma. "I'm surprised you didn't say anything about this."

"They don't need me for this one," Emma said.

The other three Gems exchanged glances.

Her grandmother brightened. "Well, at least I won't be alone this week."

A car honk was heard outside.

Olivia stood up. "That's our driver. We have to go."

"Then at least give your adopted grandma a goodbye hug."

The three departing Gems each gave Grandma Bernadette a genuine hug.

Miyuki paused next to Emma. "We can have a long talk when I come back if you want."

"Thanks. I'd like that. Be careful on your mission." Emma faced Olivia and Nadia. "That goes for all of you."

"What are they going to go do?" Grandma Bernadette asked. "Now you have me worried, young one. What does Laura have you poor kids doing?"

"Don't worry about us. We'll be fine," Olivia said.

As the three Gems left, Grandma Bernadette moved closer to Emma. "I know you girls can't tell me, but—is it more dangerous than normal?"

"This time, I have no idea."

Grandma Bernadette wondered about the meaning behind the words, then gave up and kissed her on the forehead. "How about I fix you some oatmeal mixed with nuts and berries. Healthy and good for you."

Emma didn't complain. Not today. Let her grandmother enjoy this moment since Emma had to soon take it away. Today she had to ditch school and take a flight to Montreal to see Ryan.

"You look nice," her grandmother said.

"Felt like dressing up today. That's all. It makes me feel good." Emma was telling the truth. Kind of. The clothes did make her feel good. But she hoped Ryan would find her irresistible in them.

"Since it's just you and me this week, let's have some fun. It's been a while," Grandma Bernadette said. "How about we go to your favorite seafood place for dinner. The one in Oakland."

Emma did love that place. However, by dinner-time she would already be in Canada.

Grandma Bernadette continued. "We could visit some museums. Go to the art crawl on Friday night. The aquarium. The planetarium."

Now she felt bad. Her grandmother was already planning their week together, and Emma was about to ruin it.

"You know what? I'll cancel my office hours this week. That

way I can pick you up at school and we can hit the museums before they close. Oh, young one."

"What?"

"They're performing *Aida* this Saturday night. Professor Hines has a son who works for the opera company. I know we can get tickets."

"Grandma…"

"I promise that I'm not making any attempt to hook you up with a boy. The professor's son is quite happily gay, so don't worry."

"But I can't—"

"Can't what, young one?"

Excitement still danced around her grandmother's eyes. A chance to spend time with her only granddaughter. All that hope was on full display on Grandma Bernadette's wrinkled face.

Emma couldn't do it. She didn't have the strength to kill that hope and destroy her excitement. She would have to find another way to let her grandma down.

Her phone beeped. Emma checked it. It was her email. There was now an Air Canada e-ticket with her name. The flight to Montreal via Toronto left this morning at ten thirty and Emma was expected to be on it.

Being a good granddaughter would have to wait.

CHAPTER 8

As Olivia washed her hands in the airport bathroom sink, the glass mirror showed a girl with a prosthetic nose that Olivia still didn't recognize. The girl's nose was slightly flatter and more round than Olivia's real nose. Her beautiful curly black hair was pulled back tight and out of the way, giving more emphasis to her forehead. The clothes this girl wore had a Caribbean flair, which matched her cover as a teenage girl from the Dominican Republic.

Nadia occupied the sink next to her. Her friend looked naked without her head scarf hiding her long black hair. Nadia retrieved a brush from her purse and combed her hair out, allowing it to glisten even under the flat fluorescent lighting of the bathroom.

Olivia stepped out of the bathroom and scanned the people inside the Portland International Airport terminal. She had trouble picking out Miyuki in her new disguise. But finally Olivia saw her staring at a lumberjack advertisement. Miyuki wore new round glasses to go with her super-short haircut. The disguise made it more difficult to spot her in a crowd. Which was the whole point.

"*Hola*, studying up on the local history?" Olivia asked.

"I'm not Lola. I'm Cho Ximo from Shanghai, remember?"

"No, Love. *Hola* means hello in Spanish."

"You should lose that British accent," Nadia said.

"*Gracias, señorita*. You're right. From this point on we communicate through our cover identities. No more references to our former selves. Got it?"

Miyuki responded with a flurry of Chinese words that flew right over Olivia's head.

"*Sí,*" Olivia said.

Not to be outdone, Nadia dumped a few phrases in Russian.

Miyuki's eyes opened wide. "Oh, that sounded good."

"Thank you, *comrade*."

The two girls giggled.

After they claimed their luggage, the group split up. Nadia got on her phone and used the Huber app to have a driver pick her up while Olivia and Miyuki wasted about a half-hour inside the terminal to give Nadia time to reach the Heart the E compound first. This way they wouldn't be seen arriving together. But when Olivia and Miyuki reached the taxi passenger waiting queue—it was over forty people deep.

"Flipping great. We'll be extremely late now," Olivia said.

"Relax, we'll get there," Miyuki said. "Have a candy! It's Korean and yummy."

"I don't want a candy."

"It's banana." Miyuki held the piece of candy near Olivia's mouth. "I think it likes you."

"It what?"

"I want you to eat me," Miyuki said in a high-pitched, cartoon-like voice. "My only purpose in life is to make your mouth happy. Eat me!"

"Stop it."

"Eat me!"

Olivia was weakening.

"Let me into that mouth!" Miyuki gently pressed the candy against her lips. Finally Olivia opened up and let the candy fall on her tongue. The flavor of banana flowed over it as the sugar invaded her bloodstream.

Miyuki clapped her hands in triumph, causing a few bored glances from the people in the queue.

"Don't draw attention to us," Olivia whispered.

Miyuki dropped her hands.

It took a half hour, but they reached the head of the queue and climbed into a waiting taxi. Olivia gave the driver the address and noted his eyes scrutinizing both girls through the taxi's rear-view mirror.

"This is way out there," the driver said.

Miyuki shot a look at Olivia.

"Is there a problem, *señor*?" Olivia was proud of herself. That question in English had a sprinkling of a Caribbean Spanish accent. Exactly how she was taught in Level Two Advanced Spanish during training.

"This address—you're looking at about an hour drive out of the city." The driver looked closely at them again. "It'll be expensive."

"We can pay."

"With what?"

The way the white man stared at her, Olivia knew exactly what his problem was. It wasn't about their destination. It was about who wanted that destination. Olivia wanted to tell this racist a-hole to piss off and they'd get another taxi. But they were already late to the camp, and the taxi queue was still long. Olivia forced a smile and gave him her credit card.

The driver scanned it. "I can't take this."

"It's a Visa," Olivia said.

"Not issued through a bank located inside some banana republic."

Miyuki eased into her Chinese alias. "My credit card. You accept?"

She handed him her credit card. It was a Mastercard from one of the largest banks in China.

"Can't take this one either."

Frustration heated Olivia's body. She was about to explode on this guy and lose her cool.

But Miyuki took out a wad of cash. "How much? You take us."

As soon as he saw the money, the man's eyes lit up. "Three hundred. Plus tip."

She nodded and gave him some money. "Half now. Half later."

The man put the taxi in gear and drove them away from the terminal and on-to the highway. The taxi soon took them away from Portland and deep into Oregon itself, with its deep forests and beautiful rivers. They left the interstate highway and took a series of two-lane roads that snaked their way through the lush forest.

Finally the taxi stopped in front of an open wooden gate. There was a posted sign made from some type of recyclable cardboard. It read, *Welcome Heart the E family!* The driver pulled out their luggage from the trunk, and Miyuki gave him the rest of his money plus a tip.

Olivia kept her back to the man and concentrated on her cover instead. In her mind, Olivia went over the details about the Dominican Republic she had studied. Olivia then took out her Spanish Bible. She moved her fingers over the worn leather surface, then whispered the Lord's prayer in Spanish. This was an acting technique she learned from Emma. Holding something your character owns to help the actor ground herself into that character. Olivia also reminded herself to call out in Spanish if she ever felt emotional or scared. One British reference could blow her cover wide open. She must think in Spanish. Always in Spanish.

"Excuse me. But you have never told me your name," Miyuki said.

"My name?" Olivia was confused. Why was Miyuki asking her this?

"When we met at the airport, I introduced myself as Cho Ximo." Miyuki didn't miss a beat. She was already deep into her own cover.

Now Olivia got it. Miyuki was doing this in case someone was watching them.

"My name is Camila," Olivia said with her Spanish accent.

"A pleasure to meet you, Camila." Miyuki's Chinese accent was perfect.

With new confidence, the two Gems walked up the dirt road. Their ears picked up sounds of a crowd echoing through the trees as they approached four big log cabins. The clatter of kitchen utensils and the smell of simmering vegetables came from one of the cabins. Two of the cabins turned out to be outdoor shelters with picnic tables stuffed inside them.

Olivia and Miyuki circled the cabins and came upon a giant campsite composed of hundreds of pitched tents. The centerpiece was a large wooden stage surrounded by dozens of fire-pits. On one side of the campsite, there was a line of outhouses. Not porta-potties. Old-school wooden outhouses. The campsite was flooded with teens and young adults. Most of them wore the same Heart the E lime-green T-shirts.

A young man with curly blond hair approached them. Olivia pegged him at around college age or slightly older. His skin was off white due to a lot of sun.

"You two are late," he said.

Miyuki bowed. "We are so sorry. Please forgive us."

"Got ya!" The young man broke up laughing. "I'm only joking with ya. Welcome to Heart the E's annual conference. Did you register on-line?"

"*Sí.* I'm Camila from the Dominican Republic." Olivia

referenced Miyuki. "This is my new friend Cho from China."

"We meet at the airport," Miyuki added. "I see her Heart the E bag. Knew we both going to the same place."

"Then it was meant to be," the boy with curly blond hair said. "Now you two are gonna be longtime friends. I love that. I'm Cody Kurtz."

"I recognize you! So excited to meet you." Miyuki shook up and down as she gave the boy a quick hug.

"Wow. I love that. Don't ever lose that enthusiasm."

Olivia couldn't go that far, so she only smiled at Cody. "I've watched all your Utube videos. They're amazing."

"You two are amazing. You came from the Dominican Republic to be here? And China?" Cody looked around. "We have kids from every corner of the world here, and it still blows my mind that people from all over the world still watch my videos." Cody stopped and motioned to someone. "Hey, Gabi? Can you grab two more hand-woven canvas welcome bags for our new guests?"

A Latin-American girl with brown skin emerged from the crowd and nodded before sprinting off.

"I'm so psyched about the next few weeks. We have concerts. Nature hikes. Bike races. Tree plantings. Kayak races. Climbing lessons. Bird watching. We are so merging with nature it's not even funny."

"Merging with nature?" Olivia asked.

"I should say making love to Mother Nature because she loves us. And we should love her back."

The Latin-American girl named Gabi came back and handed Miyuki and Olivia their welcome bags.

"Everything's in there," Cody said. "The schedule for the next few weeks. A T-shirt. Answers to questions. And a delicious pack of natural energy snacks to get you through your first few days. Are we loving this yet?"

"I love it," Miyuki clapped her hands.

"Me too." Olivia only managed a thumbs up.

"Sweet. Gabi will take care of you. I know I'll see you around, so until then, enjoy yourselves!" Cody gave them a large grin before easing away. Another group of teens watched a boy showing off his juggling skills. Cody pointed at him. "I love that."

Gabi stepped in front of them. "*Hola*, My name is Gabrielle, but

I prefer Gabi. I'm from Costa Rica."

"Oh, I want to visit Costa Rica someday and go surfing," Miyuki said.

What was she doing? Olivia knew for a fact that Miyuki's alias said nothing about her knowing how to surf.

"The surfing on our Pacific coast is epic," Gabi said. "Where do you usually surf?"

Miyuki sighed. "No good place to surf in China. But I want to learn someday."

"If you're ever near Jacó, come look me up and I'll teach you." Gabi's eyes switched to Olivia. "How about you?"

"Surfing has never appealed to me."

"I'm trying to place your accent. Definitely not Haitian."

"Dominican."

"Ah, *Sí. Bueno,*" Gabi said. "Let me show you to a tent."

Gabi led Olivia and Miyuki to a new row of tents on the outskirts of the camp. Gabi flipped through her computer tablet. "This one is open. Do you two want to share? I don't have enough to get you each a tent. Sorry, but since you came in late—"

"We understand. *Gracias,*" Olivia said.

"Hey, Gabi?" Cody yelled his question across the camp.

"Coming." Gabi rolled her eyes, then smiled. "We'll be serving dinner in an hour."

Gabi hurried off, leaving Olivia and Miyuki alone.

It took them most of the hour to unpack and arrange what they had brought inside the small tent. It was a tight fit.

"Bedtime will be cozy," Miyuki said.

Olivia sighed as she stood next to the tent. The only space left inside was the middle, and that would barely fit their two sleeping bags.

"Do you snore?" she asked Miyuki.

"I don't know. I'm never awake to notice."

Olivia let it go. Being Miyuki's roommate for a couple of weeks might be another mission in itself.

"Will we be outside for dinner? We should put on buggie spray." Miyuki dived into their tent.

"Hello, my name is Aylin."

Olivia knew that girl's accented voice. It was Nadia, still without her headscarf.

"Gabi wanted you to know that dinner was about to start," Nadia said. She turned toward some girls walking up and told them as well. The girls thanked her and jogged on ahead.

"*Hola*, Aylin." Olivia checked the surroundings. "Are you settled in?"

Nadia lowered her voice. "Yes. I asked Gabi if I could help with anything, and she put me right to work."

"Excellent. What tent are you in?"

"Sixty-one. I found your tent number from Gabi's tablet."

"Do you have a roommate?" Olivia asked.

"No."

Miyuki emerged with a can of bug spray. Without hesitation, the girl sprayed a cloud of deadly bug gas all over, making everyone cough.

"Are you trying to kill the bugs or us?" Olivia asked.

Miyuki waved the cloud from her face and noticed Nadia. "Hey! Now we're complete again."

"Hello, my name is Aylin. I'm from Azerbaijan." Nadia offered to shake hands.

Miyuki had to shift a few gears in her head before shaking Nadia's hand. "Oh. . .yes. I'm Cho from China."

"Dinner is starting soon."

"Good. I'm hungry."

"I'm nauseated," Olivia said.

"Why?"

"Seriously, love? You emptied a can of bug spray in my face and now I feel sick."

Nadia checked for listening ears. "Watch your accent."

Olivia closed her eyes. Nadia was right. She needed to concentrate and not let Miyuki distract her.

"*Gracias*."

Olivia waited about five minutes after Nadia left before she and Miyuki walked to the wooden stage. There was a queue of teens waiting for their food while others sat at picnic tables scattered around the stage and under the outdoor shelters.

Olivia and Miyuki entered the queue and received a bowl of tofu fried rice, a plate of garden-fresh salad, a piece of whole grain bread, and a vegan chocolate brownie. Their dinner "trays" were made of woven straw and wood. It was a meal Emma's grandmother would've loved.

Miyuki sniffed at the rice and shrugged. Olivia sighed and followed Miyuki to an empty table near the stage.

Olivia tried the fried rice, then wished she hadn't. It needed about a liter of soy sauce to make it edible. At least the salad tasted decent and the bread was fresh. Olivia would've preferred a stick of butter on it, but the only thing available was goat cheese.

"I would kill for some good Thai food right now," Olivia said.

"The rice is not too bad," Miyuki said.

"If you like the rice, you'll love the meatless pepperoni cauliflower pizza tomorrow night," Gabi said. "Honestly, I could go for some Thai food as well."

Olivia flashed her a polite smile. Gabi had heard her. Thank goodness Olivia was using her Spanish accent.

"Mind if I join you?"

"Please." Miyuki nodded.

Gabi sat down at their picnic table. She put down her "tray" and grabbed a small bottle of hot sauce. She added it to her rice and mixed it.

"Would you like some?" Gabi asked Olivia in Spanish.

"*Sí. Gracias.*"

Gabi had put a lot of the sauce on her rice, while Olivia used a restrained amount. She took a bite. The rice was hot and spicy, but delicious. She still had to take a heavy swig of water to bring down the heat, but it was worth it. Olivia gave Gabi a thumbs-up.

"Hot sauce?"

Miyuki shook her head as they continued eating.

"So you're Camila. And you're Cho?" Gabi asked.

"*Sí*, on both counts," Olivia said.

"I was in such a rush to get you two into a tent that I forgot to confirm your reservations. But I did and you're both good to go," Gabi said. "Do they have good Thai food in Santo Domingo?"

Olivia wondered why the girl was bringing it up again. "I don't know about the capital, but where I live, there's a good Thai restaurant in Puerto Plata. It caters to the tourists at the beaches. Their food is delicious."

"English is. . .so limiting." Gabi leaned to Miyuki. "Would you mind if we had a conversation in Spanish?"

Olivia's heart beat faster. She was hoping this wouldn't come up, but of course she would have to meet another Spanish-speaking person on her first day.

"Oh—no, it doesn't bother me at all," Miyuki said.

"What does your family do?" Gabi asked in Spanish.

Olivia concentrated. "They work in hospitality. My papa is a hotel manager for the Hilton beach resort, and my mother manages luxury bus tours."

"Ah, *sí*, that explains it."

"Explains what?"

"How you can afford Thai food."

"My family has been fortunate," Olivia said. "What about you?"

"I'm a proud Tica," Gabi said. "Born and raised outside Jacó. My papa is an electrician and my mother has a clothing shop."

"How long have you been involved with Heart the E?"

"Six months. Cody needed people over eighteen who spoke Spanish to help him spread the movement into Latin America. So I dropped out of college and here I am."

"You dropped out of college for this?"

"*Sí*. I believe in Cody and what he's doing. Someday we will turn the world into a better place. Don't you believe that as well?"

"With all my heart," Olivia said. "Actually, my mother pushed me into coming here because she felt if I was serious about Heart the E, I should find out everything about it before fully committing."

"Your mother is wise. All mine did was tell me how loco I am for doing this. My mom still thinks I came here to sleep with boys."

"What?"

Gabi rolled her eyes. "*Sí*, she said that to me. The world is about to melt into the sea and she's more concerned about her daughter getting pregnant by *gringos*." Gabi paused. "There's a Thai restaurant in Austin, Texas, that I loved when I could scrape up enough money to go."

"Is that where you went to school?"

"*Sí*, I'm a Texas Longhorn. Or I was. Maybe someday I'll go back to finish."

"College must be so fun."

"I liked the independence. Setting my own schedule. Going to bed when I want to. Although it's very expensive. My uncle lives in Texas so through him I was able to pay in-state tuition."

Some kids cheered as Cody Kurtz went on-to the wooden stage, holding a guitar. He switched on a microphone already clipped to a stand.

"How is everybody?" he asked.

The teens all cheered.

"Getting enough to eat?"

They cheered again.

"Those vegan brownies were made from heaven, huh?"

More cheers.

"If you didn't know already, I'm Cody."

The crowd yelled in unison, "Hi, Cody!"

Cody laughed. "I love that—um—where was I? Yeah, okay, I'm Cody Kurtz and I'm the one who founded Heart the E."

"We love that!" the crowd yelled back at him.

Cody laughed so hard he almost fell over. "You guys—that was funny." Cody pulled over a wooden stool and sat on the corner of it. "Just two announcements tonight. We got a full day of awesomeness planned for tomorrow, so lights out at midnight tonight. Why? Because mother earth needs her rest too since we're resting in her forested womb tonight. Second announcement, our poetry readings will start tonight at seven forty-five, not eight. That's a typo on the schedule."

Cody balanced a guitar on his knee. "I'm sure happy all of you came. We're gonna have a great time singing about our best friend in the universe, our Mother Earth." Cody strummed his guitar, then picked out a melody on the strings as he sang. "Our Mother Earth is calling our names. Our Mother Earth is calling our names. Our Mother Earth is calling our names...because we can save everything she craves."

The teens sang along like they'd heard this song a thousand times but still liked it.

Olivia sang along with them, faking as best she could and thinking this could be one of the toughest missions she had ever been given.

CHAPTER 9

Emma's Air Canada flight landed in Montreal late that afternoon. She followed the passengers off the plane and headed for the baggage claim. When she had been waiting for her connecting flight in Toronto, Emma called Ryan, and he was so excited she was on her way. Emma acted excited on the phone. But to be honest, she wasn't sure what to feel. Happiness? Excitement? Guilt?

Finally her bag slid down the baggage chute and settled on top of two more pieces of luggage making their third lap around the baggage claim.

Emma leaned over so she could snatch her bag off the belt.

But a man's hand beat her to it. The crowd around her was so thick that Emma couldn't see whom the hand belonged to.

"*Monsieur? Monsieur, my* bag!" Emma called out as she ran over to the area where the bag was taken, but there was no sign of it. and the people around her didn't seem to care.

"Miss?" a male voice asked. "Is this your bag?"

Emma knew it was Ryan even before she turned around. He had a line of stubble running along his strong chin, which made him look adorable, as if his cute dimple in the middle needed help. He was dressed in jeans with a nice polo shirt. She swallowed. Her heart was beating much faster than it should.

"Why yes, that's my bag." she managed to say in a cool, but playful tone.

"I think we need to search this bag."

"It was searched by customs in Toronto."

Ryan walked away with her bag, forcing Emma to chase after him. "But you're in Quebec now, Miss Rothchild. We must make sure you're not bringing anything illegal into the province." Ryan placed her suitcase across a chair and opened it.

"Hey, close that right now," Emma said.

Ryan dug around the contents and pulled out some lacy underwear. "What were you planning to do with these?"

Emma tried to grab it from him but failed.

"Ryan!"

He held it higher. "Tell me. What were you planning to do with these? Seduce our young French-Canadian boys into doing naughty things?"

"Oh my God, everyone's watching us."

Ryan dropped the underwear and picked up some shoes. "How many shoes can you pack? Did you leave any room for pants?"

Emma locked her arms around his, preventing him from going through all her stuff. "I now have you exactly where I want you."

"Is this a trap?" he asked.

"Yes. And I'm the bait."

Ryan hesitated. "I surrender."

Emma pulled him towards her. "Then I accept your surrender."

Their lips drifted closer and closer before Emma—turned her cheek away.

"You'll have to work a little harder to earn that kiss." Emma backed up.

"You look amazing," Ryan's grin shone like the sun. His blue eyes were still beautiful, his white skin a touch darker. He'd had some sun recently. "What changed your mind about coming?"

"I've been getting a lot of heat for communicating with you. Some people inside the Authority are telling me to stop it."

"What did you tell them?"

"That I know you. I know your heart. And I think you can still be saved."

Ryan laughed. "I don't know about that."

"Well, I'm sick of everyone telling me who to see. Who to talk to. If I wanna talk to you, I should be able to. "

"They're scared that I'll turn you."

"No way," Emma said. "I hate everything Venomous stands for, and I still don't understand what you see in it."

"I see opportunity. I see a future. You're seeing this in terms of black and white. Life is gray, Emma. Very gray."

"Can we just hang out and enjoy each other's company? You know, like we did at your father's place in Missouri? I'd like to hang out with that version of Ryan for a while."

"Let's make it our spring break. No school. No work. Only fun. I promise. Only you, me, and a lot of French Canadians." Ryan sealed her luggage back up and carried it. "Are you hungry?"

"Almost, but after sitting on a plane for hours, I'd rather walk around first. Any suggestions?"

Ryan drove Emma to the Montreal neighborhood known as Mile End. The late afternoon weather was gorgeous, so the two of them walked up and down the streets, enjoying all the colorful murals and other beautiful things this neighborhood had to offer. Emma pulled Ryan into a couple of local shops as she bought a few items and made Ryan carry them.

"Do you have room for these things in your luggage?" he asked.

Emma ignored his silly question. She always made room for her shopping conquests. What's the point of buying nice things if you can't bring them home?

"How's your appetite now?"

"I could eat something."

Two blocks later they came upon a small local bagel shop. The sign read *St Viateur*. The aroma of fresh bagels baking in the oven woke up Emma's hunger.

"Have you been in here yet?" she asked.

"Not yet. I've heard their bagels are good, but there are some restaurants up the block," Ryan said.

Emma's mouth watered for a lox and cream cheese bagel, the kind she used to get in New York all the time.

"Or we could eat here," Ryan said.

Emma then realized her foot was already in the doorway of the shop. She went ahead and moved inside. *St Viateur* was basically a small bakery with no dine-in seating. On one side were high stacks of flour ready to be thrown in to the next bagel batch. The other side had display refrigerators containing cream cheese spreads, drinks, and other tasty things that go on top of a bagel. In the middle was a narrow line of people waiting to order.

Emma joined them.

"There's nowhere to sit," Ryan said.

"We'll take it to go." Emma noted the packs of fresh salmon cut into flat strips for bagels. She grabbed one package and some regular cream cheese as she waited. It took a while, but Emma reached the front counter.

"What do you want?" she asked.

Ryan shrugged. "A garlic one, I guess."

Emma tossed Ryan a look.

"What? Do they not have garlic?" he asked.

"You want me to put up with your garlic breath all day?"

Ryan laughed. "How about sesame?"

"Good choice."

The old man behind the counter looked up to her. "*Oui, mademoiselle?*"

"*Bonjour*, two sliced sesame bagels, s'*il vous plaît*," Emma said in French as she flashed a warm smile.

The man put three sesame bagels in the bag and handed it to her. He smiled back with one crooked tooth and winked. "Take an extra one. For tomorrow's breakfast."

"Oh, you don't have to do that."

"When it comes to pretty girls, I can't help myself. Please take it before I give you the entire store." The old man turned to the cashier. "Ring up two bagels."

Emma put down her bag of bagels, cream cheese, and lox of salmon. She offered the woman her gold card.

"I'm sorry. Cash only," the woman said in English.

Emma realized she had forgotten to exchange her American money for Canadian dollars.

"It's on me." Ryan offered the woman the appropriate amount of money before scooping up the cream cheese and salmon. Emma thanked him before grabbing the bagels and a plastic knife.

Outside the bagel shop, they found a wooden street bench near a nice green spot. Emma sniffed her bagel. It was still warm and fresh. She broke out the cream cheese and used the knife to spread it all around her bagel.

"Is that raw?" he asked.

"The salmon?"

Ryan nodded.

"Yup. Are you scared?"

Ryan scoffed. "Set me up, barkeep. I'm not afraid of no fish." He watched Emma prepare both of their bagels. "I wish I knew more French. Luckily there are enough English-speaking Canadians around to help me when I get into trouble."

"How long have you been out here?"

"About a month and a half. I like this city."

"Is this your permanent home now or—?"

"It's kind of temporary," he said. "I rented a place farther up the road."

Emma handed him a bagel all set up with cream cheese and lox, then took a bite of her own. It tasted like heaven. Emma could just close her eyes and see the skyline of New York.

"That's really good."

Emma licked her fingers. "I know, right?"

Her phone rang and Emma checked the screen. It was Grandma Bernadette.

"Oh shit. I totally forgot."

"Forgot what?" Ryan asked.

"I forgot to tell my grandmother. She doesn't know I'm here."

"You didn't tell her you were going to Canada?"

Emma shook her head. "She thinks I'm still at school."

"Wow, Emma."

Emma wiped her mouth with a napkin. "Damn it, I was going to call her in Toronto while I was switching planes, but then I called you and totally forgot."

"My soothing voice is very distracting."

Emma grinned.

"What are you gonna do?" he asked.

Her smile melted. "What else? Tell her the truth and hope she doesn't lock me out of the house." Emma closed her eyes for a moment. Gathered her thoughts. Then pressed the green button on her phone. She did her best to prop up a smile.

"Hi, Grandma! You'll never guess what happened. I was driving to school and Ben Gooden called. He had a four-hundred-dollar airline voucher that was about to expire and he couldn't use it, so he asked me if I wanted to use it, and I said, wow, who have I not visited in a while. Well, I remember this girl who was part of my circle of gal pals in New York, and she recently moved to Montreal. And I was like—I should go visit her! So I took the voucher and got the ticket and I'm now in Montreal. Isn't that crazy, Grandma? It was all so fast, and I didn't have time to get your permission, and I feel bad about that, but I so needed this little mini-vacation, and I promise when I get back home I'll catch up on school and everything, okay?"

She almost forgot.

"I love you."

Ryan mouthed the word WOW.

Emma crossed her fingers and listened for her grandmother's answer.

"Young one—that's the dumbest excuse for skipping school I've ever heard in my life. Are you in the city now? We can meet at Amy's Grill for dinner and you can tell me the real reason you ditched school today."

"Grandma, I'm in Montreal."

"This better be the name of a new coffee place."

"No—um—Montreal, Canada. I'm in Canada right now."

Silence.

"Grandma?"

"Why the hell are you in Canada?"

"I told you. To visit a friend."

"As they say in Arkansas...that dog don't hunt," her grandmother said. "Now what's going on? Is your grandma Laura behind this?"

"I can't say."

"That's it. I've had it. I was looking forward to spending a week alone with my only granddaughter, and Laura won't even allow me that. I'm going to give that woman a piece of my mind."

"Please don't do that, Grandma."

Her grandmother paused. "When will you be back?"

"I don't know when, but I promise we'll have that dinner together soon."

Her grandmother was quiet for what seemed like forever. "All right. Be careful, young one. I love you." She sounded disappointed as if Emma had let her down.

Emma didn't like that feeling at all.

She closed her phone.

"Is she pissed?" Ryan asked.

"I'll make it up to her." Emma bit into her bagel, hoping the cream cheese and salmon would take her mind off disappointing her grandmother. Then she remembered Ryan. "So are you going to stay a high school dropout, or will you get a GED? I mean, does Venomous even have a high school?"

"Why do I need a high school diploma? I'm making money without learning geometry, history, or chemistry. Plus no gym classes. I'd say that's a win. I don't see why you're going to school. Once your father's trust fund kicks in...you'll be filthy rich."

"I want to be more than some rich girl. I want to do something to help people. And to do that I need an education. There's a lot I don't know."

Ryan scoffed. "You don't need college to learn about the world. Abraham Lincoln educated himself through books. He never went to college. You can study anything you want to online. College is bullshit."

"My grandmother says you can lose all your money, but you can never lose an education."

"Says the woman who's a college professor."

"Well, I'm going to college. Even if it's a waste of money. It's my money to waste."

"Says the girl who's been given everything in her life."

Emma stopped eating.

Ryan shifted in his chair. "That came out wrong."

"Sounded pretty clear to me."

Ryan paused. "I'm a little resentful. Not towards you just—my father—I wish things were different."

Emma remembered when Ryan's father had cut him out of his inheritance. Then, when he went to prison for his plot to starve millions of people, Ryan's father committed suicide. The Raymond Foods financial empire was broken up and seized by various governments, leaving Ryan and his mother with nothing.

"Where are you sleeping tonight?" Ryan asked.

"I made reservations."

Emma hadn't, but how hard would it be to find a hotel room in a city like this?

Ryan used a napkin to clean his hands of cream cheese. "My place is just up the road from here." He took another bite of his bagel.

Emma froze. Did Ryan want her to? Just like that? It felt too casual. Shouldn't their first time be special? Or at least, more serious? Couldn't Ryan at least be more romantic about it? Like they do in the movies?

No way. Not now. Emma wasn't ready yet.

"I'm not sleeping with you," she blurted out.

Ryan choked on his bagel. His eyes watered before he could wash it down with his drink. "Shit, I'm sorry. That's not what I meant. I mean—you can have my bed and I'll sleep on the couch. The one in the living room."

"Oh—sorry. I guess—yeah, that would be okay."

Emma followed Ryan up the stairs to his second-story condo. Once inside, Emma freshened up and changed into something more casual before flopping down on his couch. Ryan played some music. It was the Beatles of course. He retreated into the kitchen, took out two beers from the fridge, and popped them open. He offered one to Emma. She didn't want it, but took it from him anyway. There was a red maple leaf on the bottle.

Ryan offered a toast. "To new beginnings."

Emma clicked her bottle to his. And drank. The beer was smooth and not that bad.

Ryan sat on the couch with her. He talked about Montreal. How European it felt. How the locals treated people who didn't speak perfect French, yet despite this he liked the city. Emma asked him again why he was living here.

"There were some operations that needed my help. That's all I can say," Ryan said. "How was Africa?"

"What are you talking about?"

"I heard you and the girls stirred up some trouble."

"Oh my God, are you helping terrorists now, Ryan?" Emma stood up. "Because if you are, I'll go to a hotel right now."

"Relax."

"I'm serious."

"I'm not helping terrorists," Ryan said. "Venomous has people everywhere. The word circling around is that a group of teen girls basically unleashed chaos on this terrorist camp in Namibia. As you know, there's only one group that fits that description."

Emma sat back down. "I can't answer your question. It's classified."

Ryan smiled.

"How's your mom doing? Is she still in Wichita?" Emma asked.

"She's okay. I call her once in a while to check up."

"Are you still sending her money?"

"Every month. About half of what I make," Ryan said.

"Half?"

"Venomous pays very well. I'm seventeen and make three times as much as some forty-year-old guy who works in an office."

"I bet he has more humility."

Ryan took a swig of his beer and studied her. "You know, we're more alike than you're giving us credit for."

"How so?"

"We both come from money. We appreciate and understand it more than some people do."

"But you should never flaunt that money in front of people," Emma said. "We should be considerate towards people who aren't as fortunate as us."

"That's your grandmother talking."

"No, my father said the same thing. He didn't want money to define who he was. And neither do I."

"Face it, Emma. We were born into privilege. We have a huge head start on everyone else. Even though my dad took my inheritance away, I was still able to use my position—my privilege —to make a deal with Venomous. Now I'm making serious money from all the contacts I know," Ryan said. "So don't call out my privilege—or humility as you called it—when you just bought a one-thousand-dollar plane ticket to ditch school and go to Montreal just so you could hang out with a guy."

CHAPTER 10

That morning, Emma woke up in Ryan's bed. But without Ryan, who slept on the living room couch like he promised. She yawned and stripped the covers from the bed as she stumbled over to the window. Emma pulled apart the curtains and took in the city of Montreal in all its old-town glory. Ryan's place was deep in the city center itself, so Emma could see people walking and riding their bikes.

A strong baking-bread smell wafted into the room, causing Emma's stomach to rumble. She opened up her baggage, found some sweats and a T-shirt, then stepped out of the bedroom.

Emma found a shirt-less Ryan in his small kitchen, frowning at a smoldering tray of four burned pieces of dough that he must have taken out of the oven.

"Was that our breakfast?" she asked.

"That was the plan. I keep forgetting the oven settings here are in Celsius, not Fahrenheit," he said. "Did you sleep well?" Ryan's smile returned. His muscular forearms and bare chest were tight.

"So you didn't sleep well?" he repeated.

Emma realized she was gawking at him. "I did sleep well. Your bed is very soft."

Ryan took her in. Emma suddenly felt naked, but she knew she wasn't. Maybe she was being too self-conscious with a boy who was already half-naked.

"You look amazing," he said.

Emma then realized she had no make-up on. Hadn't taken a shower yet. Her hair was a mess. And she was wearing sweatpants. She was supposed to be seducing Ryan by looking sexy and gorgeous. By becoming a fantasy girl he would do anything for. It was a mistake to come out of his bedroom looking like a lazy college freshman.

"No, I don't look amazing. I just got up. I look awful. I'll go change."

"Stop it. Your face is naturally beautiful. You don't need the makeup."

"Now you're messing with me."

"No, I'm not. Girls think they need all this makeup to look great, but most of the time it's overkill."

"You're not a woman, Ryan. I hate to break this to you, but most of the time we look good to make ourselves feel good. It has nothing to do with impressing the guys."

Ryan thought about that. "Liar."

"What?"

"What about yesterday? Your hair. That tight dress you wore. The heels. The red lipstick. You were hitting the right keys on my piano. And you knew it."

Emma tried her best not to smile. "Did you make any coffee?"

Ryan grinned. "You know what? Since I can't cook, let's go out for breakfast. My treat."

Ryan took Emma to a part of the old town section of Montreal. The outdoor café had a ring of plants surrounding the perimeter. Ryan addressed the hostess in his butchered version of French, which the lady did manage to interpret and escorted them to a table. When their server arrived, Emma took over the language reins and ordered them breakfast in French.

"Are you from Paris?" the server asked in French. "Your accent is very pronounced."

"Is it? When I was younger, I stayed in Paris for a few summers. I must have soaked up the accent there."

"*Non*, you're American? Oh, your French is excellent. I knew you weren't a native Québécois. However, I did think you were from Europe. Ah, that explains the American boyfriend."

"His French isn't so good," Emma said.

The man made a face. "He comes in all the time and his French is atrocious. Tell him to use English. Montreal is a bilingual city. When he butchers our language, he's insulting all Québécois. Please tell him to stop."

Emma laughed.

"I understood some of that," Ryan said with a frown.

"I will bring your coffee, *mademoiselle*," the server said.

Soon they were drinking coffee and eating fresh croissants that were excellent. On a par with some of the French bakeries Emma remembered in Paris. She talked to Ryan about school and her classes and about Kayla, a new friend who had transferred in earlier that year.

"What do you want to do today?" Ryan said. "There's some historic sites that we can walk to from here."

"Historic sites? Sounds exciting."

"Then what do you want to do?"

Emma could tell her sarcasm was a little too strong. Besides, she was flexible today, and if that's what Ryan wanted to do…

"You know, it's a nice day for a walk, so let's go learn some history," she said.

Emma and Ryan walked down St. Paul Road, one of the cobbled streets of old Montreal. Ryan offered his hand and Emma took it.

"If you want to, we could rent a couple of bikes and ride along the mile district later," he said. "There's a lot of local shops, art places, and street murals to see there."

"You had me at local shops," Emma said. "Sounds fun. And I mean that."

"Up the hill there's a fort that played a role in the American Revolutionary war. Did you know that we invaded Canada?"

"Why did we do that?"

"You'll find out in a series of thrilling historical plaques they put near these thrilling historical buildings," Ryan said.

That made Emma smile. Her smile lasted only a block when Ryan released her hand and took out a digital music player with ear-buds.

He offered one of the buds to Emma. "Some music to pass the time?"

Emma remembered the lake and how Ryan had introduced her to the Beatles. He played all of their albums and they listened for hours. Together. Enjoying the connection that two human beings had to one piece of music. It was magical.

Emma pushed the earbud into her right ear. Ryan did the same for his left. His thumb selected a few musical choices and hit play. Suddenly Emma's ear was assaulted with the hardest, loudest, most foul noise called music she had ever heard. Emma wasn't sure if it was punk rock. Hard rock. Skater rock. But whatever it was, she hated it.

Then the music stopped.

"What the hell was that?" Emma asked. "Are you trying to make me go deaf?"

Ryan only laughed. "I couldn't resist messing with you. How about some John Lennon, post Beatles?" Ryan switched the music files. Soon John Lennon's beautiful voice sang over a piano. His words about being a dreamer. And that he wasn't the only one. The music made Emma sway back and forth with every step as Lennon's voice took over her thoughts. It was a nice surrender. Like she was gliding off the earth and floating to a more loving and peaceful world.

She then felt Ryan pulling her off the street and into a tourist shop filled with *I love Montreal* T-shirts, mugs, and bumper stickers. He pulled out his earbud and looked worried.

Emma took hers out as well. "What's going on?"

"Someone's tailing us. A white man wearing a Montreal Canadiens hockey cap. Five foot eight. Khaki shorts," Ryan said. "Did you tell anyone that you were coming here?"

"Only my grandmother. But she just assumes it's another mission, so she wouldn't say anything."

"Maybe your people found out."

Emma knew Mrs. B wouldn't put a live tail on her because of this very reason. They wouldn't want to spook Ryan.

"What if your people are watching us?" she asked.

"That's a possibility. Could also be the CIA."

"Why would the CIA be following you?"

"I stole some money from them," Ryan said.

"Seriously?"

"It was only a half million dollars, but the CIA extorted it from this wealthy Indian man who was selling North Korean weapons on the black market. Venomous owed the guy a favor, so we got his money back with a hefty service fee attached."

"And you've been living off this hefty service fee?" Emma asked.

"Asset One let me keep half of it. For him, that's very generous."

"So it must be the CIA."

"Maybe. Could also be the Canadian CSIS."

"Oh my God, Ryan. Anyone else that you've pissed off since I last talked to you?"

"Nah, that's about it."

"What do you want to do?"

"I want to spend the day alone with you. Minus the audience," Ryan said. "I could have you leave first and see if he follows you."

"If we split up, that'll tip him off that we know he's tailing us," Emma said. "Is there a bus stop near here?"

"Yeah, there's one close by. But the guy would just follow us on board."

"Good. That's what I'm counting on. Just follow me closely and do exactly what I do." Emma held Ryan's hand and went back outside. As they continued walking down St. Paul road, Emma used the glass windows of the many stores they passed by to check behind her. She could see the man with the khaki shorts and the Montreal Canadiens hat at a distance. Ryan was right. He was tailing them.

Emma and Ryan soon came upon a bus stop with four people already waiting.

"How much is the fare?" she asked.

Ryan had some Canadian coins in his hand. He whispered, "I'll get both our fares. I still don't see what prevents our shadow from joining us on the bus."

"Ryan, what did I say?"

"Do exactly what you do."

She patted him on the cheek. "Good boy."

Emma and Ryan stood in line for the bus. Emma casually scanned the windows across the street, checking their reflections for any sign that their tail was still behind them. However, Emma didn't see him. The man had disappeared. Emma didn't rejoice. She knew he was still somewhere. Still watching. Still waiting. Emma wondered if that man had ever taken the New York subway.

"What do you plan to do?" Ryan whispered.

"Do you trust me?"

"Yeah."

"Wow. That sounded confident."

"Yes. I trust you."

"Better," she said.

The bus came into view as it made a turn and lumbered down the street.

Emma squeezed Ryan's hand. The bus groaned to a stop as the brakes made one final belch of air. Emma followed the four people on board. Once she reached the driver, Emma paused until Ryan put in both fares before continuing deep into the interior of the bus. There were quite a few empty seats available, but she didn't sit down. Emma reached the second door near the rear wheels and stopped. She held on to the standing-room only bar. Ryan reached her and did the same.

"It won't work."

Emma ignored him. She peeked over at the other door. No sign of their tail.

The bus idled as it waited for more passengers. But no one came on.

The driver released the parking brake.

Finally the man with the khaki shorts jumped on board and put in his fare.

"Get ready," Emma warned.

As the man took a few steps back into the bus—

Emma jumped out of the open rear door. She ran behind the bus, then circled around it from the opposite side before running back up the front steps again.

"*Bonjour!* We already paid," Emma said to the driver in French before she dived into an empty seat. To her relief, Ryan slid in next to her.

"What the hell was that?" he asked.

The doors closed as the bus pulled away from the stop. Emma peeked out the window. The man in khaki shorts appeared bewildered as his eyes scanned the area for them.

"Well, I don't believe it," Ryan said.

"He'll figure it out eventually. But that gives us enough time to get off at the next stop, circle back to get your car, and go somewhere more secluded."

"Have I told you yet?"

"Told me what?" Emma asked.

"That you're amazing." Ryan leaned in and kissed her on the cheek.

The kiss shot through Emma like electricity, making every part of her body quiver.

She still held it together. "I know."

The buzz from the kiss lasted until the next bus stop, where Emma and Ryan got off. Holding hands again, the couple walked down the next street.

"So where did you learn that neat trick?" Ryan asked.

Emma smiled to herself. "Back in New York, my friends and I would play our version of chicken by hopping on and off the subway right before it was about to leave the station. Once in a while, a girl would get stranded and we'd have to get off at the next stop and walk back. Then we'd do it again."

"That sounds—so dumb."

"Whatever. It just saved your butt from the CIA."

"That it did."

About fifty feet in front of them, the doors of a parked Mercedes swung open as two large boulders disguised as men blocked the sidewalk.

Emma tensed up immediately.

Ryan pulled Emma behind him as his testosterone kicked in to protect his female. But from what Emma saw, Ryan would need help with these goons.

Emma heard something skid to a stop behind her. She turned to see the man with khaki shorts get off a bicycle. Emma faced the new threat. The two of them were now surrounded.

Emma's mind went into self-defense mode, sizing up her attacker and reminding herself about all the things that she could do to him that would be most unpleasant, hopefully giving her and Ryan enough time to escape.

"I've got your back," she said.

Ryan shot a look at the khaki man. "Let them take me. I don't want to get you involved."

"It's kind of late for requests."

One of the human boulders talked. "Together, our venom strikes as one."

Ryan relaxed his stance. "And the one serves the many." Ryan put his hand on Emma's shoulder. "Stand down."

"Why?"

"Because these are *my* people."

That revelation didn't comfort Emma at all. She kept her fighting stance.

"Why are you following me?" Ryan asked the men.

"Asset One is always watching, young brother. You are being

summoned."

Ryan sighed as he faced Emma. "Apparently my spring break from Venomous has ended. I might not be back for a while." He took out his keys and offered them to Emma. "You can stay at my apartment for as long as you want. Just lock up when you leave. Do you remember where my car is?"

The boulder man swiped the keys from Ryan's hand. "She is being summoned as well."

"What, why?"

"I do not have that information."

"She's my guest. I want her to be left alone."

"That choice is not permitted."

CHAPTER 11

At the Oregon campsite, members of Heart the E queued up for breakfast. This morning it was scrambled tofu eggs, more rice, veggies, wheat toast, and coffee. Olivia had to borrow Gabi's hot sauce again, and even Miyuki found the tofu eggs disgusting, sticking with the rice and veggies only.

Olivia watched Nadia from a distance as she approached Cody and some older young adults eating at a picnic table under one of the log shelters. Soon Nadia was invited to sit down and eat with them. Olivia was proud of her. The old Nadia would be too shy to approach a target like that without Olivia or one of the other Gems there to boost her confidence. Now she was doing it all on her own.

"How well did you two sleep?" Gabi asked.

Olivia had tracked Gabi down that morning to borrow her hot sauce. The girl decided to stay and eat with them.

"I slept like a baby leopard," Miyuki said.

"Me too," Olivia said. "It helps that it's so cool up here at night, makes me what to snuggle inside my sleeping bag."

"Last week it rained while we were setting up the camp," Gabi said. "Reminded me of Costa Rica during the rainy season. I'm used to the wet and the humidity, but not the cold."

After everyone had breakfast, Cody once again took to the stage with his guitar.

"Are we loving this beautiful morning?" he asked.

Some campers cheered.

"Makes it great to be alive, doesn't it?" Cody asked. "We have a lot to do today. We're planting hundreds of trees this morning for the good people of Portland. Then this afternoon we'll be visiting a wildlife rehabilitation shelter. Then when we get back here, I'll have a big surprise tonight that you'll love. But to start this day off

71

right. . .let's sing a song."

The campers cheered again.

Olivia gritted her teeth. Not another bloody song.

"How about 'Mother Nature's Son?'" Cody asked the campers.

"We love that!" they warmly responded.

Later that morning, Olivia followed most of the five hundred plus Heart the E members as they climbed aboard a fleet of busses. It took about forty-five minutes for the busses to reach Portland, and they pulled into a large city park that overlooked a major highway. A few city municipal trucks were already parked there with rows of tiny trees sitting on their rear beds. Some city workers organized a pile of shovels and picks, and a bulldozer sat near a pile of dirt.

The teens and young adults poured out of the busses, and Cody carried a portable loudspeaker.

"Is this not awesome?" he asked them. "We bought the trees, and the city is supplying us with these tools so we can plant them ourselves."

Olivia scanned the grassy park. Most of it was open and facing the highway. Planting a bunch of trees here would block out most of the traffic and add a little patch of forest in this otherwise urban area. To Olivia it seemed like a nice idea.

Miyuki handed her a shovel. Olivia took it and followed her to one of the trucks.

A city worker carefully handed her a small tree. "Can you carry that all by yourself?"

Two boys stepped in and offered to help her. Miyuki thanked them with a nod, and the three of them carried the tree to a yellow marker that indicated where each tree needed to be planted. Once they set the tree down, Olivia positioned her shovel into the ground, placed her foot on the top, and put her weight down, breaking the ground. With the help of the two boys, Olivia had a nice hole dug in the ground.

"Close, but it needs to be deeper." Gabi measured it with a wooden yard-stick. "About one more foot should do it."

"You heard her," Olivia told the boys in a strong Spanish accent.

The boys went to digging immediately.

Gabi stepped over to Olivia. "The way you order those boys

around—you'd make a good work foreman."

"I like to get things done right. Otherwise, what's the point?"

"I couldn't agree more."

Miyuki came up to them with her hands held up in mock surrender. "They're not letting me do any work."

"You two girls have them trained well," Gabi said.

Miyuki giggled. "Hey, what is the big surprise tonight? The one Cody was talking about this morning?"

"My lips are sworn to secrecy."

"Please? I'm very nosy."

"It's not a surprise if I tell you," Gabi said.

"Write it in the dirt and I'll cover it with my shovel," Olivia said.

"I'm not talking."

"Are you Cody's go-to girl?"

"We're not dating," Gabi said. "If that's where you're going with that."

"I'm not implying anything. Only an observation," Olivia said. "He trusts you a lot."

"Is there a reason he shouldn't trust me?"

"You have insulted her, Camila," Miyuki said with a grin.

"Wasn't my intention," Olivia said. "I suppose I'm jealous because Cody is so amazing and you're in his inner circle."

Gabi laughed. "Cody feels like we all are in his inner circle, but I am his go-to girl. Now he does have a few trusted people who work in the main office, but most of the rank and file are kids just like us. Some volunteers have been with Cody since he started organizing the conferences. But still—Cody is an open book. He wants everyone to feel special."

"That's a beautiful way to say it," Miyuki said.

"How did you get involved with Heart the E?" Gabi asked Miyuki.

She told Gabi her cover story, which centered on a friend from China who had seen an on-line chat Cody did on Utube. While Miyuki and Gabi were talking, Olivia watched Nadia and Cody walking alone, both engaged in some kind of deep discussion as the two of them drifted away from the crowds of teens planting trees. Hopefully Cody was giving Nadia a lot of useful information.

So far, everything was going according to plan, something that always made Olivia happy.

That afternoon the fleet of busses descended on the parking lot of a wildlife refuge and rehab center. The park was closed for the day so Heart the E could have it all to themselves.

Olivia and the other members followed Cody to a small outdoor amphitheater, it was a tight fit but they managed to stuff everyone inside it. Cody introduced the woman in charge of the wildlife refuge. She came out with a dozen wildlife workers who had various animals with them. The woman took over the presentation, explaining what they did with the animals that were brought into them. They took out a ten-foot python that required two workers to hold it.

"I love that!" Cody shouted.

Everyone laughed and clapped their hands.

As they were bringing out a tiger to show, Olivia felt her pocket buzz. She glanced down at her phone and noticed three words.

Ladies bathroom now.

Olivia leaned over to Miyuki. "Nadia wants me to meet her. Stay here."

Miyuki nodded.

"Excuse me," Olivia whispered as she stood up. The teens in her row made way for her as Olivia slipped out of the amphitheater.

As she turned a corner, Olivia almost slammed into Gabi.

"Whoa. Close call." Gabi carried two full canvas bags.

"What's that?"

Gabi set the bags down and took out a key chain. "Hundreds of wildlife refuge key chains and square buttons."

"Is this all for us?"

Gabi sighed. "Yes. Cody didn't have the heart to tell the owner we're not a bunch of eight-year-olds. He did refuse the free coloring books though."

"Coloring books? That's loco."

"They mean well. Anyway, I need to distribute these to everyone. Do you want to help?"

"Sorry, but I'm on my way to the toilet. Maybe after?"

"I'll do it when we board the busses. Help me then?"

"*Sí.*"

Gabi moved out of the way so Olivia could enter the ladies' bathroom.

Olivia scanned under the stalls for feet.

"I'm over here." Nadia stood in a corner near the sinks.

Olivia joined her. She kept her voice low. "How's it going with Cody? Saw you spending a lot of time with him today."

"He's very open," Nadia said. "For a boy, I was surprised. Cody is passionate about the environment. Taking care of nature. Reducing our footprint on the world. He's vegan. Practices with his guitar every night. Reads a lot of books about biology and nature. Personally practices non-violence. And despite his aloof appearance, he's not naive or stupid. From what I can tell, his intent seems quite genuine. I don't think any of this is an act. He truly believes in what he's doing."

"So what would Venomous want with Cody or his group? As far as the information Mrs. B gave us, his organization is a non-profit."

"Perhaps they're stealing money from it. Remember what Dr. Yes was doing at Avondale?"

"Another money-laundering front?" Olivia asked. "It's possible. That means we need to be checking the people who run the business side of his organization. Have you seen any of them here?"

"According to Cody, most of them never come to the retreats or conferences."

"I wonder why."

"Maybe I can look into that. Cody and I seem to be bonding well."

"I noticed that," Olivia said. "Well done, by the way."

"He does all the talking. I only listen."

"Well, keep it up. then. You're doing a great job. We'll rely on you to get more intelligence on Cody's office staff. Let us know if you need help."

Nadia thanked her and left the bathroom.

Olivia waited about ten minutes before leaving and joining Miyuki inside the amphitheater.

"You miss the baby rhino. It was so cute," Miyuki said. "How was the bathroom?"

"I'll tell you at dinner."

"I'm already hungry. Do you know what we're having?"

Olivia frowned. "Probably some type of grilled plant."

That night, their dinner was a choice of either a garden vegetable burger or a black bean burger grilled with all the fixings. Olivia and Miyuki both chose the black bean burger and found an open spot on one of the large tables. At least the seasoned French fries were surprisingly good and helped Olivia stomach the black bean burger. Miyuki lathered her fries in ketchup.

Nadia passed by their table with a garden vegetable burger, but she didn't acknowledge Olivia or Miyuki as she sat down with some of Cody's volunteers at another table.

Everyone at dinner was talking about the day. How awesome the wildlife refuge was and all the trees that were planted that day. Then there was a vegan chocolate cake brought out. At first Olivia didn't want to try it, figuring it tasted like grass. But Miyuki brought her a piece of it anyway. The moment Olivia tasted it, she was hooked. It was the best chocolate cake she had ever eaten.

"This is vegan?" Olivia asked.

Miyuki licked her lips. "Isn't it delicious? I want to find out how they make the icing so good."

As the Heart the E campers devoured their dessert, Gabi finally showed up to dinner. She grabbed the last garden vegetable burger on the warmer and finished off the last portion of the fries.

Olivia waved her over to them. "Where have you been? I've been looking for you everywhere."

Gabi sat down. "I had to do a last minute run to the airport." Gabi stuffed some fries in her mouth. "I'm starving."

"Who did you pick up?"

"Cody's big surprise. Their flight was canceled in London, so they had to change some flights around."

Cody climbed up on the stage. "How was that cake? Good, wasn't it."

A few cheers.

"That cake was made by Gwen Lefferts from her grandmother's recipe. Stand up, Gwen!"

A young woman stood up.

"Give her a cheer!"

The campers did what Cody said.

"Thank you for the cake, Gwen!" Cody pulled up his guitar again. "How about some music?"

A few more cheers.

Olivia forced herself not to roll her eyes in front of Gabi. Cody's songs were getting on her nerves.

Cody began one of his more familiar songs about white rabbits when he suddenly stopped. "Oh crap. I almost forgot about tonight's surprise. Do you want me to give it to you now, or after I sing?"

"Give it to us now!" some teens yelled back.

"I love that. Okay. We have two fellow Heart the E members who just came all the way from Europe. And I think you know them well because all this year they've been on my Utube channel, and they've done a huge amount of work for our movement around the world." Cody paused for effect. "I'll give you a hint. They both have red hair. They're both Irish. And they both are the most feisty couple of girls you'll ever meet."

A few girls shrieked with excitement.

Olivia didn't get it. Who were they so excited about?

"That's right, Deirdre and Fiona are here!" Cody yelled. "The Maguire sisters."

Olivia froze as identical twins Bridget and Sophia O'Malley jumped on-stage with Cody. They looked different from the girls Olivia remembered from New Zealand. They were more casually dressed than the school uniforms they'd had to wear at Avondale. They also wore the bare minimum amount of makeup on their pale faces. However, Olivia could identify their dark eyes and fiery-red hair.

"What's up Oregon!" the sisters said in unison, driving the young crowd crazy. They both smiled and waved as a crowd of members formed around the stage. To them, these girls were like rock stars.

"Who wants to kick ass for Mother Earth?" Bridget asked through the microphone in an Irish accent.

"Heart the E ya bitches!" Sophia yelled.

The young members cheered and screamed for the twins.

"We're both so thrilled to be back here," Bridget said. "Our poor father was ill so we had to make sure he was well before we rushed back here to be with our friends from around the world."

"We love ya. Honest to G," Sophia yelled.

"Fiona and I wanna try a piece of Gwen's cake while Cody leads us all in his guitar awesomeness," Bridget said. "Then Fiona and I have some things we wanna speak to ya about. Are ya ready to have a good time tonight?"

The entire campsite cheered.

Olivia felt a hand on top of hers. It was Miyuki her eyes looked worried. And if Olivia could look at a mirror, she was positive that her eyes would look worried too. Their simple intelligence mission just became more complicated.

CHAPTER 12

There was a dank, foul smell that lingered around this place. Wherever this place was.

Emma remembered being put into a van and driven to a house where the goons tied up Ryan's and Emma's hands before covering their eyes with blindfolds. Then they were back in the van and drove for maybe a couple of hours to whereever this place was.

Emma called out to Ryan, but if he was there, he wasn't answering.

Her mind flooded with questions. *What was going on? Weren't these Ryan's people? Why were they doing this?*

A door opened and footsteps slapped against the floor, which judging by the echo, told Emma that it was a concrete floor. A chair scraped across that floor before the person in question sat down.

"Hello, is someone there?" she asked.

"Yes," a man's voice answered.

"Where's Ryan?"

"He's irrelevant now. You should be more worried about me."

Emma's heart pounded faster.

The male voice continued. "I'm going to ask you some questions. Please answer them as completely as possible. Do you understand?"

"I think so."

"Do you understand?" the man yelled.

"Yes," Emma replied.

The man's voice relaxed. "Where is the Authority station in California located?"

Emma slowed her breathing and focused. She did have some interrogation training, but it was mostly on how to ask the questions, not how to lie about the answers.

"I have no clue," she said.

"That's a lie. You report and receive orders from your superiors there. Where is it located?"

"I can't tell you. It's a secret."

A quick electric shock went through Emma's body.

"Oh my God, did you just shock me?"

"Answer the question."

"I can't."

Another shock went through her body. It was a tad longer and it burned.

"Stop it."

"Answer the question and I will."

Emma hesitated.

"Are you refusing?"

"Wait a minute." She paused. "Fine, it's on Alcatraz Island. Or I should say it's under the island."

"San Francisco Bay. Where the old prison is located?"

"Yes." Emma knew it was a lie. But it was something they would have to check out first. If it stopped another shock, it was worth the risk.

"What's the name of the woman who runs that Authority station?" the man asked.

"Mrs. B."

"Describe her features."

"She's old. Very fat. Has giant horn-rimmed glasses and wears clothes that have cats all over them."

That totally did not describe Mrs. B, but Emma thought she sold it well.

"Where did you relocate the robot boy named Robert and his friends?" the man asked.

"Some place in Russia. Siberia, I think."

"Can you be more specific?"

"I don't speak Russian, so I can't remember what the name of the stupid town was."

"Do you wish to take a break now?"

"Yes, please," she said.

"No, we will continue," the man said.

"A-hole," Emma mumbled.

"What was that?"

"May I have some water?"

"No, we will continue," the man said. "Who are the Gems? Give me their real names, and tell me everything you know about each girl."

"I want some water first."

Emma felt another jolt. It made her cry out.

"We will continue. Answer the question."

"I met this group of girls at the mall. They love to go shopping. And we also love hanging out and doing each other's hair. Plus we love watching *The Bachelor*. Have you seen that show? At first, you think it'll be stupid, but as you watch it—"

"Answer my question," the male voice said with agitation.

"I'm getting to that," Emma said. "So each girl has these special talents, right? Emerald makes great pancakes. She makes them with these little peanut butter chips. . .oh my God. They're delicious. Oh, and Sapphire can do this weird thing with her tongue—"

Pain shot up Emma's back and radiated through her arms. This was a long burst and it felt like it was burning her neurons.

Emma had to take a moment.

"I strongly suggest you stop playing around and get right to the point," the man said.

Her limbs hurt. Her legs hurt. Her neck hurt. She felt a tear trying to escape her eye. A part of her wanted to give in. It would be easy to just tell him the truth. But Emma knew she couldn't. That if she did, it would not only put her friends in danger, but her grandmother as well.

She sat up in her chair and braced for it. "My code name is Black Opal. The code names for the other Gems are Emerald, Ruby, and Sapphire. They all come from different places and different backgrounds. We are a team. We are one. We do not turn on one another because we love one another. Our names don't matter. Our families don't matter. Our past doesn't matter. What matters is our commitment to each other and the world we serve. And because of that, my answer for you is fuck off." Emma tensed up, ready for the incredible shock that would rip into her body and make her scream.

But it didn't come.

The man went on. "What are your intentions towards Ryan?"

"I don't understand the question. We're just friends," Emma said. "Friendship, I guess?"

"Are you here to recruit him?"

Yes, Emma thought.

"No. I came out to hang out with him," she said. "He's a cute guy."

"Do you love him?" the man asked.

"I don't hate him."

"Have you had sex with him?"

"None of your business."

"Would you die for him?" the man asked.

Emma thought about that. It depended on the circumstances. If Ryan was trying to do the right thing by saving puppies from a burning building, then of course she would risk her life to save him. But if he was lighting the fire himself—

"Yes," she said.

With some reservations.

"Describe the head of Tokyo station. What does Mr. E look like?"

Emma settled in. This man wouldn't be going anywhere for a long time.

CHAPTER 13

Olivia thought today was actually fun. In the morning, the non-US members of Heart the E took their turns through a ropes course, and Olivia was surprised at how much she enjoyed it. However, the ropes course was easy for a girl who had already completed her training on the Authority's rigorous agility course that was modeled after British, Russian, and American special forces. Still, Olivia enjoyed helping and encouraging the other girls through the course, which was no doubt difficult for them.

Miyuki loved swinging through the ropes course so much that Olivia had to tell her to stop. Many of the girls had never done this before including Miyuki's alias.

"I can't help it," Miyuki whispered. "I was trained to be a gymnast, so my body loves to swing around things. I think I'm part monkey because I do love bananas." Miyuki then did a spectacular leap to grab a rope—and missed it. She fell into the safety net.

When the girls helped her out of it, Miyuki said to them, "I shouldn't have done that. Too confident. Don't do what I did." Miyuki lowered her head in embarrassment, but then managed a quick wink towards Olivia.

The afternoon was more chill. Olivia, Miyuki, and Gabi carried one of the campground's canoes out to the nearby lake. The water was calm as they floated out on the water, enjoying the cloudy skies and the cool wind coming off the water. Their conversation weaved from mothers to boys to Mexican soap operas and finally back to boys again.

"Cody is so cute and tall. And that smile. I could eat him up," Miyuki said.

Olivia made a face. "Oh my God, Cho. I can't believe you said that."

"You don't think so?"

Gabi laughed. "What? Do you not think Cody is hot, Camila?"

Olivia could see why girls would be drawn to Cody with his easy-going style and friendly personality along with his blond hair and hazel eyes. But honestly, Cody wasn't an introvert like Lewis was. She kinda had a weakness for the quiet boy who was comfortable with himself and didn't have to act up to make himself confident.

"Wow, girl, you're thinking hard."

Olivia snapped out of it. "Cody's a nice guy and I like him, but not in that way."

"Who's your ideal guy?" Gabi asked.

"I like the quiet ones. The guy who opens up to you and only you. It makes me feel special."

"But you're not the quiet type."

"Opposites can attract," Miyuki said.

"Opposites can drive each other loco too. I know. Just ask my last boyfriend," Gabi said. "That was a mistake."

A thought crossed Olivia's mind and she went with it. "Do you think Cody and one of those Maguire sisters are—you know?"

"Making passionate love in their tents?" Gabi asked with a grin.

Miyuki gasped and covered her mouth.

"I think so," Gabi said.

"Oh, yeah?"

"Yeah, there's something off about those two girls. I don't know if it's an identical twin thing or what but—they're so passionate about the environment, which is great, but they're so radical. Cody is a let's-live-in-peace kind of guy. But since those girls have come into the movement, Cody has been more open to doing not-so-peaceful things."

"Like what?" Olivia asked.

"Some Heart the E kids in Germany broke into a zoo and released some animals. Can you believe that? These poor animals are let go inside some strange human metropolis. They don't belong there. I don't know what those kids were thinking. If they were smart, they would have loaded them on a truck and released them back into their natural habitat. At least then those animals would have a chance to survive," Gabi said. "Still, these kids claimed that Bridget and Sophia put them up to it, but the girls denied it, and the German authorities couldn't find any evidence to charge them."

"And Cody believed them?" Olivia asked.

"Of course he did. But it wasn't just that. They've done other things like get kids to throw pies in the faces of EU politicians who oppose environmental legislation. Encourage kids to chain themselves to the entrance gates of power plants. Things like that."

"And Cody never did things like that before?"

"You've seen Cody. He loves singing songs, planting trees, and promoting an earth-friendly lifestyle. The only rallies or protests he ever went to were the ones organized by other groups. Wildlife rescue programs—that's right up Cody's alley. But the other things —" Gabi turned to Miyuki. "You heard about what happened in China, right? I've heard that was the twins idea too."

"What thing that happened in China?" Miyuki asked.

"The Xian Wi incident? The one with the tiger?"

Miyuki acted lost.

"How do you not know about that?" Gabi asked. "It was a huge scandal in China."

To Olivia, it was obvious that Miyuki had only skimmed the Heart the E information package that Mrs. B gave them all to study. And that mistake was about to blow her cover.

Olivia had to jump in. "Xian Wi was a Chinese industrialist visiting Australia to open a new joint Australian-Chinese manufacturing plant. When he went to his luxury hotel suite, he found a live tiger there. How the hell anyone got a tiger inside there, I have no idea. But they did, and this poor man had to lock himself in the bathroom while the hungry animal tried to break down the door and eat him."

"Why would the twins do that?" Miyuki asked. "How is that saving the environment?"

"It was a stunt," Gabi said. "Like everything else they do. It's to draw attention to the cause."

"What happened to the poor kitty?"

"They shot it," Gabi said. "That's what made me angry. What right do we have to sacrifice one animal to save other animals? It doesn't make sense."

Miyuki checked her phone. "We should be heading back to camp."

"Can you do me a favor?" Gabi asked. "Don't mention anything that we talked about here. It's only between friends. I don't want Cody to think I'm spreading rumors."

That afternoon, Olivia and Miyuki split up. Miyuki tagged along with a group of Korean and Vietnamese members who wanted to do a nature walk together. This left Olivia free to wander around the campsite. She noticed Nadia with a group of kids playing the card game UNO at one of the picnic tables. Olivia wandered over and found a place to sit down and watch. Soon one guy had to leave and offered his playing spot to Olivia. Now Nadia dealt the group a new hand. Olivia had a draw four card. She waited until just the right moment to slap it down.

"You awful person," Nadia said with a smile as she had to draw four more cards from the deck when she only had one left to play.

Once they finished that UNO game, the group started another.

Soon Gabi came by and began watching. "How do you play this game?"

Olivia had Gabi sit next to her as she explained the game to her.

"I love UNO!" Cody said, standing over them.

"Would you like to join us?" Nadia asked.

"I'll just watch," he said. "Are you all enjoying the camp?" Several yeses went around the table. "There's nothing like being outside and soaking up the sun and the smell of the trees," Cody said. "And sharing it with good friends. This is like heaven to me."

Olivia felt another song coming on.

"I'm so happy you could all come. We have some big things to tell you about."

"What big things?" Olivia asked.

"Huge things," Bridget said as she slipped right next to Olivia, who did her best not to tense up even though her insides were screaming *help, red alert, and oh my God she's going to kill me* all at the same time.

All the teens around the table became excited and peppered Bridget with questions about what "Deirdre" thought about alternative energy, global climate change, Japanese whaling, her vegan diet, all kinds of issues. The Venomous operative had done her homework. Bridget's answers were intelligent and thought provoking. Olivia was impressed. Bridget even looked the part of Deirdre by not using any artificial products in her red hair. It was all natural. One girl asked Bridget how to set up her own Utube channel like theirs because they loved their videos.

"What about my videos?"

"Oh my God, I love yours too, Cody!" one girl said, embarrassed.

"He's kidding," Bridget said. "Cody has three times the Utube followers Fiona and I have."

"You two are catching up fast. How long have you had your channel up? Less than six months?"

"We don't keep track of that. Fiona and I only care about our earth. We have this huge love for it. So much so that we need to fight to protect it. And if Utube will give us a platform to do that, we'll use it."

Everyone nodded.

The fan-girl continued to gush. "Well, you both are amazing Utubers."

"So what brought you here?" Gabi asked Bridget. "What is it about Cody's message that spoke to you?"

"Oh, that's such a good question," the fan-girl said.

Bridget thought about it, then reached out and touched his arm. "I'd have to say it was Cody's heart."

"Awww," the fan-girl said.

"Cody's heart is in the right place. I love how he sees the Earth and what we need to do to fix things."

"But you and Fiona are right. We need to take the fight to them," Cody said. "The people who are responsible for the mess they've made of the earth."

"Cutting toxic emissions from factories and motor vehicles will only get us so far," Bridget said. "We have to do something about the people in power. That's what we're going to talk about tonight. Heart the E is going to fight the power."

That night, Olivia joined all the Heart the E members as they gathered around the stage and waited. Soon Cody walked on-stage with his familiar guitar and sang more songs that everyone knew the words to. Even Miyuki began singing along with everyone else.

Olivia faked it. She had to. She was sick of these songs. It reminded Olivia of church. How everyone would sing the same, familiar hymns because you were supposed to, not because your heart wanted to sing them. Or maybe it was Olivia's heart that wasn't into singing them. Either way, Olivia felt like an outsider trying to pretend she was a believer.

Cody finished up his last song, a folk song by some guy named

Woody Guthrie, before he announced…

"Let's give it up for Deirdre and Fiona!" Cody yelled as he surrendered the stage to the twins and their fiery red hair. The sea of teens and young adults cheered.

Bridget took the microphone first. Her eyes scanned the crowd. "Heart the E is an amazing group. Why? Because this is the best cause in the fecking universe. Saving our Mother Earth from muppets who either through self-interest or stupidity want to destroy her green grass. Destroy her blue skies. And destroy her crystal-clear oceans."

Lots of boos from the audience.

"Straight up. The Earth needs our help. And that's why I love this group because we are the only pro-Earth group out there who gives young people like us a real voice to tell those polluting Mother Earth to stop."

Cheers from the audience.

"To tell all those muppets denying global warming to wake up. To tell those politicians who deny they're hurting our planet to wake up. To tell those corporations who deny their role in poisoning our environment to wake up." Bridget's eyes lit up. "We are the future. And that future we want must be fought for. Straight up—Mother Earth can only tell us she's hurting. She can't fight for herself. We must do it for her."

Many young adults in the crowd nodded. They dug what she was saying.

"Tell 'em, Fiona darling." Bridget stepped away as her sister took the microphone.

Sophia's eyes burned with passion. "Yer bang on, sis. We need to get fecking mad!"

The crowd mimicked her words and nodded to themselves.

"We need to do more than live what we preach. We must act. Tomorrow there's a chairman of a big oil company giving a speech to some business muppets in Seattle. Ya know what we're gonna do? We're going up there to make that *gobshite* realize that we don't need his oil in our oceans anymore. His oil kills our fish and kills our birds. Let's go up there to Seattle and tell 'em we don't want their fecking drilling rigs anywhere near our oceans."

The audience cheered again.

"What do ya think, Cody darling?" Bridget asked.

Cody climbed back on the small stage. "I love that!"

CHAPTER 14

Emma felt exhausted. They had been at it for hours, the man asking her hundreds of questions about the Authority, and Emma trying her best to either lie or dodge around the question. Her body felt numb. The electric shocks were quick, barely half of a second. But they were enough to keep her body awake and on a constant edge. Her mind was also jumping around, sometimes wanting to just give out the information, while at other times wanting to fight that urge because Emma was terrified that she would say the wrong thing and get someone killed.

Emma didn't know how long she could keep this up. The situation was eating away at her sanity in small pieces, like flakes of rubber from a tire. This man knew what he was doing. She assumed that he could keep this up for days. And Emma knew that she wouldn't last that long.

However, Mrs. B had given Emma a golden ticket. A piece of real information that Venomous could use to their advantage while casting Emma in a favorable light if she supplied it. But Mrs. B warned Emma not to hand over this golden ticket unless it was absolutely necessary. Or if she needed that one final nudge to get invited into the Venomous clubhouse.

Emma didn't want to give up that ticket.

At least, not yet.

The man interrogating her was silent for a moment or two. She was wondering if he was thinking up a new way to torture her when the heavy main door opened and his chair scraped across the concrete floor.

Emma relaxed. He must be taking another bathroom break.

That idea was dropped when Emma heard a large clatter of footsteps entering the room. Emma felt her wrists and ankles being freed. Next, they stood her up and kept her from falling as she was being moved out of the room. Maybe they were going to let her go.

Or maybe they were going to kill her.

Emma wondered if fighting these guys was worth it. If she could take off the blindfold, she would have a fighting chance of getting away.

Well—Emma reasoned that if she was about to die—then she would take that fighting chance.

As they guided her down the hall, Emma dove forward and barrel-rolled across the cold floor. She jumped to her feet and ripped off the blindfold.

She tried to focus. The lights were bright and it was hard to see, but two dark forms were closing in, so—

Emma did a bicycle kick into the first guy, bringing him down. Someone grabbed her right arm. Emma's training kicked in. She twisted her body to the right, bringing the man holding her arm with her. This got him off balance as Emma hooked her foot around his leg and brought him down to the floor.

Her vision was clearing up. Emma could see two more Venomous goons near an open door.

She pushed through her fear and ran at them.

One of the men shoved her through that open door while the second pointed a pistol at her.

Emma was desperate. She thought about kicking it out of his hand, but before she could act—the man retreated behind the doorway.

This reaction made Emma pause.

The two men she had put on the floor were back on their feet.

Emma braced for a new attack.

But all four men kept their distance behind the metal door as it was shut tight.

Emma couldn't believe it. All she managed to do was get herself put into a new room.

She looked around and saw a boy strapped to a chair with a blindfold.

It was Ryan.

Emma ran over and took off Ryan's blindfold. His eye was black and there was dried blood on the corner of his lips.

Despite this, Ryan smiled. "I knew it was you."

"Oh my God. What happened to your face?"

"It's okay. Everything will be alright."

"Seriously? They gave you a black eye, Ryan. Is this how Venomous treats its members?"

"There's always a reason for everything we do," he said. "Are you alright? Did they hurt you?"

"They shocked me with electricity. Besides that, I feel great."

"They shocked you?" Ryan thought about it. "Sometimes we use that to keep a person awake and off balance."

"Well, it worked. I'm freaking upset and ready to kill you."

"I had nothing to do with this."

"Did you tell them about me? I thought this was a truce, Ryan. We were only going to hang out together."

"I'll straighten this out. Promise. They'll listen to me."

"For some reason that black eye tells me no."

"Will you be patient?"

"Go to hell. You got me into this mess. Now get me out of it."

A motor above them whirred as a large monitor emerged from a door in the ceiling. As it clicked into place, the monitor flickered on, revealing a man wearing dark sunglasses with thick white frames. He had extra-long blond hair that hung straight down each side. The man's square face contained no emotion. Resting on the back of the man's chair was a beautiful black falcon. It stood proudly behind its owner.

"I apologize, Asset of the ninety-fifth order. It was necessary… to test you for…security purposes." The man's eyes took forever to move over to Emma. "This is Black Opal, I presume. Asset Ninety-Five has told us so much about you. My apologies to you… as well. We had to validate your intentions. Impressive. If you had revealed…any useful information about the Authority, I would have labeled you a traitor…and had you killed on the spot. Someone too willing to offer up secrets…can-not be trusted by anyone."

"I'm not here on an operation. I only wanted to spend time with Ryan."

Asset One didn't smile or frown. His face was unreadable to Emma. "So we have observed. Very well. Asset ninety-five, you may take a leave of absence…from your duties."

Ryan hesitated. He was surprised. "Thank you, Asset One."

"Perhaps Black Opal would enjoy…a tour of our training facility. The location is quite…pleasant. And private."

"That's most generous, sir. I will make the necessary

arrangements."

"Excellent," Asset One said. "Ah…to be young again."

Asset One faded to black. The motor whirled once again as the monitor rose back up into the ceiling. The door popped open. Four Venomous goons entered and lined up against the wall. They waited for a command.

Ryan stood up and straightened his blood-stained shirt. He lifted his chin as he approached the four men. "You'll go to my condo and carefully pack Black Opal's belongings for travel. I'll text you a list of my items that you'll pack as well."

All four men nodded.

"I'm not going to a Venomous training camp," Emma said.

Ryan sighed. "If I read my boss correctly, I think this is one of those offers that you can't refuse."

"Then I'm a prisoner now."

"You're still my guest," Ryan said. "And from now on, I'm not leaving your side." Ryan addressed the men again. "One last thing. Asset One-two-five, did you administer my interrogation?"

One of the four men stepped forward. "Yes, I did."

"I recognized your voice. You did an excellent job. Very thorough."

"Apologies for the eye. I was only following Asset One's orders."

"I understand."

Emma recognized the man's voice. That goon was the one who had interrogated her as well. Emma had a strong desire to clip electrodes to the man's coconuts and let him experience the wonders of electricity for himself.

"Is something wrong?" Ryan asked.

Emma let it go. She was being released and traveling to a Venomous facility with Ryan. As far as her mission went, so far, so good.

"It's nothing."

Ryan's face didn't buy her answer. He stepped closer to Asset One-two-five. "Did you administer both interrogations?"

"Yes," the man answered.

"Did you use electric shocks on this girl?"

"It's a technique that has proved most effective against females," he said, unemotional. "Would you like me to apologize to her as well?

"That won't be necessary."

Emma wanted to flip both of them off, but before she could entertain the idea—

Ryan punched the man in the face. Hard. He fell back against the wall.

"Hand me your pistol," Ryan said.

One Venomous goon complied without hesitation. Ryan held the butt of the pistol and slammed the handle across the side of the interrogator's head. As the man collapsed to the floor, Ryan continued to whale upon the man's body with uncontrolled fury.

The other three goons did nothing to stop it.

When Ryan was done, the man was still breathing. Still alive. He moaned in pain as blood oozed down his lips and mouth.

Emma couldn't believe what she just saw. She had never seen that level of violence from Ryan, and it shocked her.

Ryan was breathing hard. He paused to catch his breath, then handed the pistol back to the other goon. "You three will retrieve our luggage from my condo. But first, this man needs medical attention."

CHAPTER 15

It was a new morning as everyone sang and socialized inside the caravan of Heart the E busses that drove the four hours to Seattle, Washington. Stepping off the bus, Olivia was surprised to see a parking lot already roped off. It was directly across the street from the restaurant where the chairman of the oil company was speaking. Police cars were already in position as officers stood watch over the area.

"Did they already know we were coming?" Olivia asked.

"*Sí*, Cody filed a permit with the city so we can legally protest," Gabi said.

"That was quick," Miyuki said.

"The twins have been planning this protest for a while."

"I've never done one of these before," Olivia said. "What do you do?"

"You hold up a sign and yell whatever everyone else is yelling. But don't throw anything or the cops will bust us."

Olivia liked that advice as Gabi and some of the other volunteers passed out signs that had been made the previous night. The one she gave Olivia read *Big Oil = Dead Oceans*. Once everyone had a sign, Cody and the other members began to chant slogans in unison.

"Save our oceans! Save our fishes! Save our birds from these sons of oil riches."

Across the street, men and women dressed for business went in and out of the five-star restaurant. They watched the protesters with only a passing interest. Many of them were used to seeing such demonstrations in Seattle.

The Heart the E members repeated the chants for about ten minutes before Cody broke out his guitar, and they sang protest songs for a good half hour. Then the group went back to the chants.

Olivia wondered what the point of all this was. It was obvious to her that the people inside the restaurant who came to see this oil chairman speak didn't care what any of the protesters thought. Nor did their demonstration seem to change their minds into not—

Something struck Olivia's back. It was a small rock that clattered against the pavement. She swung around to see who threw it at her.

Miyuki waved at her from behind the engine cowling of one of the busses.

Olivia checked her surroundings. The Heart the E members were doing another chant at the restaurant. But Gabi was right next to her and would notice her absence.

Olivia took a step back and knocked over her empty water bottle. That gave her an idea.

"Hey, I'm going to get us more bottles of *agua,*" Olivia told Gabi in Spanish.

"Do you need any help?"

"No, *gracias.*"

Olivia wanted to run, but she walked calmly over to the busses and got behind the engine cowling with Miyuki.

"That hurt," Olivia said. "Did you have to throw such a big rock?"

"Oh, sorry, I have limited choices inside a parking lot," Miyuki said.

"So what's so urgent?"

"I sit by this girl on the bus who works as a volunteer in the main office. We talked all the way here about Bridget and Sophia." Miyuki lowered her voice. "She tells me that the twins showed up in Oregon about nine months ago. Cody liked them and took them under his wing. Through his help the twins built their own Utube channel with over one hundred thousand subscribers, mostly teen members from Heart the E who came over from Cody's channel."

"We already know about that, love."

"She also told me that the twins helped Cody raise thousands of dollars in new funding, plus helped him recruit more European members. That new funding could be from Venomous."

"And those new members they recruited could be Venomous operatives," Olivia said. "But that still doesn't tell us why

Venomous is going through all of this trouble. Is it to launder money? Or are they using Cody and his organization for something else?"

"Do you think Cody is working for them too?" Miyuki asked.

Olivia paused. That hadn't occured to her. Cody seemed genuine, but it was possible. "You're right. We can't rule anyone out."

Miyuki jingled a set of keys.

"Where did you get those?"

"I lifted the girl's keys to the main business office so we can snoop around."

"That's brilliant!"

"I'll slip away and get the keys copied here in town; then I'll put them back in her tent where she will conveniently find them again," Miyuki said.

"Then tonight you and I can sneak out and take a closer look at those financial records," Olivia said.

"How's that water coming?" Gabi asked out of nowhere.

Olivia swallowed her surprise as she turned to Gabi. Did she hear any of their conversation? Olivia had no choice but to pretend that she didn't.

"Sorry, we were gabbing and I totally lost track of time."

"It was my fault," Miyuki said. "I was looking for the water bottles too, and we began talking."

"The water bottles are in the back of our bus. I'll show you." Olivia climbed on board with both Miyuki and Gabi in tow. She grabbed a paper tray of new water bottles and handed it to Miyuki. Olivia then took another tray of bottles. As the three of them stepped off the bus, Bridget and Sophia were there.

"Your timing is grand," Bridget said. "We need ya to help us. We're taking these cans of motor oil and pouring it over the top of that oil guy's head."

Sophia held out her phone to Miyuki. "And you'll record it so we can put it on-line."

It was bad enough that Bridget and Sophia were this close to her and Miyuki. But now they wanted them to do some political stunt.

"I can't do that," Olivia said. "They'll throw me out of the country."

"So what?" Sophia asked. "Ya get to go home early. That's a

small price to pay for making a grand statement towards Big Oil."

"Haven't ya heard anything we've been saying? We have to fight back," Bridget said. "Ya can't be a warrior for Mother Earth unless you're willing to sacrifice a few things."

"We've been kicked out of a lot of countries," Sophia said. "Believe me, it's not a big deal."

Bridget flashed her sister a look before speaking. "It's up to ya, darling. If what we do in this group isn't important to ya, maybe you should think over why ya joined."

"Does Cody know you're doing this?" Gabi asked.

"Straight up. Cody has our backs one hundred percent."

"I'll help, then."

"Oh, that's grand. What about you two?"

"I'll record it," Miyuki said.

This felt all wrong to Olivia. Her danger mode was on full alert. This could be a trap or something that could blow their covers wide open. However, Olivia didn't seem to have a choice.

"I'm in," Olivia said. "What's the plan?"

* * *

Olivia reluctantly followed Sophia and Bridget as they left the main protest and snuck through a few back alleys so they could enter the restaurant's main kitchen by way of the delivery door in the back. Once inside, the five girls slipped inside a cramped unoccupied office in the kitchen.

"Now, Fiona and I will distract everyone while ya take this pan full of oil and place it upside down on top of that CEO's head like a grand little hat," Bridget said.

Olivia glanced at the cheap aluminum baking pan full of motor oil. She still wasn't happy about this.

"It's your plan," Gabi said. "Shouldn't you two share the risk too?"

"Get off the grass. Are ya scared?" Sophia asked.

"We have to do whatever it takes to make our point," Bridget said. "And this will certainly do that."

"I believe in what you're trying to say. That's why I'm here. But a true leader—leads. She doesn't hide behind others."

Olivia couldn't agree more. She was liking Gabi more every day.

Sophia glared at Gabi so intensely that Olivia feared they would go at it right here in the office.

"We never hide," Bridget said. "Do we, Fiona darling?"

Sophia took the pan of oil away from her sister. "Feck no. Let's dump this bitch."

"When the muppet begins his speech, you three will run through the restaurant and cause a commotion. Stay away from where the man is speaking, that way if there's any security or cops around, they'll be focused on you three and not Fiona and me when we enter and get behind the CEO to give him his present. Any questions?"

No one answered.

"Like my sister said, let's dump this bitch."

CHAPTER 16

Richard Fernway the third, the CEO of the petroleum giant North Am Group, began his speech a few minutes after noon. His audience were all members of the Seattle Association of American Business Leaders. They rented the five-star restaurant for a private luncheon to welcome this head of industry to Seattle. They were hoping to convince Richard and others like him that Seattle, Washington, hadn't been overrun with liberals and hippies like Portland had. That the Seattle-Tacoma area was still friendly to corporations and other CEOs like Richard who were looking for new places to build things. In Richard's case, these business people were keen on a new oil refinery that Richard wanted to build somewhere in the Pacific Northwest. The closer it was to Seattle, the cheaper the gasoline prices would be. And that was why Richard was here. He liked to be wooed and courted by those who needed him.

It was when Richard got to the part of his speech about his dog biting his sister when three girls, possibly in their teens, emerged from the kitchen and began yelling, "Big Oil kills fish." The noisy children raised their fists and kept repeating the same phrase over and over as they weaved through all the lunch tables. It was obvious to Richard they were protesters. Young people didn't want to put in the work anymore to better themselves, so now they wanted to tear down those who made something of themselves.

Richard stopped speaking and waited for security to do their work so he could continue. But then something dropped on top of Richard's head and he felt something running down the sides of his face. The smell gave him an immediate clue. It was motor oil.

Richard stepped away from the podium and covered his eyes so the oil wouldn't irritate them. His ears picked up more chants, this time much closer as more voices yelled, "Big Oil kills fish!" and,

"Save our oceans!"

Someone guided Richard to the side and took off his "oil hat" before wiping his face with a wet towel. It was his assistant Peggy. With his face clear of oil, Richard glanced at the chaotic scene in front of him. Two girls with the most reddish hair he'd ever seen were near his podium with their fists in the air as they yelled their chants. Finally, two security guards put an end to it by tackling the girls to the ground.

Several of the shocked business people asked Richard if he was okay, and he joked with them about the entire situation. It was all ridiculous and wouldn't change a damn thing about how he was going to run his business.

"Come out of there, now!" a policeman yelled as he held his pistol towards the ground, but ready to go at a moment's notice. The officer was up against the wall, right next to a door labeled *Supply Closet*.

Richard hoped the policeman would have to use deadly force. That would teach these left-wing nut-jobs to stop harassing normal people with their insanity.

After a second policeman joined the first one on the opposite wall, the door opened slowly as a black girl emerged from the closet with her hands up. She began spouting some Spanish nonsense at the officers. Richard wondered why a black girl would be speaking Spanish anyway. Soon the officers made quick work of the black girl, putting the cuffs on her before escorting her quickly out of the restaurant. She was the last of the nut-jobs. Now Richard could finish his speech—if he could remember where he left off.

CHAPTER 17

Olivia tensed up as the police officer pressed her body against his SUV. Then he forced her to spread her legs.

"Anything I need to know about?" the officer asked.

Olivia concentrated on not blowing her cover. *Keep thinking Spanish.* Soon her broken English came out in a Spanish accent. "I do not understand, officer."

"Any drugs, weapons, or needles on you? Anything that will either stick or poke me when I search you?"

"No, officer."

The officer did a quick pat-down. When a female officer finished searching Miyuki, she was motioned over to do a more personal pat-down on Olivia. She repeated the same question about drugs or weapons.

"No, ma'am," Olivia replied.

The female officer's search was more rigorous, and Olivia found it very uncomfortable. However, it was soon over as all five girls were escorted to a waiting police van. A huge cheer erupted from across the street as the Heart the E protesters celebrated their five brave heroines.

"We love you, girls!" Cody yelled from his megaphone as the crowd behind him echoed his sentiments.

Olivia wished she felt like a hero, but right now she felt like an idiot. She shouldn't have let the twins force her and Miyuki into doing this. Now they were headed to jail and who knows what after that? Would their cover identities hold when the police checked their IDs? Would they get flagged by the FBI? Would this end their mission and alert the twins and Venomous that they were on their trail?

Olivia climbed inside the van as the back doors closed.

After going through the booking process, Olivia found herself stuck in a holding cell with Gabi, Miyuki, and the twins from hell. The men in the holding cell across from them would whistle and yell for them to take off their clothes.

Olivia tried her best to ignore them. What worried her were the twins being this close to her. Would they notice the fake nose and the subtle changes to her appearance? Or would they notice that Miyuki's long hair had been chopped off and pair the two of them together? Olivia had already experienced how vicious these twins could be, and if they figured out the truth inside this confined space—there would be a bloodbath.

"Was it worth it?" Gabi asked, sitting on a bench next to Olivia. Miyuki had wisely chosen the opposite corner of the cell, putting herself as far away from Olivia as she could. However, it did put her closer to Sophia.

Bridget leaned against a far wall. "Oh, swingin' Jesus—did ya not see all the news people monitoring the protests? They all shot video of us leaving in handcuffs. People will know what we did."

"And what was that, exactly?"

"An act of defiance," Sophia said. "An act that shows those we fight against that we're serious about changing our world. They'll be afraid of us now."

"Cody talks a lot about ya. Gabrielle, isn't it?" Bridget asked.

"Why must people be afraid of us?" Gabi asked. "When Cody started Heart the E, his goal was to educate and spread the word about environmental responsibility to other young people like himself. It's a youth movement. A culture movement. It's not a political one."

"How long have ya been in the movement, Gabrielle?"

"Cody told us about six months," Sophia added.

"That's right," Bridget said. "Roughly the same time as us."

"I've watched and studied every video Cody has made on his Utube channel since he was sixteen years old," Gabi said. "On those videos he explains to the members what Heart the E is really about. The core of what we are and what he wants us to be. It's a noble idea that made me want to join. But what you girls are trying to do—it doesn't fit with what Cody wanted this group to be."

"That's rather amusing since Cody has been on board with this idea from the very beginning. Honest to G."

"I don't believe you," Gabi said.

Sophia jumped to her feet. "Are ya calling my sister a liar?"

Bridget held her hand in the air and her sister sat back down. "Do ya have a problem with us, Gabrielle?"

Gabi crossed her arms. "You could say that. I think you're taking advantage of Cody's relaxed nature so you can use the organization's resources for your benefit."

Olivia could feel the tension inside the prison cell. Gabi didn't know what these girls were capable of. Picking a fight would be a giant mistake.

"If ya don't like what we're doing, then why did ya volunteer to help?" Bridget asked.

Gabi flicked her eyes to Olivia. "Because I don't abandon my friends."

Hearing Gabi say that was strange at first, but then when Olivia thought about it—yeah, they were friends.

"Aw, that's grand." Bridget's attention turned to Olivia. "You've been quiet. Do ya share the same opinion about us?"

Olivia shrugged. "If Cody approves of what you're doing, then I support it."

"Thank you," Bridget said. "What's your name again?"

"Camila."

"Camila," Bridget repeated.

"Where ya from?" Sophia asked.

"Puerto Plata. It's in the Dominican Republic," Olivia said.

"I've seen ya somewhere before." Sophia glanced at her sister. "Doesn't she look familiar?"

"Bejesus, Fiona, ya think ya know everyone on the planet."

"Piss off. I'm being serious here." Sophia leaned forward. "Do ya travel much, Camila?"

Olivia shook her head. "This is my first time in a foreign country."

"So that would be a no," Bridget said.

Sophia didn't seem too convinced as her eyes focused on Olivia.

"These girls are trash," Gabi said to Olivia in Spanish. "We don't need bitches like them messing up our movement with the wrong attitude. Sorry, but that's how I feel."

"Don't apologize. I shouldn't have gone along with their stunt," Olivia said in Spanish. "I agree with you."

"Then we should convince Cody to kick their freckled rears out of the organization."

"What are ya two muppets saying?" Sophia asked.

"None of your business," Gabi said in English.

Sophia glared.

"Keep looking at me that way, *señorita*," Gabi said. "And you and I will have a serious problem, *sí?*"

Here we go, Olivia thought. These girls were about to get into it, and there was nothing to stop—

A guard came into the cell-block. This made Sophia and Gabi back off each other. He got out his keys and unlocked their jail door.

"Come with me. You're all being released."

CHAPTER 18

When the private jet she was on leveled out, Emma's blindfold was removed. The jet's windows revealed a large pillow of clouds passing below them with a clear blue sky on top. Emma could smell the all-leather interior. Her soft, marshmellow-like passenger seat hugged her body and provided plenty of legroom. The jet itself was first class.

However, Emma's heart wouldn't stop beating like a drummer on cocaine. Even her breathing was fast as if Emma were running a sprint every fifteen minutes.

The jet was well-stocked. Ryan had had chocolate-covered strawberries brought on board as well as some fresh bagels with salmon lox and cream cheese. So far the boy was treating her like a princess.

"What's wrong?" Ryan asked her during the flight. "What did I forget?"

"You forgot that my father died in a plane crash," Emma said. "Flying isn't exactly my favorite thing to do in the world."

"I wish there was another quick way to get to our training center, but there's not."

Emma squeezed his hand. "I'll be okay. I'll get through it."

"Would feeding you chocolate-covered strawberries help?"

"It wouldn't hurt," Emma said.

Ten hours later, the private jet finally landed. Ryan escorted Emma down the stairway. Emma squinted at the bright sun but used her hand to shield it as her eyes took in the new surroundings. It was a small airport with only one hangar and a runway that ran parallel to a long sandy beach, which looked out over the ocean waves. The temperature was mild and reminded Emma of Hawaii.

"Are we in the Pacific?" she asked.

"I can't tell you," Ryan said.

"Caribbean?"

"Still can't tell you."

The jet was met by a large ATV, big enough for four people plus cargo. The flight crew loaded their luggage as Emma and Ryan climbed in the back.

Their ATV driver, a young man with brown skin, turned around. "My name is Omar. It's a pleasure to welcome you back to the island, Asset Ninety-five."

"Thanks, Omar," Ryan said. "Please take the scenic route for my guest."

Omar drove the ATV along the paved trail. They passed by groves of coconut and pineapple trees. Emma even noticed a few banana trees as well. To her, that indicated this place was near the equator, but again she wasn't sure.

Omar stopped the ATV in front of an iron gate with four lines of barbed wire running along the top of it and a heavy fence that ran along the perimeter of whatever facility they were about to enter. The gate opened slowly, and the ATV headed inside the facility. As Omar followed the paved walkway, Emma noticed a sprawling campus-type environment with hundreds of busy people.

One class surrounded a square and studied two people engaged in hand-to-hand fighting.

Another class stood in a line and practiced knife throwing at wooden posts that were moving.

Yet another class circled a giant cage as they watched a student standing inside it wearing a protective dog-attack suit. Sure enough, a pit bull was sent in for the attack. The student struggled with the dog before it was called off by its master. The dog retired from the cage.

Next, there was a mighty roar as a full-grown lion was released into the same cage.

"Oh my God. Seriously?"

Ryan traced Emma's eye line. "Oh, yeah, that class is scary. Makes you confront fear. That guy's lucky. When I did that, they sent in a large grizzly."

"What happened?"

"I wrestled with it," Ryan said.

Emma didn't believe him.

"Okay—more like—it sat on top of me and I almost died. But

you know, after you meet face-to-face with a six-hundred-pound bear—there's not much more out there to be scared of."

"This is true," Omar said.

"Have you gone through it yet?" Ryan asked.

Omar nodded. "Mine was an alligator. I wrestled with it and ended up breaking its neck."

"That's excellent," Ryan said.

"Why did you have to kill the poor thing?" Emma asked.

"It was either him or me."

When they drove closer to the cage, Emma could hear the student banging on the locked door as he pleaded to get out.

The instructor kept his hands folded behind his back. "Face your fear. Face it like a man. You never run away from danger."

The lion grabbed the student and flung him to the floor of the cage.

"Look into the cat's eyes. Let him know you are not afraid of him!"

The student yelled in terror as he got to his feet and ran around the cage. "Help me!"

The large cat grabbed him again and tossed him across the cage like a big plaything.

Ryan shook his head. "I don't think he's going to pass."

Omar laughed.

"You people are crazy," Emma said.

The ATV tour continued as the vehicle passed by the shooting range. There was a clatter of machine-gun fire. The sudden series of pops from an automatic pistol. And the swoosh of a rocket-propelled grenade followed by the explosion.

"Take us to the beach," Ryan said to Omar. He glanced at Emma. "Sometimes the training areas can get a little noisy."

Omar took a different series of paths. Soon they were stopped on another beach. The ocean waves rolled up and touched the beach before drawing back.

Ryan escorted Emma off the ATV.

"Asset Twelve has prepared two bungalows inside the instructors' living area," Omar said. "I'll take your baggage there. Is there anything else I can do for you, Asset Ninety-five?"

Ryan thought about it. "Can you have some refreshments brought to us?"

Omar nodded before speeding off.

"So everyone here is in training?" Emma asked.

"Yes, Omar for instance. He's a student too. Notice how I can give them all orders because they haven't received a ranking yet."

"How does it go again? You're ninety-five, and that means—?"

"I'm a Venomous asset ranked or placed at the order of ninety-five. The lower your number, the higher in rank you are. Operatives with high ranks are usually placed in charge of the large operations."

"So when an operative does well, they get promoted to a higher rank. And if that operative does bad, they lose a rank."

"No, that operative would lose their life. Venomous doesn't tolerate failure often," Ryan said. "Wanna do some surfing? I can have one of the students bring us our bathing suits."

"You're from Missouri. What do you know about surfing?"

"Enough to get me in trouble. What about you?"

"One of my friends has been showing me, but I don't feel confident enough to do it without her," Emma said. "Besides, don't you have to work?"

"My job is to answer all of your questions."

"Questions about what?"

"About Venomous. You should know everything about an organization before you join."

"I've said nothing about joining."

"Yet, you're curious," Ryan said. "You could have asked me to take you home. I'm sure Asset One would have let you under the circumstances. Yet—you didn't say that. Why not? I think it's because you're curious and you want to know more."

"Maybe I'm trying to trick you. How would you know?"

Ryan stared deep into her eyes. "Because you haven't lied to me once. I know I haven't been honest with you always. But you—you've never lied to me. I trust you, Emma Rothchild. I trust you so much that I'm trusting my very life to you. I bet my life that you do want to know more. That you'll give this all a fair shake. Because if my boss finds out that you've deceived me, you'll be killed. And I'll be killed for being stupid enough to trust you."

CHAPTER 19

That night Olivia couldn't sleep. The protest at the restaurant. The twins recruiting her to take part in their stunt. Sophia almost recognizing her in jail. And then she learned through Cody that their stunt had been broadcast on CNN and the BBC World Service, which meant Mrs. B had seen it. Being featured on worldwide television wasn't exactly part of a spy's goal of not drawing attention to herself. This entire day had stressed Olivia out so much that she couldn't sleep. Her brain kept jumping from one worry to another. A complete circle of worry that made Olivia feel miserable as her stomach endlessly churned. Olivia liked to anticipate problems and fix them before they happened. But that was the difficult thing about being an operative, you had to be able to embrace uncertainty and roll with things as they happened.

It was a concept Olivia was still trying to manage.

Inside their tent, Miyuki was curled up inside her sleeping bag, making a cooing noise in her sleep. It sounded like either a sleeping cat or a noise a dove would make. Olivia wasn't sure. Whatever it was, it didn't help her sleep. Olivia checked the time and it was almost four in the morning.

She had to pee.

Olivia tossed on some shorts and emerged from the tent. Throughout the campground there were lights placed in strategic positions. All of these were powered by the sun during the day and stayed lit for most of the night, although their brightness was limited. Olivia managed to reach one of the outhouses and—

As she stared at the floor inside it, Olivia noted her bare feet. She had forgotten to put on her shoes.

Olivia cursed at herself. God knows what was on the floor of that public outhouse. But the sleepy part of her brain was willing to risk this if it meant Olivia would be back in bed sooner rather than later. Olivia went inside the outhouse and did her business.

She then cleaned her hands at a washing station before rubbing on some hand sanitizer and starting her way back to the tent.

In the dim light, she noted another girl heading for the outhouses. Olivia slowed her pace to see who it was. Finally the girl passed under one of the lights. It was Gabi.

Olivia relaxed. She thought about talking to Gabi to see if she had any more information about Cody's odd relationship with the twins. But running into her after she used the toilet at four in the morning would seem a little too convenient. So Olivia planned to wait in the shadows for Gabi to use the outhouse before continuing to her tent. However, that idea changed when Gabi bypassed the outhouses and kept on moving at a brisk pace.

Olivia wondered where she was going in such a hurry, especially at this hour.

She followed Gabi, keeping to the shadows as the girl passed by each light source. Soon Gabi left the Heart the E's giant campsite and took the access road. At that point, she switched on a small light from her phone because this part of the forest was pitch black. Olivia used Gabi's light source to follow her without revealing her presence.

A few minutes later, Gabi reached the main road and continued her early morning hike. Olivia reached the road and felt the stones under her bare feet. Maybe she should have slipped on her flip flops before going to the toilet. Despite her feet hurting, Olivia went down the road and kept Gabi at a safe distance in front of her.

It was another ten minutes before Gabi reached a local twenty-four-hour convenience store. She went in and a loud ding went off to let the clerk know that someone was entering.

Olivia hid behind one of the fuel pumps. She wanted to follow Gabi inside, but that door alarm would also alert Gabi to her presence. Explaining the outhouse encounter was one thing. Explaining an encounter at a local convenience store at four in the morning would be a difficult sell.

Olivia scanned the large windows that looked into the store. She had lost sight of Gabi and wondered what she could be doing inside. Maybe Gabi wanted a Twinkie or some not-so-natural sour cream and onion potato crisps to satisfy a late-night food craving. That would explain a lot.

Through the large window, Gabi came back into view near the magazine stand. She took out an entertainment news magazine and flipped through a few pages. When she was done, Gabi put it back on the rack and disappeared again. Only to reappear at the register with a couple of candy bars. The clerk scanned them and Gabi paid. Then she headed back down the road towards the camp. Olivia followed her until she made the turn back to the access road that led to the campsite.

Olivia sat on a stump and rested her naked feet, which were sore thanks to the long walk. She took out her phone and switched on the photo light to examine her feet. She had a few new blisters. None of them were bleeding...yet.

Olivia lowered her feet on a patch of cool grass and took a moment to think. That was an obvious late-night snack run made by someone who wasn't totally vegan, as Gabi had led them all to believe. But that didn't mean anything. Every girl had a secret craving for something that wasn't good for them. Emma had her chocolate donuts. Nadia couldn't resist chocolate truffles. And Olivia adored her lemon-cream biscuits, especially with tea.

However, there was one thing Gabi did that bothered her. The magazine rack. Why did she go there?

If Gabi was bored, she would've read that magazine for much longer than she did, or at least she would've scanned the other magazines as well. But she didn't do that. Gabi went up to one specific magazine, thumbed through it quickly, then put it back down before picking up her candy bars and leaving.

Olivia touched her sore feet. She didn't want to...but she had to go back to the store.

The front door alarm buzzed. The clerk inside worked on a display of crisps on sale. Olivia smiled at him before zig-zagging casually through a couple of aisles while glancing at a few things. She took her time but finally reached the magazine rack. A copy of *That's Entertainment* was still there on top. As Olivia reached for it—

"Hey, you!" the male clerk said.

Olivia withdrew her hand.

"Where're your shoes?"

Olivia felt the cold floor under her bare feet. "I left them in my tent."

The clerk scoffed and pointed at a large sign near the entrance.

No shirt. No shoes. No service.

"Oh, I'm sorry. I didn't know about your rules. You see, I'm from the Dominican Republic and—"

"Like I give a shit. Those are the rules. Go tell all of your tree-hugging young commies up in that camp of yours to dress like normal people when they come inside our store. We get sick of that shit, you know?"

What a rude bastard, Olivia thought. Treating her like she was trash while he looked like someone who needed instructions for using a box of cereal. Still, going all the way back to camp to grab her shoes didn't appeal to Olivia. She was already here and wanted to examine that magazine as soon as possible. But this man probably wouldn't allow that.

Then Olivia remembered her cab ride with Miyuki. How she took out that wad of cash to make that racist driver shut up and just do his job. Maybe that was the way to go here.

Olivia approached the clerk. "I understand. But it's late and I don't want to go back to camp to get my shoes now."

"Tough shit."

"Are you allowed tips?"

The clerk glanced at her, then pointed at a tip jar with a couple of one dollar bills inside.

"What if I contributed to your jar? Would that make a difference?"

The clerk shrugged. "Depends."

Olivia dug into her pocket for her wallet and realized it was still inside her tent. She checked her other pocket and found some change. But it was only two dollars and a dime. It was all the money she had.

Flipping hell.

Olivia slipped one dollar into the jar.

The clerk scoffed. "One dollar buys you one minute. You'd better hurry."

Olivia thanked him and headed straight for the magazine rack. She found the *That's Entertainment* magazine and opened it. She flipped through the pages until a small envelope fell to the floor. Olivia picked it up, then carefully unsealed the envelope using the edge of her long fingernails, trying her best not to damage whatever was inside the envelope. Olivia checked the large circle mirror above the aisles.

The clerk had gone back to re-stocking the crisps display.

Olivia removed the contents of the envelope. There were two pieces of paper. One had a message written in Spanish.

Targets S and B now at compound. Assessing the situation. New possible targets. Please identify.

The other piece of paper had three very well done pencil sketches of Olivia, Nadia, and Miyuki. It now made sense to Olivia. This was a drop. A place where a spy would drop off and receive information from her handlers.

Gabi was an intelligence operative.

CHAPTER 20

That night, the sounds of the surf came rolling in from the ocean as Emma walked with Ryan across the sand. In the distance was a large fire-pit raging with orange flames.

"Who's going to be there?" Emma asked.

"Mostly new recruits. The ranked operatives don't like mixing with those who have yet to take the oath."

"The oath?"

"The oath of loyalty to Venomous. It's quite a ceremony. Hopefully, you'll get to see one while you're here. Maybe your own."

"I'm still looking around the store. If I want to buy something, I'll let you know," Emma said.

As they reached the lit part of the beach, Emma noted about one hundred kids laughing and hanging out around the fire. Actually, they were older than her. Maybe early twenties? They were the same type of college-aged kids Emma would see walking around the UC Berkeley campus when she visited her grandmother's office. One girl with tanned white skin noticed Ryan and approached him. She wore a two-piece bathing suit, but it was so small and tight it didn't hide what was under it. She flipped back her long dark hair.

"Hello, my name is Christina," the girl said.

"Ryan."

Christina's eyes lingered just a little too long on his chest.

Emma stepped in front of him. "Hi, I'm Ryan's girlfriend, Emma."

"Oh—your bathing suit is so pretty," Christina said to Emma.

"Thanks. I like your hair. It's so long. It takes a long time to wash that, I bet."

Christina nodded.

114

Emma kept her smile.

An uncomfortable silence developed.

"Did you two meet here during training?" Christina asked.

"We met somewhere else," Ryan said.

"It's classified," Emma added.

"We're here on personal business." Ryan clarified.

"Asset Ninety-five, welcome to the island."

Emma twisted towards the voice. It was a middle-aged woman with green eyes, short dark hair, and a brownish shade to her skin that was similar to Nadia's. She was tastefully dressed in beach attire, yet the woman had nothing to be ashamed of, her body was still in great physical condition.

Christina immediately took a knee near Ryan. Emma didn't understand why.

Ryan turned towards the woman. "It's good to see you again, Asset Twelve."

The middle-aged woman came over and gave Ryan a hug and a kiss on the cheek. "Asset One has told me everything." The woman whistled at the people on the beach. "Your attention is required."

The crowd of young people gathered around her and listened.

"This is Asset Ninety-five, one of my best students ever to come out of this facility. Let him be an example to you all how a young member of Venomous is expected to behave," the older woman said. "Welcome him."

The young men and women around them suddenly spoke in unison. "Welcome, Brother. Together, our venom strikes as one."

"And the one serves the many," Ryan said.

The young people responded, "So say we all."

"Asset Twelve?" a young man asked.

"Go ahead, Albert."

The young man pointed at Emma. "That girl did not say the greeting."

Asset Twelve slid her green eyes over to Emma. "That girl—is not one of us."

The recruits glanced at each other.

"Her code name is Black Opal. She is a member of that Authority group called the Gems."

The young recruits talked among themselves. They recognized that name.

Emma stood a little taller. She and her friends were famous. Well, among spies, anyway.

"Do you want us to kill her?" the young man asked.

Emma took a step behind Ryan.

The older woman smiled. "Under normal circumstances, I would have had this girl killed the moment she set foot on my island. However, Black Opal is to be treated as a guest. Asset One has given the order himself." The woman's cheeks lifted into a smile. "So please join us as we celebrate life and the future of our recruits." The woman and her recruits went back to their fire-pit.

"What was that about?" Emma asked. "Why does everyone want to kill me?"

"C'mon, Emma. how many profitable operations have the Gems messed up for us?" Ryan asked. "You should expect some resentment for taking money out of our pockets."

Emma noticed Christina was still kneeling. She tapped Ryan on the shoulder.

"Christina, you don't have to do that," Ryan said.

"Please forgive my lack of respect, Asset Ninety-Five. I didn't know you were ranked."

"I'm not offended. Please stand."

Christina hesitated, then stood up.

"Now, can you show me where the beer is?"

Soon Ryan brought back two bottles of beer with a slice of lime on top. Ryan showed Emma how to push the lime inside the bottle, plug your thumb on top and tip the bottle upside down so the lime would float up to the bottom of the bottle. "It distributes the lime juice equally."

Emma tried to do the same thing with her bottle, but she didn't quite hold her thumb down, and the beer squirted all over the place, making them both laugh. She drank the beer and it tasted good.

"Where did we leave off?" Ryan asked.

"You mean—before we were kidnapped, tortured by your goons, then invited to a secret training island where people are purposely sent into cages to be attacked by lions and tigers and bears?"

"Oh my."

Emma laughed.

"We were listening to music together," Ryan said.

Emma glanced around. "Sounds like Asset Twelve is controlling our party music for tonight." Emma drank some more beer.

Ryan took out his MP3 player and plugged in some ear-buds. He held one of them out to Emma. "Together, we've always listened to our own music, remember?"

Emma did remember. At his father's party in Kansas City. At the lake near his home. Walking down the streets of Montreal. No matter what the world offered, they would always listen to *their* music. Emma took the ear-bud and pressed it inside her ear. Ryan came in close to her face as he placed the other bud inside his ear. Emma was close enough to smell the beer on his breath and the hint of his cologne. It smelled very good.

Ryan pressed play. The opening beats of "Sgt. Pepper" thumped inside her head. Emma was in the groove immediately, bobbing her head to the music. Ryan watched her with a large smile on his face.

The beach party around them faded away as Emma and Ryan focused on each other's eyes and the Beatles.

They finished their beers and Ryan picked up two more. No one else bothered them as they continued to hang out and listen to music together.

The alcohol was gentle and slow.

Before she even realized it, Emma had placed her cheek against Ryan's neck. They listened to about ten songs before either of them said a word.

"Your hair smells exactly like it did in Missouri," he said. "And it's so soft."

"I like your neck. I might take it home with me."

Ryan smiled.

Emma felt his fingers running through her hair, and something deep inside her stirred. The beer had removed the layer of protection that dampened the urges. It also didn't help that Emma's mission was to seduce and flip Ryan by any means available. She knew Ryan's weakness. His Achilles heel that would open him up like a rose.

It was her.

"Strawberry Fields" came on. It started slow. Inviting. Easing you into it before the music gently picked up the tempo. It was like the alcohol. A transition so seamless you didn't notice it was happening.

The actor in Emma, the girl who played the role of the seductress for Mrs. B, slipped her hands behind Ryan's neck and swayed her body close, letting the music dictate her moves as Ryan watched her.

She moved closer and closer.

Then brushed against him as his eyes fixated on her.

Emma leaned in, hovered over his lips, but made herself stop. She wanted Ryan to come to her.

Ryan did.

He gripped her waist and kissed Emma on the lips. She returned the favor.

Soon they were making out as "She loves You," blasted through their ears.

CHAPTER 21

It had been two days since Olivia sent the selfie of her and Gabi to the special MeLocker account the Authority secretly used for incoming intelligence pictures. Since then, the Gems were keeping a close eye on Gabi as well as the twins. It wasn't unheard of for an intelligence agency to put eyes on their operatives to make sure they hadn't flipped or become compromised in one way or another. Gabi could be a Venomous agent sent to watch the twins or back them up if needed. But so far nothing had raised any alarm bells.

Olivia's last two days were filled with more nature hikes. More tree-planting excursions. Composting classes. Vegan cooking classes. Bird-identification classes. And of course—more sing-alongs.

It was during one of these sing-alongs when Olivia received a text from Nadia.

Join me. Bus near outhouses. ASAP.

Olivia left Miyuki alone to keep an eye on Gabi as she hiked her way towards the outhouses. After pretending to use the facilities, Olivia did a quick check of the area before leaping up the stairs of the parked bus. She went all the way to the back where Nadia was waiting.

"I received a message from Mrs. B," Nadia said, sliding her thumb across the screen to wake up her phone.

It was a voice message. Nadia played it back.

Listen carefully and then delete this. We've identified Gabrielle as a Mexican intelligence operative. We've reached out to her government and they've confirmed our mutual suspicions about the Heart The E group becoming radical. We've also agreed to combine our resources in this

119

investigation. Your orders are to introduce yourselves to Gabrielle. Tell her that —Santa Ana says hello from the Alamo. This phrase should get her attention.

That night, Olivia found Gabi sitting around a campfire with Cody, the twins, and some other Heart the E campers, roasting marshmallows and putting them in between pieces of milk chocolate and two graham crackers. They called this gooey mess a s'more. This camp was the first time Olivia had ever eaten one. They were messy but out-of-this-world delicious. Olivia wished she could stay and have another one, but there were more important things for her and the Gems to do tonight.

"We should totally have a retreat in Costa Rica sometime. I bet everyone would love that," Cody said, his warm smile on display twenty four seven.

"I would love to help organize that," Gabi said. "Even if it's only for the kids in Central America."

"What a grand idea," Bridget said. "We could have camps like this all over the world. Bridget and I can help set one up in Europe. Gabi could help us with Central and South America. Cody has the US and Canada. We just need to convince some of our international students to maybe set up some in their home countries."

"World domination," Sophia said.

"A world of peace and love for the earth. That's my dream," Cody said. "Our generation can do it. We can be the ones who save this world for future generations."

Olivia thought that was a wonderful idea—in theory. The more missions Olivia went on, the more reality taught her that the world was more complex than she thought. It was hard to get adults to agree on anything—let alone preserving the world they lived on. Olivia wanted to believe in Cody's dream. But in reality, she wasn't sure if even Cody was being honest with everyone.

Olivia did plan on breaking into Heart the E's main office using the key Miyuki had copied to find out more about who was giving the group money. But when she found out about Gabi, Mrs. B put a hold on the break-in until Gabi was told the truth and could help them. Now it was time to get Gabi on board.

Olivia tapped Gabi on the shoulder. "Can you help me?" she said in Spanish. "One of the posts came out of the ground, and now our tent has collapsed. I can't figure out how to fix it."

"*Sí*, no problem. I'm a tent wizard."

Gabi jumped up and followed Olivia towards the tent area.

Olivia stopped. "Do you mind if we swing by the toilets first? I have to pee."

Gabi didn't mind. They made a detour to the outhouses. A guy came out of one of them, squirted some anti-bacterial gel on his hands, and wiped them before leaving the area. There was no one else around. Olivia approached one of the outhouses but didn't open the door.

She faced Gabi instead. "I need to talk to you."

"About what?"

Two of the outhouses opened up. Miyuki and Nadia stood on opposite sides of Gabi.

Gabi noted the two girls. Her eyes squinted and her jaw tightened.

"Santa Anna—"

Before Olivia could get the words out, Gabi slammed her against the outhouse door and stuck a large knife to her throat.

"Back away," Gabi ordered. "Or I'll treat her like a Thanksgiving turkey."

CHAPTER 22

Olivia could feel the metal touching her skin as Gabi, her new friend for the last few weeks, held a knife to her throat. Gabi's eyes were fixed on her, like an animal fixed on the kill. It was a big switch from the friendly, carefree young Latino woman sitting at the campfire.

"Don't flinch. Don't call out for help," Gabi said. "Tell your friends to back away. Now."

"Can I finish what I was—"

There was pressure against Olivia's throat. She couldn't tell if it was the knife or Gabi's finger-nail.

"Quiet," Gabi warned.

Olivia complied.

"Who are you working for? Who gave you that name?"

"Santa Anna says hello from the Alamo," Nadia said.

Gabi's eyes blinked.

"We on the same team now!" Miyuki said in a positive, upbeat tone.

Gabi looked confused.

"May I say something?" Olivia asked softly in Spanish.

"*Sí*," Gabi said, keeping the knife to her throat.

"I'm Emerald. This is Sapphire and Ruby. We work for the Authority."

Gabi scanned Nadia and Miyuki.

"We've been sent here because Deirdre and Fiona are Venomous agents. Their real names are Bridget and Sophia O'Malley. We think they're up to something bad, and we're here to find out what," Olivia said. "How about you?"

Satisfied, Gabi put away the knife and backed away from Olivia. "I knew the twins were most likely spooks working for someone

122

else. But I didn't know it was Venomous. Then this is a credible threat."

"What threat?" Nadia asked.

"What did my people tell your people?"

"Only that you were investigating Cody and the organization," Olivia said.

Gabi paused. "An unidentified source told my government that members of this group are planning to launch an attack on the G20 summit in Mexico City. I was sent here to investigate."

"This group?" Nadia asked. "Attacking the G20 summit? I find that hard to believe."

"I agree," Gabi said. "I've been around this group longer than any of you. Most of these kids aren't very radical. They love nature and eating vegan burgers. I haven't detected anything that leads me to think they want to hurt anyone."

"What about the oil executive and that tiger attack in China?" Miyuki asked.

"That's Deirdre and Fiona. Cody has empowered them, and they're running amok," Gabi said. "From what I've observed, I wouldn't be surprised if they took over the entire movement and kicked him out."

"From what we know about them, the twins are capable of that and much more," Olivia said.

"They both loony-tunes crazy," Miyuki added.

"Your source said they were targeting the G20 summit," Olivia said. "Maybe Venomous is using this group to hide their attack."

"Kidnapping the leaders of the G20 and extorting their governments for money would be a classic Venomous operation," Nadia said.

"Tonight we planned on going over to the Heart the E business office in Portland to have a look around," Olivia said. "Would you care to join us?"

Gabi sighed. "You won't find anything there. I broke into that office my second week here and found nothing of interest. Cody's office people are clean, and I checked out their fundraising and sponsors. They were all legit."

"Damn it, thought that would make things easier on us," Olivia said, her natural accent leaking out.

"I knew it," Gabi said with a grin. "Half British and half Jamaican, right? That Spanish accent of yours wasn't Dominican.

You learned that accent in Mexico City. Although, I did detect of few Argentinian pronunciations as well."

"She's good," Miyuki said.

"My friend was from Argentina," Olivia said. "But we both lived in Mexico City. She taught me Spanish."

"What do we do now?" Nadia asked. "Wait for the twins to make the first move?"

"If they're planning anything," Gabi said, "they'll have to put it into motion soon because the summit is in two weeks."

"Then we'll keep up the surveillance and see what cracks open," Olivia said. "Unless anyone has a better idea?"

No one did.

CHAPTER 23

Emma woke up that morning feeling like she could take on the world. She stood up and stretched. Her body felt rested and rejuvenated. Emma parted her bedroom drapes and peeked out at the ocean waves still rolling along the sands of the beach. Emma looked around her private bungalow. Her clothes from the past week had been laundered and hung with great care. Her purse and other personal effects hadn't moved an inch overnight. She'd placed one of her blond hairs over the top of her purse and it wasn't disturbed. Neither was the blond hair she stuck across the closet door and frame. It was an old-school spy trick that Mrs. B showed them. The disturbed hair would let you know if anyone had searched through your things while you were out.

Emma had to admit that Venomous was treating her very well for being their sworn enemy. The last six days with Ryan had been —wonderful.

She picked up her phone and flipped through the week of pictures…

Ryan on a jet ski. At first, Emma had held on to him as they both raced across the water. Ryan then showed her how to pilot the jet ski. Of course, Emma already knew how to use a jet ski thanks to her many weekends with her dad at Cabo San Lucas. But holding on to Ryan's tight bod was worth the extra instruction.

There was a picture of her and Ryan with their snorkeling gear on. The island did have a nice coral reef that was overrun with saltwater fish in the most vibrant of colors. The two of them had spent most of that afternoon there.

She swiped her thumb.

There was a picture of Emma dancing near the fire-pit. Ryan must have taken this one. He'd taken another picture of her smiling into the camera. Wow—Emma was surprised how happy she looked. She was almost beaming into the camera.

Another picture. Ryan with a sniper rifle. That day they'd taken turns on the range, firing at targets. She had never used a rifle before, but Ryan showed her how to aim using a scope. How to use the ground and your elbow to steady the rifle. How to hold your breath right before squeezing the trigger. She wasn't as good as he was. But it was still nice to have him close to her, whispering his encouragement, his warm breath touching her cheeks as he gave instructions.

Emma swiped again.

This time they were on a boat. Ryan smiled as he held up a large fish that he'd just caught. The ocean had been nice and calm that day, but Emma wasn't as much into fishing as Ryan was. She did suntan on the deck instead. Still, Ryan seemed to love having her around for company, and since fishing involved a lot of waiting, they were able to talk to each other.

Emma put away her phone and got dressed.

She stepped out of her bungalow and went over to Ryan's. She knocked on his door.

No one answered.

An ATV drove past and did a U-turn. Omar brought it to a stop near Emma.

"Are you looking for Asset Ninety-five?" he asked. "I saw him in the outdoor training quad."

"Oh, okay," Emma said. "The outdoor training quad?"

"The outdoor training area. That area I drove you through when you first arrived." Omar pointed. "Down this path. Turn left. Go down the steps. You'll see it ahead of you. I would take you there myself, but I'm hauling this trash to the incinerator, and it smells like someone died."

Emma thanked Omar and followed his directions. She reached the training quad and didn't see Ryan anywhere.

Emma sighed and kept on walking down one of the paths. While she trekked through the quad, many of the Venomous "recruits" eyed her like she was someone famous. Someone worth staring at. But Emma had to keep telling herself that these "fans" would kill her if Asset Twelve had her way.

Finally, Emma heard Ryan's voice and traced it back to one practice square. Christina, the young Italian girl from the beach party, faced off against him in some kind of physical contest. They were both wearing gym clothes.

Ryan lunged towards Christina. She jumped out of the way and tried to kick him. But Ryan knocked her leg away, then grabbed her waist as she tried twisting him off. Ryan let go and stepped away.

"That's wrong. Stop."

Christina did.

"Don't twist like that. You won't be able to break off your attacker that way," Ryan said. "Here." Ryan took up his position again and wrapped his arm tightly around Christina's torso.

Emma's body tensed up. It was getting angry. Or was it jealous? Whatever her body was doing, it wasn't happy where Ryan's hands were in relation to that girl's—

"Have you had breakfast yet?" Emma asked.

Ryan looked up and grinned. "Not yet."

Her question didn't make him release Christina. That bothered Emma. Didn't he realize where his hand was? And that his girlfriend saw where his hand was?

"When did you get up?" Emma asked.

"I woke up early. Decided to take a walk on the beach."

Emma pointed. "Isn't the beach over there?"

"I kidnapped him," Christina said. "I saw him on the beach and asked if he could help me with a few moves. I'm taking my karate final today."

"Well, that was nice of Ryan," Emma said, not meaning it.

Ryan turned back to Christina. "Okay. Let's try that again. Now, instead of twisting, flip me over by—"

Christina moved quickly and tossed Ryan over her head, laying him out on the dirt.

"Like that?" she asked.

"Yeah, do it that way," he said, smiling. "I think you're ready for your final."

"Thank you, Asset Ninety-five."

Before Emma could jump all over Ryan for helping Christina with her wrestling moves, a two-person ATV came into view with Asset Twelve behind the wheel. She noticed the three of them and pulled her vehicle to a stop.

"Good morning, ma'am," Christina said.

Asset Twelve nodded. "I like to see my students taking the initiative. Embracing the new day early and with vigor." Her eyes then rested on Emma. "Laziness is a habit of a weak mind."

Emma didn't appreciate the jab.

"Black Opal is still on Montreal time. She'll adjust," Ryan said.

"Do you let your boyfriend speak for you? Or do you have your own mind?" the woman asked.

"I slept in because we were up late last night," Emma said. "But he's right. I'm still adjusting to whatever this time zone is."

Asset Twelve climbed out of her vehicle. "Is that what you're good at, Black Opal? Excuses? The Gems have quite a reputation. But when I look upon you—never mind."

"What is it?"

"I shouldn't bring it up."

"But you already have, haven't you?" Emma asked.

Asset Twelve arched her back. "To be honest, you strike me as the average American blonde who loves kittens, her parents, and seasonal high school dances." The woman moved towards Ryan and slid her arm around the back of his neck. "Besides the obvious, I don't see what you see in her, Ninety-five."

Emma's stomach burned. *Besides the obvious?* Was this woman insinuating that Emma was only good for making babies?

"With respect, Asset Twelve. You're only judging Black Opal from the outside," Ryan said. "Inside, she's much stronger than you give her credit for."

"Do you remember Jacqueline?" Asset Twelve asked.

"Yes, of course."

"Jacqueline told me that the blonde girl once had a gun to her head inside an elevator. The girl was ready to pull the trigger and revenge her father's death." Asset Twelve looked to Christina. "Jacqueline had to kill her father, you understand. It was business. Anyway, inside the elevator, this girl hesitated. She was in the perfect situation to kill Jacqueline and get her revenge. But this girl couldn't do it." Asset Twelve gave a large smirk toward Emma. "Jacqueline told me you cried like a little girl."

The scene flashed in front of Emma's eyes. The fancy office elevator. Jacqueline's crazy eyes daring her to kill. Emma's sweaty palm gripping the pistol. Her finger resting on the trigger. The rage and anger inside her heart. Emma wanted to kill her, but Jacqueline was defenseless, and Emma's mind wouldn't let that go. Wouldn't allow her to justify murder. Was that justice? Would her father want her to kill for him? Emma still wasn't sure what that answer was, or if she'd even made the right decision that day.

Asset Twelve tilted her head. "You're weak, Black Opal. You don't have the stomach for this business."

"Was Jacqueline your friend, ma'am?" Christina asked.

"We were lovers."

There was a great pause as everyone absorbed that.

Ryan swallowed. "Sorry, I didn't know."

"Your lover was a psycho," Emma said. "Maybe I should have killed her."

"Black Opal," Ryan warned.

Asset Twelve kept her cool. "Don't protect her, Ninety-five. Let your girlfriend be her own woman." Asset Twelve took a couple of steps towards Emma, facing her down. "Go ahead. What else would you like to say about my friend?"

The anger swelled up in Emma's throat. The pain of her father's death. The fire inside her to find out who had killed him.

"Okay. Let's start with Jacqueline's short spikey hair. It looked like a porcupine died on top of her head," Emma said. "She also put on too much makeup, and she bit her nails so bad that she had to wear gloves all the time. Oh, and she never used enough deodorant. Either that or she should've taken more showers. With soap."

Instead of getting angry, Asset Twelve laughed. "Such childish insults. Your high school claws are well-sharpened. However, you've made my point. You're nothing more than a high school prom queen. A white rich girl given everything in her life with no concept of how the real world lives."

"Shut up."

"Your eyes are so red. Our island infirmary can supply you with eye drops if you need them."

"I think it's time for some breakfast," Ryan said, almost pulling Emma away.

But she shook him loose.

"I do believe she wants to stay and play. Very well. Shall we see if my hypothesis about you is correct?" Asset Twelve stepped back. "Ninety-five?"

"Yes, ma'am?"

"Attack your girlfriend. Break her leg."

"What?"

"You will do exactly as I order. I want you to break her leg."

Ryan's frustration showed in his face as he hesitated.

"Are you refusing?"

Ryan was quiet.

"Refusing a direct order will not be tolerated. Your pain receptors will be activated."

Ryan didn't move.

"Very well." Asset Twelve pulled out her phone and tapped on some type of app.

Ryan buckled to the ground, holding himself tight as Emma dropped to his side.

"What is it?" she asked.

Ryan gritted his teeth and couldn't speak.

"His pain receptors have been activated," Asset Twelve said. "They will send pulsating electric shocks through his nerves until he complies."

Ryan lay on his side. His eyes watered from the pain.

Emma climbed back to her feet. "Stop it!"

"Not until he complies with my order."

Emma glanced at the woman's phone.

"You would be foolish to try," Asset Twelve said. "I'm too skilled for you to handle."

Emma didn't care. She launched a palm strike against the woman's arm. But the woman and her arm were gone. Asset Twelve was already behind her. Something pressed against her back, shoving Emma to the ground. But Emma picked herself back up and went into a fighting stance.

Asset Twelve slipped her phone securely into her pocket and crouched into a fighting stance.

Emma didn't hesitate. She launched a series of kicks and palms strikes at the woman just as fast as her skills could manage.

The older woman blocked every one of them.

Asset Twelve grinned. "You have the energy. You have sound techniques. But you're too predictable."

Emma didn't know what else to do. She'd given this woman everything she was trained to give. And even a few things Miyuki and Nadia had showed her. Well, there was one thing she hadn't tried.

Emma took a few steps back, then ran at the woman again. This time Emma did a hand-stand and used her forward momentum to fling her legs over the woman's shoulders. She then clamped her thighs together before taking them both to the ground. Emma then rolled to the side and used her thighs to form a tight head-lock on Asset Twelve. Either she would give up the phone, or Emma would choke her to death.

A shadow appeared over Emma. It made her look up into Ryan's eyes.

"Let her go," he said.

"Why? I have her right where I want her. Pretty good for a prom queen, huh?"

"Look behind you."

When she did, Emma caught the gleam from a six-inch blade. Asset Twelve held the knife in her other hand, the blade ready to plunge into Emma's back.

Emma released her thighs, allowing Asset Twelve to stand up, brushing the grass and dirt out of her hair.

Asset Twelve then studied Emma for a long moment. "Where did you learn that?"

Emma took a moment to catch her breath. "A friend of mine... she's a gymnast."

"I see. Most impressive. Perhaps I've misjudged you."

"You think?"

Asset Twelve smiled.

"What ship is that coming into the harbor?" Christina asked.

Ryan and Emma looked downhill towards a small port. A small cruise ship was steaming into a spot.

"That's Asset One's ship. He's here," Ryan said.

"Oh yes, I almost forgot the reason I came over here," Asset Twelve said. "Tonight, you and Emma have been invited to join us for dinner on board the *Falcon's Claw* by Asset One. I would wear something appropriate."

CHAPTER 24

Olivia woke up that morning feeling like she could take on another day of camp. Today there was nothing officially planned. Everyone in camp was encouraged to do whatever they wanted, so some members took canoes over to the lake. Others went back to the ropes course. A few took time out to be alone with a book or their phone to catch up with their friends at home.

Gabi was at one picnic table, making sketches of the camp as Olivia watched. Cody sat alone on a camp chair, picking on his guitar. He wasn't playing full songs, just going over a few chords. Gabi watched him and began a new sketch of Cody and his guitar. Olivia was fascinated by how Gabi filled in the shadows and the textures of the sketch. It was amazing how the girl's eye could pick up so much detail and transfer it on-to the paper. Gabi had a real talent for art, and Olivia wished she had the same creative genes as her new friend.

"I love that!" Cody said, seeing the picture for the first time. "I didn't know you were an artist, Gabi."

"You never asked."

Cody examined his portrait. "This is wonderful. May I keep it?"

"Sure. I just enjoy doing it. Sketching always puts me in a good mood." Gabi finished up the sketch and gave it to him.

"This is amazing, Gabi. Thank you."

Olivia caught a glimpse of Sophia and Bridget approaching their table.

"Time for another group meeting," Bridget announced as she came uncomfortably close to all three of them.

"Didn't we have a group meeting last night?" Cody asked.

"We have to start preparing things tonight."

"For what?" Olivia asked.

"Can't we just chill tonight and have some s'mores. Pretty soon our conference will be over and all these fine people will have to go home."

"Cody darling, did ya forget about our big send-off event?" Bridget asked.

"Oh yeah, the one where I was gonna order pizza for everyone?"

Bridget tilted her head. "Ya forgot, didn't ya?"

"He does that a lot," Sophia added.

Cody frowned. "I guess so."

"Mexico City? The summit, remember?"

Gabi shot a look at Olivia.

"Oh, right. You wanted to protest that."

"We should protest it. The G20 is responsible for, like, ninety percent of the world's pollution," Bridget said. "We can hop on our busses and go down there to Mexico and show 'em how we feel about their fecked-up policies about the environment. It's the perfect opportunity before everyone leaves."

"Going to Mexico—that sounds complicated. Why not go to Mount Rainer and do some more hiking. Or what about Crater Lake again? I love hiking there."

"Crater Lake is fine with me," Gabi said.

Bridget sighed. "Fiona and I already have the trip set up. Ya don't have to plan a thing. All ya have to do is get on a bus with your passport."

"Oh yeah, I like plans like that," Cody said.

"It's gonna be grand," Bridget said. "We'll get on worldwide television for sure."

"Are you girls planning another stunt?" Cody asked. "I don't know if that's a good idea. It's like—Mexico is a foreign country. They might throw us in a real prison. Like prison we can't pay bail for."

"Yeah, nah, don't worry. No stunts. This is only a protest in support of our world."

"What kind of logistics are we talking about?" Gabi asked. "Do we have permits? Do the Mexican federal police know that we're coming?"

"Bejesus, chill out," Sophia said. "We've got this all handled."

"Straight up, we went through the Mexican embassy and got the necessary permissions," Bridget said. "So yes, they know we're comin'."

Gabi touched Cody's arm. "I don't like this. What about the anarchists who show up at these things? We could easily get swept up in a riot or a mob protest. We're not about violence, are we?"

"Oh yeah, no, of course we're not. I wouldn't want that. If something like that started, we'd have to leave. No violence. We're only there to stand up for the earth. We want to force those leaders to look at us and hear what we have to say. That's all."

"Are you sure you don't want to go hiking instead?" Gabi asked.

Cody frowned. A part of him wanted to.

"Heart the E is a movement," Bridget said. "We must show the world who we are. Eating pizza and hiking won't do shit towards changing this world for the better."

"Yer bang on," Sophia said.

"Deirdre's right," Cody said. "We should try to do more."

"So our big send-off is on?" Bridget asked.

Cody thought about it. "Yeah, let's do it."

Bridget hugged Cody tight. "That's grand. So grand."

Gabi looked down at the table, trying to hide her disappointment.

Olivia felt the same way, but they still had a job to do. She turned towards the twins.

"When do we leave for Mexico?"

CHAPTER 25

Inside her bungalow, Emma checked herself in the mirror. She looked clean and presentable in a blouse, cute shorts, and dressy sandals. It was perfect for a dinner in the tropics or whereever she was.

There was a knock at her door. Emma opened it to reveal Ryan. He was dressed for the Oscars' red carpet with a black suit and light blue tie with matching handkerchief. His hair and face was perfectly groomed and handsome. When he saw Emma, his smile faded.

"Wow, you're all dressed up," Emma said.

"And you're not," Ryan said. "You can't wear that."

"What's wrong with this?"

"Asset One is old-school. He doesn't invite people over to have a barbecue and a couple of beers. He puts on a five-course meal with servers who brush the table to pick up crumbs while you're eating. Please tell me you have something more formal to wear."

Emma sighed. This boy didn't know her like he should. "Ryan, I've traveled all over the world with my dad since I was a kid. This girl knows how to pack for every occasion. Give me ten minutes."

"Ten?"

Ryan was right.

"Make it twenty."

Emma went back into her bedroom and got to work. She lost the blouse and shorts, then changed into a black cocktail dress she'd packed for formal emergencies. She kicked off the sandals and slipped on the emergency black pumps. She did a double-check of her makeup before stepping back out to the living room in under twenty minutes.

"That's perfect," he said.

"Of course it is. Ready?"

Ryan offered his arm, and Emma took it as they headed outside.

Omar waited with Asset Twelve in a large ATV. The older woman wore a plum-colored dress with matching lipstick and eye shadow. The colors looked sensational against her darker skin. Ryan helped Emma into the ATV before jumping in back himself. Omar followed the twisty route down towards the docks.

Ryan leaned in so only Emma could hear him. "When you meet Asset One, let him do all the talking. Don't say anything unless he asks you a question. And don't stare. It bothers him."

"Speak only if he asks me a question and don't stare. Sounds simple enough."

"I'm serious. Don't stare. He's killed people who have done that."

"Killed them?"

"Don't make fun of the way he talks either. He's killed people for that too," Ryan said. "Asset One is a little self-conscious."

"A little? Seriously, is there anything else I can be killed for?"

"Yes…talking about Asset One behind his back," Asset Twelve said with a smirk.

Emma glared at Ryan, who sat back in his seat. They both stayed quiet until the ATV reached its destination.

The Falcon's Claw floated next to the large wooden pier it was tied to. Up close, the small cruise ship was gigantic compared to the millionaire yachts Emma remembered seeing in places like Martha's Vineyard and Monte Carlo. The cruise ship seemed like overkill for one man, even if he was the head of one of the most infamous criminal enterprises on the planet. Unlike a normal cruise ship, the entrance ramp was guarded by six men, who bristled with weapons. The leader of this group cleared them to board the ship.

Once on board, the three were greeted by the *Falcon's Claw's* captain, who was in full dress uniform. Even the members of his crew were dressed like they were on the luxurious White Star Line of *Titanic* fame. They followed the captain through a set of two massive wooden doors that emptied into the biggest living room Emma had ever seen in her life.

The walls of this "living room" went higher and higher to form a gigantic atrium. From what Emma could tell, this part of the original cruise ship was probably the main atrium where tourists would stare up at the giant skylight that formed part of the roof of the ship. But now it was a giant room for only one man.

Oil paintings with gold frames were hung on the walls. The furniture was made of gold and leather. Expensive Persian rugs sat on top of a dark oak wood floor. And the centerpiece of this "living room" was a row of eight golden falcon statues. Each statue had its own pedestal.

Emma drifted over to one of the falcon statues. They were all painted gold. And their eyes—the bird's eyes were sparkling. Emma couldn't believe it. Were those real rubies?

"Those are my most…precious possessions," a male voice said.

Emma jumped back as a man with long blond hair and white glasses moved out from the shadows. He was already inside the room and observing them.

Without skipping a beat, Asset One moved to the statue and caressed the top of the bird's head. "Sky's sarcophagus…is made of solid gold. The rubies…are quite real," he said. "You were drawn to them. Which means you have a good eye…for beauty, my dear. Each one of my falcons has given me such…wonderful companionship."

"You mean there's a dead bird inside that?" Emma asked.

Ryan froze in place. Apparently, that was the wrong thing to say.

Asset Twelve revealed a wicked smile. Most likely hoping that she'd be ordered to kill Emma on the spot.

Emma wanted to kick herself. She had insulted the man's beloved pet and didn't even wait for him to ask her a question. Yeah, she was about to die.

"Um. . .I meant no disrespect, sir. I'm sorry about your feathered friend. I bet he was a lovely bird."

Asset One didn't smile, nor did he frown. "My feathered friend…I like that term. These were friends who have passed away. I wanted to honor them…like the Egyptians did their pharaohs. Precious, are they not?"

"They're beautiful."

"Speaking of that. Your father must have been so proud… seeing you enter a room."

Emma's heart twitched for her dad. He was proud of her. At least, that was what he would say to her. It was a nice thing for the man to say.

"Lovely. Very lovely." Asset One turned to Ryan. "You have excellent taste."

"Thank you, Asset One."

"Where's your falcon now?" Emma asked. "The living one?"

Ryan gripped her shoulder. "Asset One, please forgive my friend. She tends to speak quite a lot."

Emma jerked her shoulder away and fired off a look at Ryan.

Asset One referenced the top of the atrium. Emma craned her neck. Right under the decorative skylight was a beautiful falcon perched high above them.

"His name is Sunchaser. He enjoys watching his prey…before he kills it."

Asset Twelve stepped away from Emma.

Ryan hesitated. His eyes bounced from the falcon to her and back.

Emma felt the vibe in the room change. She thought the man was joking.

"Has she seen…most of the island?" Asset One asked.

Asset Twelve moved over and joined her boss. "Only the parts I wished her to see."

"Enough to tip our hand?"

"Of course not."

"Still, we've been most welcoming to her," Asset One said. "To continue…I think we need a commitment."

"What kind of commitment?" Emma asked.

Asset Twelve smirked. "He means that you have your foot in our door…yet Asset One wonders if we should let you come in or cut your foot off."

"Your analogy is amusing," Asset One said.

Ryan stepped forward. "I think Black Opal will be a great asset to us."

"I've already heard your sales pitch." Asset One's unemotional eyes slowly moved to Emma. "But I have yet…to listen to hers."

CHAPTER 26

On the top deck of the *Falcon's Claw*, Emma and Ryan joined Asset One and Asset Twelve for dinner under the clear night sky as the ship's lights made the ocean shimmer around them. Sunchaser floated above the ship as the falcon did lazy circles in the air. On the large outdoor table, the four of them were served a full-course meal. The best of the best. A seafood salad. Then a French onion soup that was the best that Emma had ever tasted. Next was the main course. Steak, lobster, and optional crab legs so fresh they seemed to have jumped out of the sea.

Emma skipped the crab legs for messy reasons. She worked on the steak and some of the lobster since the shell was already pre-cracked. Asset Twelve used a lobster bib as she ripped into her crab legs with relish. Her fingers and hands quickly became dirty with crab flakes.

Ryan followed Emma's example, deciding to stick with the controllable steak and lobster. When Ryan reached for his drink, Emma noticed a slight quiver in his hand. The boy was nervous but trying not to show it. Emma couldn't blame him. This woman and this man made her nervous too.

"I'm looking forward…to the Copa America cup. Brazil has another strong team," Asset One said.

"Colombia will take it all," Asset Twelve said.

"Colombia? Interesting. Their team is young…never have they been in a tournament like this one. Their chances of winning would seem…daunting."

"The odds are thirty to one, I believe."

"Thirty to one?" Ryan asked. "Those are terrible odds."

"Agreed," Asset One said.

"They were so terrible that I placed a quarter-million-dollar bet on Colombia," Asset Twelve said.

"A quarter of a million?" Emma asked.

Asset One sat back, watching his female comrade. "I can see the ace…hidden under your skirt."

The older woman flashed a satisfied grin. "Asset Seventeen has most of the Copa America referees in his back pocket. I predict there will be some—irregularities—in the officiating."

Asset One motioned one of his men over. "Inform Asset Seventeen that I'm expecting a generous…contribution to my bank account when his team wins the cup."

The man nodded and left.

"You mean Asset Seventeen didn't inform you of his plan?" Asset Twelve asked.

"He's slipping. If the man's not careful…he'll fall right through the ice…and drown." Asset One motioned to one of the servers wearing plastic gloves. That man came over, took a fresh crab leg, and cracked it open. He spooned out all the meat, then returned to standing in place.

"Has anyone here tried ice fishing?" Asset One asked.

Everyone shook their heads.

"As a child, I enjoyed walking across the ice…picking a good spot. Digging into the surface and dropping in my lure. I would sit there for hours. Relaxing. Enjoying the quiet. The cool breeze off the ice…as it played with my hair. You see, there wasn't much to do…in my Norwegian village during the winter."

"There was no ice to cut through, but I loved fishing in the lake our family had in Missouri," Ryan said. "There were a lot of catfish and bass. When I was younger, my father and I would go out on a boat together. Then when I got older, he got busy and we stopped fishing together." Ryan concentrated on his steak. Emma knew that Ryan's father was a touchy subject, but she was glad he was able to talk about it.

"Your father was an arrogant and greedy man," Asset One said. "Willing to risk his reputation and…his entire Raymond Foods empire on a scheme…to make money off of starving people."

"And it destroyed him."

"Precisely. Don't allow his foolishness to influence your future. You're smarter than he was, Ryan. One day you'll be successful… beyond your wildest expectations."

Emma remembered that Raymond Foods story a little differently. "But Venomous used Ryan's father and his food empire to extort money from the governments of those starving people."

"Technically...we didn't extort any money because you and your friends blew up Jacqueline's plan," Asset Twelve said. "And she paid the price for that."

"How sad. Would you like a hug?"

Asset Twelve fired a look at Emma.

"Ladies, we're here to enjoy...this beautiful evening. Not to dwell on the past," Asset One said.

Emma and Asset Twelve exchanged glances, then went back to their meals.

Asset One used his fork to spear a chunk of lobster and whistled. Soon, Sunchaser swooped in and snatched the piece with his beak and soared into the night sky.

A large Venomous goon approached the table. "Message for you, sir."

"Why must you interrupt...our dinner? We have yet to serve... the chocolate torte."

"The captain thought it was important, sir. It's about the information you sent to Odessa."

Asset One used a napkin on his hands before placing it to the side. "Yes, I see. I'll look at that now."

The goon handed him the message, which Asset One opened. As he read it, Emma watched as the man's lips gently formed a shallow grin.

"Give this to Asset Twelve," he said.

The goon took the message over to her, and the woman began reading.

"I don't believe it," she said.

"What is it?" Ryan asked.

"I had my people in the Ukraine...check out the information that Black Opal gave to us. It's all true."

"That slimy bastard," Asset Twelve said. "Fifty million dollars. How brazen."

Emma smiled on the outside, but inside she was relieved. The golden ticket that Mrs. B gave her had apparently worked. It was the "commitment" that Asset One demanded from her.

"So Asset Eleven is a double agent?" Ryan asked.

"He is a triple agent," Asset One said. "Working for us, the Ukrainians, and the Russians...while pocketing vast sums of money in over twenty separate bank accounts."

"May I invite him to the island?" Asset Twelve asked with an edge.

"Yes. Please have a discussion about his future...in our organization."

"His limited future?"

"Indeed."

"What type of retirement package shall I give him?" Asset Twelve asked.

"The shark reef will be most appropriate. Send me a link to the video stream. I do enjoy watching wildlife...interacting within their native habitats." Asset One then gave orders to the goon, who quickly left the deck.

Emma's gaze then fell on Sunchaser. The falcon perched on one of the nearby deck rails while his beak ripped through the lobster meat with relish. She wondered if the bird had ever tasted human flesh.

"Tell me, Ryan. How are the twins? Are they making progress?" Asset One asked.

Emma shook off her bird-watching and listened.

Ryan's eyes jumped to Emma, then back to Asset One. "Do you want to discuss that here?"

Asset One took a drink of wine, then licked his lips. "Emma will be part of our family soon. Today she gave us fifty million dollars...on a platter. It's a most welcome gesture. A gesture that should be rewarded with openness. Let's not hide things from our new friend."

Emma stopped eating. Asset One knew her name. "Um, I told Ryan that I'd think about it. I haven't decided anything yet."

"Emma, I know why you are here. I know what the Authority wants you to do. But I want to speak to you about...what you want to do. Ryan is monitoring the progress of assets One-three-zero and One-three-one. Like you, they're two remarkable young women...who are instrumental in my plan."

"And what plan would that be?" Emma smiled innocently at Ryan. The boy hesitated and shifted in his chair as if his body subconsciously didn't want to spill the beans.

"The Medusa operation," Asset One said. "A plan to kill the top twenty world leaders. Chop off their heads...and their countries will die. Or in our case...allow a series of power vacuums that Venomous...can take advantage of."

Emma placed down her fork. "Those twins are going to assassinate twenty world leaders?"

Asset One leaned back in his chair and looked upon Emma like she was the most naive person on the planet. "Dear child...who do you think ravages the resources of this planet for fun and profit? Who exploits human beings...in factories and sweat-shops to make piles of money. Why...it's the people you work for."

Asset One whistled again. Sunchaser flapped in for a soft landing on his long padded glove. He offered him some lobster and the falcon ate it greedily from the man's hand. "Have you heard of the Century Group?"

"No," Emma lied.

"They are among the richest families in the world. They fund the Authority. They use it to manipulate governments. They use it to exploit this planet...for their own selfish purposes." He fed Sunchaser more lobster. "You see us as the criminals? We are the survivors. We take money from the governments and institutions that...make money off the people and the planet. Are we strict? Yes, of course. Are we hard? Yes, we must be disciplined to fight against such...powerful adversaries. But are we all that different? We all want money, Emma. We don't lie and pretend that...we're above such things. However...the Century Group pretends that they're above all their money and power. They pretend to know... what mankind needs."

Sunchaser used Asset One's arm as a bridge to the table. The falcon waddled over to the plate and helped himself to the goodies.

"Have you found that to be true, Ryan?" he asked.

Ryan sat up straight. "My father was a slave to money. He let it manipulate him into doing stupid things. He thought it made him better than everyone else. But it just made him more of a monster. In the end—when he lost it all—he lost himself. Killed himself like a coward because his vanity couldn't take living with the failure anymore." Ryan's focus fell on Emma. "You're like me. When it came to our family's wealth, we both wanted to do something that mattered." Ryan leaned closer to her. His eyes were serious. "Think about this for a moment. After you've inherited your father's empire, you'll become a powerful young woman. A woman who can change the world and shape it into whatever she wants."

Emma laughed. "You're crazy. Seriously, I have zero power in my life right now."

"Why do you think the Authority recruited you, Emma? They knew you were about to inherit a fortune. They knew you were beautiful and captivating. Your father taught you how to act around adults. How to handle yourself at parties. You are someone who can make others like and follow you."

Emma rolled her eyes. "When I first came to California, everyone at school called me the Ice Queen. Where was all this—charisma—I'm supposed to have? I sure could have used it then."

"The Century Group wants you under their control...because they see you as a possible threat," Asset One said.

"Seriously?"

"Your family was once part of the Century Group. Now you stand to inherit your father's wealth...they'll want you to sign your father's assets over to them...for safe keeping."

"They'll steal it from you," Ryan added. "Like my father did to me.

"This is ridiculous," Emma said, dropping her fork on the plate. "I want to be an actor. The theater is all I care about. It's not about the money. It's not about the stupid corporation. I only care about fulfilling my father's last wishes. That's all."

"You promised your father that you would look after the companies and all the people who worked for them, didn't you?" Ryan asked.

Emma was quiet.

"So you do care about preserving...your father's legacy," Asset One said. "I admire your loyalty to him."

"I can do both. I can be an actor and own a corporation. A woman can do anything she wants."

"Bravo, Emma, bravo. You can have it all. Power, money, the acting career you desire." Asset One paused. "Celebrities have real power. They can mobilize an army of fans to do whatever they want...with a simple tweet. A smart young woman with that kind of following...along with the money...and with the connections that Venomous can offer—your personal power will have no limits."

"I've said it before," Ryan added. "You don't need the Authority to make yourself feel good. You can help shape thousands of people's lives on your own."

A smile began to crack Asset One's stoic face. "Think about the future and your place in it. I believe you'll realize that...you've been helping the wrong side."

CHAPTER 27

For most of the morning, the members of Heart the E were packing up four busses for their big Mexico City road trip. Those who didn't have passports had to stay and take care of the camp while everyone else went. Olivia and Miyuki helped one group of young adults load up a bus with water, snacks, and other items they would need for their trip.

"Can you two girls help me for a sec?" Gabi asked.

Olivia and Miyuki left the other members to finish loading as they followed Gabi behind the large kitchen cabin, where Nadia was waiting.

"Should we put a stop to this when we cross the border?" Gabi asked. "I can have the Mexican authorities in Juarez arrest Bridget and Sophia for conspiracy and terrorism charges. Then get them to talk under interrogation."

"We have no evidence," Miyuki said. "So far, they've done nothing wrong. They're only planning to protest the summit."

"Are you bonkers?" Olivia asked. "They're Venomous agents. Of course they're planning to do something. We know that for sure."

"But what?" Nadia asked. "Have you ever seen the level of security at those events? Bridget and Sophia would need an army to break into that summit."

"Your friend Sapphire is right. These kids wouldn't physically attack anyone," Gabi said. "We should assume the twins are using the protest to get close enough to the summit to put another plan in motion."

"What about planting a bomb? Or firing off a rocket-propelled grenade at the compound?" Olivia asked, her mind churning out plenty of disaster scenarios. She couldn't help herself.

"I'll contact my government and have them arrested," Gabi

said. "We shouldn't take any chances."

"Right, play it safe. I totally agree, love. In the meantime, we should all keep a close eye on Sophia and Bridget. Don't let them out of your sight, even for a moment."

"What if they go to the restroom?" Miyuki asked.

"Peek under the stall," Gabi said.

All the girls giggled.

An hour later, the Heart the E caravan of busses got underway. They went eastward through most of Oregon before they cut southeast through Boise, Idaho. Then they made their way southeast through Utah, just clipping the southwestern end of Colorado before heading south through Albuquerque and most of New Mexico. It took the caravan twenty-four hours to reach the US-Mexico border in El Paso, Texas.

It was cool that morning as the busses waited in a line of traffic to enter Mexico. It was a moderate wait, but finally the first bus reached the checkpoint. Olivia and Gabi made sure they were on the first bus, mainly because they wanted a front-row seat to what would happen next.

Soon, two Mexican border officers came aboard and checked everyone's passports. When they reached Bridget, the officer asked her to get off the bus.

"Why do I have to get off?" Bridget asked, concerned. "Is there something wrong with my passport, officer?"

"No, *señorita*," the border officer said. "We do random personal searches. See the female officer outside, please."

Bridget took a long look at the officer, then glanced at the half a dozen Mexican border officers waiting outside the bus. She huffed loudly as she stood up.

"Take your purse and luggage with you, please."

"Are you searching those too?"

"Standard procedure, *señorita*. They will be returned to you."

Bridget groaned as she marched down the front steps of the bus.

Gabi nudged Olivia with excitement. "Pull the window down."

Olivia pushed in the tabs to their bus window, and it slid halfway down. Now they could see and hear everything.

"This is fecking rubbish! I want my lawyer!" Sophia yelled as four border officers fought with her down on the ground.

"What's going on?" a boy on the bus asked. "Are Fiona and Deirdre getting arrested?"

The discussion spread throughout the bus.

Olivia whispered to Gabi, "Brilliant, they've already pulled Sophia from the other bus."

"Why are ya putting handcuffs on my sister?" Bridget yelled, her eyes on fire. "Why are ya arresting us?" Bridget tried to run for it, but a female officer tackled her to the ground.

"Whoa!" the boy inside the bus shouted.

Bridget fought with the officer as six more Mexican border officers swept in to subdue these two teen girls.

"Leave her alone!" the boy on the bus shouted.

The other Heart the E kids on the bus began booing and yelling at the officers to leave the twins alone.

"Hey—you guys, let's keep it down," Cody said loudly so everyone on the bus could hear him. "We don't know what's going on yet." Cody carefully walked down the steps to talk to one of the officers.

Gabi grabbed Olivia's hand. "Let's go be nosy." She pulled Olivia down the aisle of the bus and out through the front steps. They stood behind Cody as he was talking.

"But I don't understand, what did they do to get arrested?" Cody noticed Gabi behind him. "I'm not getting through to him. Can you—?"

Gabi spoke with the border officers in Spanish. They told her that the two sisters possessed fake passports and must be held for questioning. Gabi repeated that to Cody.

"Oh no, that's not good," he said.

Sophia was grunting like a wild animal as seven men loaded her into a federal police panel van.

As they put handcuffs on Bridget, she yelled, "The Irish embassy is gonna hear about this, ya bitches!"

Soon Bridget was in the van too as it drove off with its emergency lights flashing.

Cody looked worried as he ran his fingers through his blond hair. "I don't know what to do. We should wait for them, right?"

"Mexican courts can take forever," Gabi said. "It might be a few weeks before the twins even see a judge."

"If we wait for them, we could miss the whole G20 summit," Olivia said.

"Oh man, I don't want this to be a spoiled trip for everyone," Cody said. "Yeah, you're right. I'll stay behind."

"Cody—let me stay behind," Gabi said. "I have a friend who lives in Juarez, so I can stay with her and make sure Bridget and Sophia get everything they deserve."

"Are you sure?"

"Don't worry about it. Don't I take care of everything for you?"

"But without you—oh, man—who'll help me with the protest? Bridget and Sophia set all of this up, and I haven't done anything like organizing a protest before."

Gabi referenced Olivia. "You have Camila here. She's a natural-born leader. And that Azerbaijan girl Aylin? She's been very helpful to me. Let them help you with the protest."

Cody didn't look too sure.

"We can do it, Cody," Olivia said.

"Really?"

Gabi added a nod to help.

Cody thought about it then his body relaxed. "If Bridget and Sophia need a lawyer or anything, just call me or the office, and the organization will take care of it."

"I will." Gabi turned to face Olivia. "I guess this is goodbye."

"Goodbye for now," Olivia corrected her as they both hugged.

"It's been a pleasure working with you," Gabi told her in Spanish.

"I've enjoyed it too," Olivia answered in Spanish.

Gabi smiled and switched back to English. "Take care of Cody. If you don't, I'll come find you."

Cody laughed. "I do need a lot of supervision." He offered Gabi a hug and she took it. "Thanks for taking care of this. I owe you one."

"*Mucho gusto.*"

After the hug, Gabi and Cody lingered for a moment, each holding the other's hands. The friendliness and comfort between them was clear.

As was something else.

Gabi seized the moment and kissed him on the lips.

Olivia was amazed. Gabi just did it. Like didn't ask for permission or let the guy make the first move. That girl wanted to kiss him and that's what she did.

There was no way Olivia could do that with Lewis. Not like

that.

Gabi separated her lips from Cody's. "I've been wanting to do that for a long time."

Cody's eyes were saucers. He whispered, "I loved that."

Gabi laughed as she walked away, waving to both of them as she headed for the pedestrian border crossing.

Cody stood there. Not moving. Not making eye contact with anyone. He acted stunned like Gabi just hit him with a brick.

"C'mon, lover boy." Olivia helped Cody back on the bus.

As the bus caravan drove deeper into Mexico, Olivia and Nadia went over all the plans for the G20 protest that Cody could remember from what the twins had told him. According to Cody, there was some dude they spoke with from the Mexican embassy in Austin, Texas, although he couldn't remember the dude's name.

"But who is our contact in Mexico City?" Nadia asked, trying to make sense of it all.

"We need someone who works for the government in Mexico City, not Austin," Olivia said. "Didn't anyone write this stuff down?"

"Like I said." Cody sighed. "Deirdre and Fiona handled everything. They had the contacts. I guess I should have been more involved with the planning."

"Where are we staying?" Nadia asked. "Do we have a hotel lined up or a campground we're using?"

"I don't know." Cody placed his hands on both sides of his head and pushed like he was popping a zit. "This is going to be a disaster."

"Maybe we should go back to Oregon," Olivia said.

"Hey, Deirdre and Fiona went to jail so we could do this," Cody said with a sudden burst of guilt. "We can't pull out now. We owe it to them to do this."

"Yes, we do owe it to them," Nadia said, still playing her alias well. "We can figure this out. Can you think of anyone else the twins might have mentioned about the trip? Any other organizations? Allies? Friends?"

"Not a clue," Cody said.

"I don't see a choice," Olivia said. "If no one knows where we're going—"

Miyuki leaned over and pushed up her glasses. "The bus drivers know where we're going, don't they?"

Nadia and Olivia exchanged looks. *Why didn't they think of that?*

"That's a great idea, Cho." Cody stood up in the aisle and made his way forward towards the older volunteer driving their bus.

The three Gems followed him.

"Hey, Randy-man, where are we going?" Cody asked the driver.

The driver showed him an address that was on his phone's GPS. "Fiona said it was some warehouse."

"Why are we going to a warehouse?" Cody asked.

"Deirdre said it was owned by a Mexican importer who was a large supporter for the organization. He was setting up three hundred beds so we could all stay there for the night." The driver paused. "His last name was—Geraldo? Hernandez? Hermanez?"

"Dude—I forgot about Mr. Hermanez," Cody said with a smile. "I'm such an idiot."

"Who's he?" Olivia asked.

"Mr. Hermanez supports a Mexican environmental group that has been wanting to work with us. I bet Deirdre and Fiona got in contact with him about both our groups protesting the G20 summit together."

"Having a partner in Mexico with the same agenda would make sense," Nadia said.

"Hey, Mr. Hermanez might be willing to help us get the twins out of jail too," Cody said.

"Let's focus on the protest first," Olivia said. "Once we get to the warehouse and meet this Mr. Hermanez, we should be able to figure out the game plan."

Hours later, darkness fell on the Mexican plain as the lead bus pulled off the main road and followed Bridget and Sophia's directions to a small town on the outskirts of Mexico City. The headlights of the bus washed over a warehouse with a single truck bay. The driver pointed it out to Olivia before parking in front. The other busses followed suit.

Cody and the three Gems got off the bus. Olivia scanned the area. It was dark. No street-lights. And no one was out front.

"That's strange. There's no one here to welcome us," Olivia said.

Cody shrugged. "Mr. Hermanez must be inside." He walked right up to a door and opened it. Light poured out from the inside of the warehouse as Cody continued through. The Gems followed.

"Hello?" Cody called out. His voice bounced all over the empty cement floor and metal walls.

Olivia noted there were no beds. No tables. No chairs. Nothing at all except the lights burning above them.

"Oh shit," Cody said. "Maybe we were wrong."

"Who leaves their warehouse lights on?" Olivia asked. "Especially when the warehouse is empty?"

"And unlocked," Nadia added.

Olivia's stomach tightened. Something didn't feel right. "Let's go back to the bus."

Even Miyuki was nodding her approval.

"I'll call Maggie at the office." Cody pulled out his phone. "She must have Mr. Hermanez's contact info. We'll straighten this all—"

A gun-shot rang out from outside the warehouse.

"What was that?" Cody asked.

The three Gems checked with each other. *Yes, that was gunfire.* Next, there were people screaming outside the warehouse.

Cody drifted over to the door.

"Don't open that!" Olivia yelled.

"Should we hide?" Miyuki asked.

At that moment, an electric motor engaged the large bay door as it lifted all on its own. Olivia checked around the warehouse. There was nowhere to run to. Nothing to hide behind. There was a catwalk running around the perimeter of the warehouse, but it was too late to try to climb up to it.

Halfway up, the bay door revealed armed men with their faces covered with handkerchiefs. They were shouting orders to the Heart the E members in Spanish while gesturing with their automatic rifles. The teens and young adults from the busses were being herded inside the warehouse itself.

"How many bad guys do you see?" Olivia said to her team.

"Six in the front," Miyuki said.

"I count ten near the busses," Nadia said.

"What weapons do we have?"

"I have tranquilizer darts," Nadia said.

"Me too," Miyuki said.

"I have some flame-thrower lipstick. But I can't use that inside a crowd," Olivia said.

Cody didn't understand a thing these girls were saying. Hell, he didn't understand anything that was going on. "Who are these people? Are they, like, bandits or something?"

The armed men finally crowded everyone inside the warehouse. Olivia, Nadia, and Miyuki herded themselves with Cody and melted into the crowd. So far, Olivia counted a total of twenty men. Twenty against three. Very bad odds. But what did they want?

When Olivia's dad had worked for the British embassy in Mexico City, he was warned that kidnappers sometimes operated in the rural areas of Mexico, snatching up people who had money because their families could afford to pay the hefty ransoms.

Nadia and Miyuki crowded around Olivia.

"What do you think?" Nadia asked.

"Kidnappers?" Olivia asked.

"Perhaps, but how did they know we'd be here?"

"Maybe Mr. Hermanez isn't such a nice man," Miyuki said.

"This was a trap?" Nadia asked.

"Three hundred young people from all over the world would make for a big juicy ransom," Olivia said.

The electric motors engaged one more time as the large bay door came back down, trapping everyone inside the warehouse. The armed men formed a perimeter around the Heart the E members. Some of the men had access to the upstairs catwalk too. Wait, now Olivia counted thirty men. This was insane.

Olivia felt her phone buzz with a text. But before she could dig into her pocket to grab it—

Two teen girls with flowing red hair appeared on the catwalk. Bridget and Sophia O'Malley leaned against the metal handrails as they looked down on everyone.

Olivia's heart sank.

Nadia's worried eyes met hers as she touched her friend's shoulder.

Miyuki only said two words. "Mother trucker."

CHAPTER 28

Olivia's mind filled with questions. *What were the twins doing here? What were they really up to? How did they escape police custody?*

Unfortunately, those unanswered questions didn't seem to matter as reality trapped them inside a warehouse with Bridget and Sophia on top of a catwalk, along with thirty armed men who Olivia guessed were Venomous goons. It was the situation Gabi and the Gems were trying to avoid.

So much for that idea.

Olivia then remembered her vibrating phone. She checked the screen. It was a series of texts from Gabi…

Twins escaped from custody. Took a police car. Found near airstrip. Twins could be anywhere. G20 security alerted. Federal police looking for them. Be careful.

Olivia stopped herself from rolling her eyes. Gabi's timing sucked. However, her new friend could still save their butts. Olivia's fingers began typing a plea for help when—

A gun-shot rattled the warehouse as the bullet ricocheted two feet from where Olivia stood. Nadia yelped as she grabbed Olivia's arm. Other teens screamed.

Olivia froze. Her eyes rose to the catwalk, where Sophia was looking down at her through the sight of a sniper's rifle.

"All right, ya muppets—drop your fecking phones on the floor," Bridget said, not messing around.

The kids and young adults all looked around, either too confused or too scared to comply.

"Bejesus, do it now, or we'll be shooting all of ya!"

Phones clattered against the cement floor.

Olivia and Nadia both had their phones out, ready to text, both thinking the same thing.

"You three girls." Bridget pointed directly towards Olivia and company. "Come forward."

Olivia casually slipped her phone back in her jeans as she walked forward—

Another gun-shot stopped Olivia cold. That bullet was only a foot away from her.

"Now what did we forget to do?" Bridget asked, acting like she was a kindergarten teacher.

Olivia hesitated, then took out her phone and dropped it on the floor. Nadia and Miyuki both frowned and did the same.

"Good girls. Now, come forward."

Olivia, Nadia, and Miyuki moved away from the pack of Heart the E members huddled together in the middle of the warehouse. Sophia followed them with her rifle.

"Ya know, Sophia, those girls do look familiar," Bridget said. "Enlighten me again, where have ya seen 'em before?"

Sophia lowered her rifle, but still kept it aimed. "New Zealand. They went to Avondale with us."

Bridget's face brightened. "Oh my God! Hello, roommate! Do ya remember me? Because I sure remember you all." Bridget squinted. "What's up with the disguise? That new nose and forehead of yours is fecking atrocious."

"Makes ya look like a retarded person."

"Sophia—that's mean. It just makes her look stupid." Bridget touched her chin as she examined the other two Gems. She pointed at Miyuki. "You've cut your long hair short, and those new glasses look horrid." Her finger went to Nadia. "And you—ditched the headscarf. I approve. Your long black hair is bloody gorgeous. Is it gorgeous, Sophia?"

"It's lovely."

"It is," Bridget said.

Cody emerged from the crowd. "Hey, guys, what's going on? Did the Mexican cops release you or—?"

Bridget's face softened. "Oh, Cody. Ya handsome—gullible twerp of a man. Do ya not see the sunshine that's right in front of ya, lad?"

"Is this another one of your stunts?"

"Bejesus, Cody," Sophia said. "Pull your head out of your arse, would ya? We don't care about the fecking earth."

"The earth will be just fine without us," Bridget said.

Cody looked so confused.

"Ya poor muppet," Bridget said. "Ya believed us, didn't ya?"

"I don't understand. Why did you join our group? To sabotage it?"

"They wanted to use your group," Olivia said. "Isn't that right, love? Use it as a cover to carry out a terrorist attack on the G20 summit."

Cody's eyes were saucers. "Whoa, are you kidding me?"

Bridget raised her hands in alarm. "Oh no, Sophia! Our evil plans have been ruined. Shoot, if it wasn't for Beyonce and her Scooby Doo crew, we would have gotten away with it too."

Sophia chuckled.

Olivia was nervous but kept pushing herself to speak. "I'd surrender now. The Mexican authorities already know you're up to something. They've increased security at the summit, and every police officer in Mexico is on the lookout for two red-headed bitches."

There was a collective gasp from the crowd.

Bridget laughed. "That hurts. I thought we were roommates. You know, best friends forever."

"Can I please kill her?" Sophia asked, her eye looking back through the scope of the rifle.

"Patience, Sophia, darling. We're coming up to the best part." Bridget leaned against the railing and flashed the biggest smile the girl could muster. "The part where I tell my roommate that this—" Bridget motioned to everything around her "—is all bullshit. A fantasy. A ruse. A game."

"What game?"

"You're on-to it, Olivia, darling. That's the name ya gave me at Avondale, right? Surely a smart girl like you can figure it out."

Olivia thought about it. Suddenly Nadia grabbed her arm. The two friends eyed each other. They both came to the same conclusion.

"Do you understand what she's saying?" Miyuki asked.

"Venomous never planned to attack the G20 summit," Olivia said.

"Getting warm," Bridget said.

"They used Cody's organization not to hide a terrorist plot—but to lure us into investigating it."

Nadia turned to Miyuki. "Venomous knew the Authority would send us because the twins were involved."

"Getting warmer," Bridget said.

"*We* are the target," Olivia said.

Nadia closed her eyes.

Bridget clapped. "Congrats. Ya win the box of chocolates."

"Then why didn't you kidnap us back at the campsite?" Olivia asked. "Why all this lot?"

"Sophia and I were all game for it, but those weren't our orders. Asset One thought ya could be persuaded to surrender willingly and without a fuss."

"He thought wrong," Miyuki said, getting herself ready to kick some butt. "You want to try us again? We would love a rematch."

Sophia shouldered her rifle, then jumped down from the catwalk and landed on the floor. She arched her back as she stood up.

"I'm game," she said.

"Take it down a notch, Sophia, darling," Bridget said. "Ryan will kill me if I screw this up."

Nadia shot Olivia a glance. Her friend could only shake her head.

"Let's get down to it," Bridget said. "Basically—ya three girls surrender to us right now, or we'll shoot everyone inside this warehouse. Boys?"

The men on the catwalk aimed their automatic rifles down at the crowd as the men on the floor backed up. The crowd of teens and young adults gasped, and some began to panic.

"Wait a second," Cody said, walking forward towards Sophia. "We can work this out."

In a flash, Sophia grabbed Cody and threw him down to the floor. She produced a pistol and pressed it against his head.

"Cody will be the first one, then," Bridget said. "So do ya surrender? Or do we start spraying the place with bullets?"

Olivia was frustrated. There wasn't much she could do. The Gems could try to escape, but even if they did get out of the warehouse, they would be leaving Cody and three hundred innocent people at the mercy of those two crazy-ass girls and their small army of killers. The Authority based its entire existence on the goal of preserving human life above all costs. Mrs. B would expect them to follow that goal.

Even if it meant sacrificing their own lives.

"If you release everyone, including Cody, then we'll surrender to you," Olivia said.

Bridget tilted her head. "Yeah, nah, like I'd trust your word on that."

"Let half of them go."

"Sophia, darling? Go ahead and shoot Cody."

"Wait!" Olivia yelled. "Flipping hell. Fine. We surrender. We surrender."

CHAPTER 29

Emma and Ryan sat alone on the beach. Above them, the night sky was freckled with stars. It was amazing how deep and complex outer space looked. Due to all the urban light pollution, Emma could never see the sky this clearly at her grandma's house. But out here, they looked marvelous, and Emma wanted to lose herself inside that field of tiny lights.

But her head was swimming with thoughts. Thoughts about her dad. Thoughts about her friends. Thoughts about her future.

Could her friends stop the twins from attacking the G20 summit? Emma wished that she could warn them, but if Asset One caught her trying to help her friends, then her mission would be over, and she and Ryan would suffer the consequences of the man's wrath.

No, her friends would take care of everything. They didn't need her as much as Emma wished they did. The only thing she had control over was…Ryan.

The boy had a good point. What would she do when she received her father's estate at the age of twenty-five? Being that old seemed so far over the horizon, something Emma shouldn't have to worry about.

Did Emma want power? Not really. But she always wanted to be an actress, and that part of her did want to be famous. She had already been planning that part of her life when her father died and Grandma Laura showed up, making her life much more complicated. Now she was on a mission to flip Ryan, someone who was more than a target. He was a friend.

A close friend.

A boyfriend.

Was he really her boyfriend?

She remembered the kissing on the beach.

How gently Ryan had held her.

How his voice made her relax.

How he trusted her.

To flip him, Emma would have to break that trust. Use his feelings for her against him.

Emma wasn't sure if she could do it now. She was scared that her mission was about to unravel and force her into choices she didn't want to make.

"What are you thinking about?" Ryan asked, reading her eyes.

"Your boss is right," Emma said. "I don't know much about the people behind the Authority. I assumed we were doing the right thing based on what everyone there had told me and by the missions we've been on. But I don't know what's going on behind the scenes. I've never met anyone from the Century Group. I don't know about their motives or if they truly believe in what the Authority is doing."

Emma held her legs together.

"I mean, are we hurting or helping mankind? I don't know." Emma thought about it more. "My grandma Bernadette never trusted the Authority. She called them fascist capitalists. She didn't want me to join them."

"This is the grandma you live with, right?"

"Yeah, on my dad's side."

"What then made you decide to join?"

"My mother. She worked for the Authority. I guess she died for the cause, and that's when my father left the group."

"Sounds like he was disillusioned. Did you ever talk to him about it?"

"No, I never knew about the Authority. All I knew growing up was that my dad worked inside his big skyscraper, and Mom worked for the US government. That's what they told me, anyway." Emma turned to face the ocean again. "My grandmother said that my dad would turn in his grave if he knew I joined the Authority."

"That should tell you something right there," Ryan said. "We all make mistakes. I know I did. Believe me, that doesn't mean you have to keep making the same mistake twice."

Emma leaned on Ryan. "Can't we both just leave together? Turn our backs on everyone else while traveling the world together.

Is that so bad?"

Ryan touched his forehead to hers. "You make it tempting."

Emma could feel his warm breath on her face. His presence so close to hers.

Ryan lowered his voice to almost a whisper. "The only way I can leave Venomous is by destroying it. But why do I have to? With you as my ally, we could take over Venomous. You heard Asset One, he wants to set you up for success. Almost like a queen. A powerful queen. We could take it over, Emma." His voice rose in strength. "We could take over Venomous and make it bend to our will. Then I wouldn't have to keep looking over my shoulder."

There was a fire in the boy's eyes. He was serious and determined. She liked it when Ryan was this way. It was sexy and seductive. Like the two of them could conquer the Universe.

But her mind was stressing out again. Too much information mixed with too many personal emotions—Emma needed more time to process this.

"I don't know, Ryan."

"It's perfect timing, Emma. This is like you see in the movies. It's our destiny."

"I need to be alone."

Ryan hesitated as if he didn't quite get what she said.

"I need time to think."

"What is there to think about? Asset One is offering you the moon, Emma. All you have to do is reach out—"

Emma pressed her fingers over his mouth. Ryan stopped.

"I need to be alone," Emma said slowly as if she were talking to a two-year-old.

Ryan gently squeezed her fingers and kissed them. "Okay. Good night. Do you remember the deck number?"

Asset Twelve had had their things moved over to the *Falcon's Claw's* more luxurious accommodations.

"Deck seven. I'll figure it out," Emma said.

Ryan let go of Emma's hand and stood up. He walked down the beach towards the ship all lit up in the distance.

Emma eased her back down on the cool sand. In the darkness, she could barely make out the churning white waves as they rolled over the beach. But their sound was still soothing to her ears as her mind continued to pick at her problems.

What if she quit the Gems but didn't join Venomous? Was that possible?

Asset One hinted that it could be possible. Maybe Emma could somehow take Ryan with her. Maybe after she left the Authority, Ryan could be convinced to leave Venomous too. Would that be possible?

Emma could see she was in a difficult position. If she left without joining Venomous, Ryan might suffer the consequences because he had convinced Asset One that he could flip her. Ryan hadn't exactly told her that, but she thought it was obvious since Asset One was treating her so nicely.

Emma sighed. She didn't know what to do.

The waves continued to roll in, licking the beach smooth and clean.

Soon a human body rose from the water. It was Asset Twelve.

The older woman wore a bikini that clung tightly over her athletic body as droplets fell from her wet hair. The woman approached Emma and stopped.

Emma didn't say anything.

Neither did Asset Twelve.

The woman turned to watch the surf.

Finally, after a few more waves splashed in…

"Can I help you?" Emma asked.

The woman didn't flinch. "Do you swim, Emma?"

"Not really."

"I find a late night swim calming. It allows one to relax and release the toxins that have built up inside one's body during the day."

"Thanks for the health tip."

"You should try it," Asset Twelve said. "A swim might free your mind enough to point you to an answer to your problem."

"My problem?"

"Yes, the one you wear around your neck like a string of pearls. Your decision to join us or not. To betray your friends or not. Either way, you must be committed. Venomous does not want members who are not fully committed. Defeats the purpose of an effective organization."

"No offense, but I'd like to be alone."

"Don't we all." Asset Twelve sat on her knees as they sank into the sand.

This woman—Emma wanted to slap her silly.

"Have you decided?" she asked.

"Can I ask a question about Asset One?"

"You can ask. But I might not answer."

Whatever.

"Will he kill me if I don't join Venomous?"

Asset Twelve leaned back and took in her question. "You've been presented with an opportunity. If you refuse, he'll allow you to leave. The limited information you've acquired about our island will be of little use to your masters since I'll change everything after you leave." The woman stretched her legs out to sit. "However, I have a feeling you might leave your masters as well."

She read Emma's mind like a web page. The woman was either a psychic or a witch. Emma's money was on the latter.

Asset Twelve continued. "Maybe you should quit the Authority. One should only follow those they truly believe in."

"What if I did that—could I then be with Ryan?"

"Asset One doesn't govern his assets' personal lives unless they put the organization at risk. However, that question can only be answered by him."

"So I should go ask him?"

"If you feel it's worth the risk."

"Worth the risk?" Emma asked.

"Most likely Asset One won't kill you. However, he can be a difficult man to read."

A difficult man? Emma had seen Asset One kill Jacqueline by activating a surgical implant that caused her to have a heart attack and die. All because she was sloppy. The man didn't blink an eye or react to it at all. Even when they discussed it at dinner, Asset One had no emotion about it. At least Asset Twelve was pissed at her and the Gems for setting Jacqueline up for failure. But Asset One couldn't have cared less about his former operative dying.

What if Emma said the wrong thing? Would Asset One order Sunchaser to dive down and pluck her eyes out? Would he shoot her? Tie her up and dump her off the ship and let her drown? Emma's mind was too creative in this macabre way of thinking.

Emma sighed. Maybe she should've gone to see *Aida* with her grandmother after all.

The sound of a helicopter echoed in the distance.

Emma wondered who was coming to visit them now.

CHAPTER 30

A loud and constant chop-chop-chop sound drifted into Olivia's brain as it woke up from its deep slumber. *What is that sound?* Her mind tried to grab on to it. Tried to make sense of what was going on. She then noticed a breeze hitting her face like they were moving. Soon her eyes peeled open enough to see something flashing. The objects appeared to be giant pillows or clouds—but they were flashing in and out of existence.

That can't be right. Things don't disappear in and out of existence, Olivia told herself.

She shook her head to wake up faster.

Her eyes then settled. They were in the air. It was dark outside, but something was flashing against the cloud layer they were flying through. Olivia's aviation-geek brain kicked in and recognized the chop-chop-chop sound. They were in an old Huey helicopter. The ones made famous by America's Vietnam War. And that flashing against the clouds was the white light on the tail of the helicopter.

The side door was wide open, allowing Olivia to see out of the helicopter.

Olivia focused her eyes. She could see the dark cockpit, its panels dotted with illuminated switches as two pilots were at the controls. Inside the spacious—yet sparse—cabin of the helicopter were the twins belted into two seats facing backward into the cabin, which joined the cockpit. Bridget was listening to her phone using headphones. By the way she was moving her lips and bouncing her head, she was listening to music. Sophia had a light on over her head as she was reading a book by some guy named Lovecraft. On the floor next to her, Olivia saw Nadia and Miyuki. They were out to lunch. Their wrists and ankles were tied. Olivia tried her wrists —yes, they were tied as well. As were her ankles.

Flipping hell, Olivia remembered. *Those bitches drugged us.*

After the Gems surrendered at the warehouse, Bridget had made them drink a can of soda that knocked them unconscious. How long did they keep them sedated?

Olivia glanced at Bridget again. The girl noticed and took off her headphones. She tapped Sophia on the shoulder. Sophia inserted a bookmark and put her novel up. She pointed at Olivia. This prompted two large hands to clamp down on her shoulders.

Olivia craned her neck back and saw a large Venomous goon looking upside down as he held her in place. She then noted a second goon sitting near Nadia and Miyuki.

Bridget yelled something at Olivia. But the helicopter was too loud to understand her, so Bridget came over and crouched next to her.

"How well did ya sleep?" she asked, yelling over the helicopter noise.

"Sleep? I was unconscious. There's a difference," Olivia said, matching her volume. "Where are we going?"

"What was that?"

"Where are we going?"

"Somewhere fun for us. But for you three, I think it will suck hard," Bridget yelled. "I hope you're alive long enough for us to catch up. We haven't seen each other for, like, a year or two." Bridget leaned uncomfortably close to Olivia. "I've missed ya, roommate. You're all class. I love Sophia to death, but she's not like you. I've missed our stimulating conversations about life."

Olivia couldn't say the same. Bridget was only a sociopath with better social skills than her sister.

"I miss our conversations too," Olivia lied. "Maybe you could put in a good word for us so we can stay alive."

"Yeah, nah. When it comes to our boss, I can't make any promises," Bridget yelled. "But I'll see what I can do."

"Don't be an *eejit*, Bridget," Sophia yelled. "She'd throw ya off the fecking helicopter if ya gave her a chance. Let's toss 'em off into the sea and be done with 'em."

"We can't show up empty-handed. Then Asset One will throw us off a helicopter."

Sophia got into Olivia's face. "Can I just wound her a little? Slice off an ear or break a bone or two?"

Bridget sighed. "Not without orders, Sophia darling."

Sophia's eyes were consumed with anger as they bored a hole

into Olivia's face. "Our father's in prison because of ya. Don't think we've forgiven ya for that."

"Glenn Joyce was a terrorist," Olivia yelled over the helicopter noise. "He's not even your real dad."

Olivia felt a hard slap across her face.

"Take that back ya gobshite, or I'll toss ya out of here myself," Sophia yelled. "And to hell with our fecking orders."

Bridget grabbed her sister and spun her around. Bridget's eyes made contact with Sophia's. Her twin sister was breathing hard as the anger was eating her up inside. But after a long stare into Bridget's eyes—Sophia's breathing slowed. Her clenched jaw relaxed. It was like Bridget was putting a mental spell on her sibling. Bridget leaned in and whispered into her sister's ear. That took Sophia's anger down a few notches, and she sat back down in her chair.

Bridget knelt next to Olivia again. "Sorry about that. It's been a long trip for everyone," she yelled. "But if ya talk about our father like that one more time—then I'll rip every strand of that lovely black hair right off your scalp."

Bridget returned to her seat and put her earphones back on. The goon behind Olivia removed his hands.

As far as Olivia could tell, Nadia and Miyuki were still out cold on the floor.

Olivia closed her eyes. Their situation looked hopeless.

When she opened her eyes, Olivia was distracted by a wink from Miyuki. She had one eye closed and one eye open as if she were faking unconsciousness. That eye referenced something behind her back. Olivia followed it to see Miyuki's wrists. The rope around them was frayed and weak from a piece of thin old metal jutting up from the floor of the aging helicopter. Soon her wrists would be free. If she could get her hands to her ankles, then Miyuki could break free. So if Olivia could provide a distraction—

"I need to pee," she yelled.

"Bugger off," Sophia yelled back.

"I'm serious, love. I need to pee like an elephant."

Bridget took off her headphones. "What does she want?"

Sophia shrugged.

"She needs to take a piss," the Venomous goon behind Olivia yelled over the helicopter motor.

Bridget knelt next to Olivia again. "We should be landing soon.

Can ya hold it?"

"I'm pinching it off, love. But it hurts. One more bump and I'll pee all over myself."

"Can you make do with a beverage can?" the goon asked. "I've got an empty one here."

"Did anyone tell ya to speak, ya muppet?" Bridget yelled at the goon. "Besides, she's a woman. The logistics of such a thing are quite different than for a bloke, so until ya get a vagina for Christmas—why don't ya just shut your trap."

Bridget stood up and searched the cabin, pulling open storage compartments. The second goon stood up and got out of the way as Bridget searched around him as well. Soon, she found a small metal pan and brought it over.

"Might have to pee twice, but it's better than a damn can," Bridget yelled. "I'll help ya with your shorts."

"What about them?" Olivia referenced the two male goons.

"You—muppet—sit over there."

The first goon sat on Bridget's old seat.

"Both of ya—stare at each other until I say stop," Bridget yelled. "If I see one of ya peek over here, I'll snip off your fun stick."

The two men sighed and did as they were told. They were not too thrilled about taking orders from a couple of teenage girls.

Olivia and Bridget worked together on the logistics. Soon Olivia filled the metal pan, and Bridget tossed the contents out the open door, careful not to have it splash back into her face.

"Is that all of it?" Bridget yelled over the engine.

Olivia nodded.

Bridget helped Olivia with her shorts. "I thought ya was more full than that."

"Maybe it's because I'm nervous," Olivia yelled.

"Pants are on," Bridget said. "Okay, lads, ya can stop gawking at yourselves now."

The first goon got up from Bridget's seat and prepared to move over when—

Miyuki jumped up behind the man and shoved him. The goon fell forward into Bridget, his weight pushing them to the floor next to Olivia.

Sophia was on Miyuki quick, forcing her to fight off a few karate strikes as the two squared off. But the second goon stood up behind Miyuki, ready to grab her.

Olivia tried to yell a warning over the noisy cabin, but Miyuki didn't hear her.

As the second goon lunged forward to grab Miyuki, he tripped over something and banged his head against the floor. The reason was Nadia. She was awake now and had rotated her body so she could use her bound ankles.

This lifted Olivia's spirits. They had a chance now.

Miyuki made a move on Sophia and flipped the girl over to the opposite side of the helicopter, away from the open door. But the first goon was back on his feet. He positioned himself near the open door and removed a large knife from its sheath.

Miyuki braced for the new attack.

Sophia tried to get up and help—but Nadia kicked her over and began to harass her as best she could.

Olivia thought that was brilliant. When Bridget tried to get up, Olivia used her legs to sweep them under Bridget, causing her to fall again.

Meanwhile, the goon with the knife made several thrusts towards Miyuki, trying his best to stab her. She danced around his attacks and kicked him in the arm. But the man kept a firm grip on the blade. When the goon came back with another knife thrust towards her chest, Miyuki spun him around and kicked him so hard in the back that he went right through the open door of the helicopter.

Miyuki froze. She hadn't meant to do that.

At that moment, Sophia got behind Miyuki and shoved her right out the open door too.

"Miyuki!" Olivia heard herself call out.

She was gone.

Bridget was back on her feet. She spun around and kicked Olivia in the stomach. This caused her to wheeze and struggle to get air back in her lungs as she laid her cheek on the cold floor.

Olivia felt tears coming on. The pain of getting kicked wasn't bringing them on. It was seeing one of her friends just die.

Did that just happen? Olivia asked herself. *Is Miyuki dead? I can't believe she just died.*

"Someone get me a knife," Sophia yelled.

This brought Olivia back to reality. Why did Sophia need a knife?

Sophia stood on the edge of the open door as she looked down.

Olivia squirmed and shimmied her way towards the open door for a better look. A seatbelt from Sophia's chair was pulled tight as it ran out the open door. On the end of that belt was—Miyuki—she was clinging on to it for dear life as the helicopter bounced around the sky.

"We can't kill them," Bridget yelled. "Pull her back inside the helicopter."

"Bugger off. I'm done following orders." Sophia pushed her sister out of the way as she looked around the cabin for a knife. When she reached the other side of the helicopter, Nadia began kicking Sophia again. Bridget came over and knelt right on top of Nadia to stop her.

Sophia found a small knife and ran over to the door with delight. She began sawing the knife back and forth over the seatbelt, Miyuki's literal lifeline.

Olivia had to do something. Despite her stomach hurting, she did her best to shimmy and shake across the floor towards Sophia. If she could at least get her legs over there—

Sophia stopped her sawing, then pointed the end of the knife towards Olivia. "Come any closer and I'll stab ya in the chest. I've got time to kill ya first, then deal with your friend out there."

She was right. Olivia was as vulnerable a target as Miyuki was thanks to being tied up. But she couldn't let Miyuki die. If Olivia had to risk her life—then so be it.

But before Olivia could commit to her decision—the helicopter went through a series of drops as a wave of turbulence hit the aircraft.

Bridget stood up and held on to a handle as the cabin rocked back and forth.

Olivia found herself being shaken around and pushed dangerously close to the edge of the open door.

Sophia fell on her butt; then she got back up to continue working on the seatbelt.

Another wave hit and the helicopter dropped again.

This tossed Bridget against her seat.

Nadia rolled towards Olivia, and they banged against each other. Luckily they didn't roll out of the helicopter.

"Sorry!" Nadia yelled.

"It's alright, love," Olivia yelled back. "We need to work

together anyway."

"Is Miyuki still out there?" Nadia yelled.

"Sophia?" Bridget yelled.

Olivia looked over at the seatbelt she was working on. The seatbelt was still there, but Sophia was gone.

Olivia scooted across the floor as best she could for a better look.

Miyuki swayed back and forth as she still held on to the seatbelt, trying to use it to climb back up into the helicopter. Below her, Sophia clung desperately to one of the helicopter's landing skids. She must have fallen out.

Bridget looked down, the wind flicking her red hair everywhere. "Sophia—hang on! Don't let go!"

Sophia gritted her teeth as she held on tight to the skid.

Bridget glared at Olivia. "Tell your friend to help save my sister, or I'll kill all three of ya right now."

"Reach for my hand," a familiar voice yelled from outside. Miyuki had stopped trying to climb up into the helicopter. She had lowered herself towards the landing skid, gripping the seatbelt in one hand while stretching out towards Sophia with the other.

Olivia didn't have to tell Miyuki anything. She was already trying to save Sophia. Not because of a threat to her friends. But because it was in her nature to do the right thing.

"I can pull you up," Miyuki yelled.

Sophia hesitated as if she didn't quite believe Miyuki.

"Oh monkey balls!" Miyuki yelled in frustration. "Reach for my hand, or you'll die."

"Do what she says, Sophia darling!" Bridget yelled, very concerned.

Sophia's scared eyes latched on to her sister's.

"You're not dying in front of me, ya daft cow," Bridget yelled. "Now take the girl's fecking hand."

Sophia paused, then stretched her arm out.

"More!" Miyuki yelled.

Sophia adjusted herself on the landing skid, then stretched out again.

Their fingers touched.

Miyuki stretched out more, her face squinting from the strain. Then their hands came together to form a good firm grip. But Miyuki didn't have the arm strength to pull her up.

"Use the seatbelt to pull them both up," Olivia yelled.

Bridget had the co-pilot assist her. Soon they both pulled Sophia and Miyuki up into the helicopter cabin. The co-pilot helped Bridget tie Miyuki back up. Then they tied the three Gems together. And then tied them to the bench the goons were sitting on.

Bridget examined the setup. "That should hold ya."

"What happened to him?" the co-pilot asked, referencing the second goon still out cold on the floor.

"The muppet tripped and hit his head. I guess we should see if he's alive."

The co-pilot checked his pulse. "He's alive."

Bridget shrugged. "Like he was any help when he was awake. When do we land?"

The co-pilot glanced at his watch. "Should be any minute now. I'd better get back." He climbed back into the cockpit.

Bridget hesitated. Sophia was strapped into her seat and her face looked overwhelmed. As if the girl had seen a ghost. Or her short life flashing in front of her eyes. Bridget came over and knelt beside her sister. The two locked eyes with one another, each one of them speaking in a language only they understood. Soon, tears came down Sophia's cheeks, and Bridget hugged her.

Olivia glanced out the open door. Their helicopter had descended below the clouds. They were low enough that Olivia could see the ocean shimmering in the moon-light. Soon they skirted along the coast of some type of dark land mass until they came upon a small cruise ship, its lights reflecting off the ocean.

They had reached their destination.

CHAPTER 31

That morning onboard the *Falcon's Claw*, Emma left her room on a private mission to get some answers to her questions. Questions that had been haunting her mind for days, and there was only one person who could answer them.

Ryan would be freaking out now. Telling Emma she would get killed for doing this. But Emma wasn't stupid. She knew Asset One wanted to recruit her. He wanted to use her money and her "power" to fight against the Authority. So why would Asset One kill her before he could exploit her?

Emma approached the huge double doors made of wood, the entrance into Asset One's residence. Two armed guards were watching her.

"I want to see Asset One," she said.

"Asset One is not to be disturbed," one guard said.

"Those are his orders," the other guard added.

"What's he doing?" Emma asked. "Is he sleeping, having breakfast, watching a movie—?"

"He is not to be disturbed," the one guard repeated.

"Well—I want you to disturb him. Tell him it's important."

"It's never that important," the other guard said.

A man's voice came over a speaker…

Allow her to pass.

The heavy double doors unlocked and swung open automatically.

The two guards moved out of Emma's way as she went inside.

The heavy doors closed and locked behind her.

Emma looked around the gigantic atrium. She didn't see Sunchaser or Asset One anywhere.

"Um. . .hello? May I speak with you, sir?"

Emma didn't get a reply. Her heart began racing as she tip-toed further into the giant room.

Then she heard a flapping noise as Sunchaser dived down from a secluded hiding spot up in the atrium. He landed on one of the falcon statues near Emma. The falcon blinked at her with curiosity.

"Hi there, Sunchaser. You're such a pretty bird. Do you know where your owner is?"

The falcon tilted his head and blinked. The bird stretched out its wings and picked at a spot with its beak.

"I take that as a no."

A door opened. Asset One came out wearing a robe with Japanese writing all over it as he tied the rope-like belt together.

"Oh my God." Emma turned away. "I caught you in bed, didn't I? I'm so sorry. I can come back some other time."

Asset One calmly raised his hand to stop her. "Please. Have a seat."

Emma sat down. Asset One took a large chair near the statues of his bird friends. Sunchaser flew over and landed on the man's arm, which had a glove on it. The man seemed to always be wearing it.

Asset One petted Sunchaser as it studied her. "What can I— help you with?"

"I don't know how to say this—" Emma began.

"You have questions. So ask them."

Emma hesitated, then pushed the words out. "If I decided to quit the Authority, you know, just walked away from it, could I continue to see Ryan?"

"Of course. You may take as much time as you need before committing to us."

"What if I don't join Venomous either?" She checked for his reaction. But Asset One's face betrayed nothing. Emma continued. "I'm already committed to taking care of my dad's corporation. I won't back out of that promise. But I don't want to commit to anything else. The Authority. Venomous. I want things to settle down in my life. You know, be a normal teen. Go to school. Go to dances. Hang out with my friends."

Asset One didn't answer.

"It's nothing against you or Ryan. I just need to focus on school. I want to graduate. Maybe go to a college with a fantastic theater program."

"You have dreams—you wish to follow them," Asset One said.

Emma nodded.

"Tell me. Do you know how—your mother died?"

The sentence made Emma freeze.

"Not really."

"Why hasn't the Authority told you?" Asset One asked. "Don't you deserve to know? I wouldn't keep such information—from you."

Emma sat up. "Does that mean you know?"

"Perhaps you should call your handler. What's her name? Ah, yes—Mrs. B. She runs the Gems project, does she not?"

Emma was surprised. "I never told you that."

"You held up well under interrogation. But we asked you a few questions—that we already knew the answers to. It was to test you. But I digress—you should call Mrs. B—ask her about your parents. Know the truth about them."

Asset One was right. Why hadn't Grandma Laura been straight with her from the beginning? How could Emma decide her future if she didn't know about her family's past? A past only her grandma seemed to know about.

"My phone was confiscated," Emma said. "I'll need it to call her."

Asset One pressed a button. "Bring our guest's satellite phone to my residence please."

A female member of the crew came in with the phone.

"Give it to her."

The woman did just that, then waited.

"That's all."

Emma examined her phone. There was something stuck to the back. "What's this?"

"It's a location scrambler. We don't want your Authority friends —to get a fix on our position. Otherwise, it should be in—perfect working order."

Emma sat up and built herself up before dialing Mrs. B's number. It took a while for the sat phone to find a network satellite in range, but once it did, the phone dialed the international number. After a few clicks and transfers, the line began ringing. Soon a familiar old voice greeted Emma's ears.

"It's about time I heard from you," Mrs. B's stern voice said. "What's your progress, Black Opal?"

Emma hesitated. Then just let go. "Why did my dad leave the

Authority?"

"Could you please repeat that? I'm not sure I heard you clearly."

"I said—why did my dad leave the Authority?"

There was a pause on the other end. Mrs. B was gaining her composure back.

"We can't discuss that over the phone. What's your status? Do you need assistance?"

"Yes, I need your assistance in answering my question. You said my dad quit the Authority because he was broken up over my mother's death. But was that all of it? Was there something else that you're not telling me?"

"Why? Has someone told you something different?" Mrs. B asked. "Where are you calling from, Black Opal? Are you in danger?"

"No, I'm being well taken care of."

"By whom? Are you with Ryan now?"

"Yes, I'm with Ryan. And his boss."

Mrs. B paused. "Is his boss in the room with you now?"

"Yes."

"What have you told him?"

"Nothing. They even interrogated me. But I didn't say anything," Emma said. "Let's get back to my parents. You said my mother died in South Africa on a mission. How did she die? What's the story?"

"I can't tell you that. It's classified. However, she did die a hero."

"That's not what I asked. How exactly did my mother die?"

"I'm sorry. That information is classified."

Emma could feel tears build up in her eyes. One ran down her cheek and she brushed it to the side. "What did you do to my poor father? What did you do that broke his heart? It was more than my mother's death. There's something more, isn't there? He turned his back on you as well as the Authority. Why? Why did he do that?"

Mrs. B paused. "You sound upset and overwhelmed right now. Please let us know where you are so we can help you."

"Answer just one of my questions. Honestly. Without all the classified bullshit."

"This is neither the time nor the place to have this discussion. However, I'm willing to have that conversation with you once you're safe and—

"We will have that conversation now. Or I'm done with all of you."

"Black Opal, you don't know what you're saying. Calm down and listen closely—"

"Unless you tell me now, I can't be responsible for my actions."

"What actions?" Mrs. B asked her voice tense. "Emma, don't betray me. If you betray me or the other Gems, the consequences for you will be severe."

"Then tell me about my parents."

"I refuse to be threatened like this over the phone, young lady."

"Stop the bullshit or I'm done. Seriously, I'm done."

Mrs. B paused again. "Come back to us, and we'll—"

Emma killed the call.

CHAPTER 32

Mrs. B placed the handset to her powder-blue phone back down and sat back in her office chair. The older woman closed her eyes tight while her mind added up the facts and presented her some possible scenarios—all of which she wasn't satisfied with.

She punched the call button on her intercom. "Let me know the second Mr. O has Black Opal's location."

The speaker answered, *Of course, ma'am.*

"I mean it. The very second he knows, I want him to report. Also see if you can reach any of the other Gems."

We made an attempt fifteen minutes ago, and no one answered.

"Then try again," she said. "Get Aardvark in here." Mrs. B punched the button again to unlock the intercom. She turned back to her laptop and brought up the recent intelligence reports from Mexico and Oregon before scanning through them again.

A rush of air sounded as the seal to Mrs. B's office door was released, allowing it to be opened. Aardvark stepped inside.

Mrs. B stayed focused on her laptop screen. "You don't have to stand there."

Aardvark found a place on the large comfortable sofa as Mrs. B finished looking at the reports.

She pushed away from her laptop. "Right now, I'm not sure if Emma is still playing her part or if she's been flipped. And ever since the Gems arrived in Mexico City, we haven't been able to contact them. Some of our people watching the G20 summit reported there was no sign of the Heart the E protesters. It was like they all had vanished."

Aardvark's thumbs were busy on his phone as he typed out a response and hit enter.

You are worried that Emma has compromised the mission.

"That's the problem. I don't know. She's a great actress. That phone call could have been for show. However, my gut tells me she was serious."

Perhaps Ryan Raymond and Venomous have put ideas in Emma's head to lead her astray.

"If Emma told them what we were up to, Venomous might have set up a trap for the other girls."

Perhaps that trap has already been sprung.

Mrs. B punched the intercom button again. "Has Black Opal's call been traced yet? Why is it taking so damn long?"

Mr. O is coming on your video chat screen, ma'am.

Her wall monitor flickered to life as an older Indian man appeared.

"What the hell is going on?" Mrs. B asked.

"We've pinpointed the satellite that Black Opal used to place the call," Mr. O said. "However, we suspect the phone had a location scrambler on it. We were unable to pinpoint her exact location."

"That is unacceptable."

"Calculating the time of the call with the orbit of the satellite, we have managed to find out the general area of where the call originated. It was somewhere in the Indian Ocean."

Mrs. B exchanged a frustrated look with Aardvark. "That's not helpful, Mr. O."

"I wish we could be more accurate."

Perhaps she was calling from a secret Venomous facility.

Aardvark's mind as sharp as always.

"Do we have any information on Venomous installations in that area?" she asked Mr. O.

"We know of two in East Africa. One in the UAE. And another one in Yemen. We have no intelligence that matches the area of the Indian Ocean in question. There's also a strong chance the scrambler gave us that location because the real location of the call could be one of the facilities we've mentioned."

"Yet you don't know that for sure."

"It's a strong chance. But I can't be certain of that, no."

"Then we are still guessing, gentlemen."

The intercom came on again...

Call for you, ma'am. It's the director of Mexican Intelligence.

Mrs. B sat up, glancing at Aardvark with hope. "Put him through immediately."

Mr. Valdez? Mrs. B is on the phone now.

"*Hola*, Señor Valdez," Mrs. B said.

Hola, Mrs. B. I'll get to the point. One of my operatives planted a tracker on one of your girls so we could monitor their visit to our country. You can understand our precaution, especially under the circumstances.

"I understand completely, Mr. Valdez. Please continue."

Gracias. We tracked the bug to a remote warehouse on the outskirts of Mexico City. There, the federal police found a few hundred kids from the Heart the E environmental group who were detained by a dozen or so kidnappers. Those men fled—excuse me—I must put on my glasses to read this next section correctly. The report also says that the kids told the police that the kidnappers took orders from two former members of the group. A pair of Irish twins named Fiona and Deirdre. The kids also said these twins took three girls when they left. From what my operative has described, I think these twins took your three girls.

Mrs. B frowned, flicking her eyes towards Aardvark. She was now certain that Venomous had all four of the Gems.

Currently, we have lost contact with our tracker. Our detection net has a limited range, so it's most likely that the girls aren't in Mexico or in Central America. But if we gave you the frequency, your satellites could pick the tracker back up.

Mrs. B sat up. "That's good news. We would welcome that cooperation."

In exchange, the Mexican government wants the Authority to bring those twin girls back to Mexico to face assault charges on federal police officers.

"Agreed. And please send my personal thank you to your government."

Mr. Valdez gave her the frequency of the tracker bug, which was then sent off to Mr. O and his threat assessment division. After finishing up the small talk with the head of Mexican intelligence, Mrs. B hung up and her mind began calculating scenarios again.

"The Gems must be still alive," she said. "If Venomous wanted them dead, they would have killed them in that warehouse."

Aardvark typed on his phone again.

Now we wait for Mr. O to find them.

"The waiting is always the difficult part of this job."

Would you like some tea?

"Might as well. I won't be sleeping tonight as it is."

While Aardvark left the room, Mrs. B closed her eyes and tried to relax.

Aardvark then returned with some English breakfast tea and a vanilla biscotti.

"Did you already have the kettle on?"

Aardvark nodded.

"You know me too well." Mrs. B finally relaxed as she drank her tea and enjoyed the biscotti. It was fresh from the cafeteria and quite delicious. The sugar and tea boosted her mood.

Aardvark sat back down on the couch. They both waited for developments.

They didn't wait long.

Mr. O on video chat, ma'am.

The wall monitor flicked on with Mr. O on the screen.

"Any news?"

"We found the tracking device. The signal is coming from a small cruise ship anchored near an island in the Indian Ocean."

"That's in the same general area as Black Opal's phone call. They must have all four of them." Mrs. B stood up with her cane and walked around the room with nervous energy. "I assumed Emma was only referring to Ryan's handlers. However—what if—Ryan brought her to see Asset One. That man moves around constantly, so we never get a chance to pinpoint his location."

Aardvark began typing. *For Asset One, a ship would be convenient and secure. Such a cruise ship can go almost anywhere in the world without crossing borders or checkpoints.*

"Exactly."

"A cruise ship at that island is rather odd," Mr. O said. "It's a private island. There's nothing there that supports tourism or tourists."

"Then I would say confidence is high that Asset One is on that ship." Mrs. B's mind whirled with possibilities.

It would be difficult for one of our mobile strike teams to reach them that far out to sea.

Aardvark was correct. If they were on land, it would take only twenty-four hours to drop in a strike team.

"Mr. O, what military units are in the Indian Ocean right now?" Mrs. B asked.

"I have our daily report right here. Stand by."

A digital map of the Indian Ocean and surrounding regions appeared on the monitor screen. Targets on the map began blinking. The cruise ship had a large Venomous logo on top of it.

"There are two submarines—one Russian and one Chinese—each taking up positions to monitor an American naval exercise near the Persian Gulf."

American ships appeared on the map along with the submarines.

"The Persian Gulf is too far from that island," Mrs. B said. "Besides, convincing the Americans that Venomous is important enough to divert their navy—"

"There's also a Royal Navy squadron en route to the Gulf to join the exercise," Mr. O said.

A British flag appeared south of the Persian Gulf.

"How far away are they from that island?" Mrs. B asked.

"If they changed course and headed south, their aircraft could intercept the cruise ship in a few hours."

"Did you say aircraft?"

"Yes, that Royal Navy squadron has one aircraft carrier."

Finally, the wind had changed. Mrs. B sat back down and smiled to herself. She pressed the intercom button. "Call MI6 in London. Inform Mr. Montgomery that I have a target he might be interested in."

Aardvark looked confused as he typed on his phone. *Excuse me, ma'am, but why would MI6 force the Royal Navy to abandon its exercise with the Americans to go after one intelligence target?*

"It depends on how big the target is. And I know for a fact that Mr. Montgomery has wanted Asset One's head on a spike for at least a decade."

CHAPTER 33

Emma placed the satellite phone on a nearby end table. The anger and frustration with Mrs. B had gushed out of her like a hole in a dam. Emma wiped her wet cheeks and eased down onto the cushions of a nearby sofa. Mrs. B didn't budge. Didn't she realize how serious Emma was? How desperate she was to know the truth? She had to have it, especially now when there was such an important decision for her to make.

The woman was selfish. Mrs. B only cared about the organization, not the people who were in it. Even her granddaughter was expendable for the greater cause. A cause with an agenda that Emma realized was more murky and unclear to her.

Were they the good guys? Was the information she was given about the Authority true? Did this Century Group want the world to be a safer place? Or did they need a secret organization like the Authority to change the world so they could profit from it?

Sunchaser flapped his large wings and sailed down from the atrium. He landed on the arm of the empty chair next to Emma. At first, she leaned away from the falcon.

"He feels your pain," Asset One said.

Emma relaxed a little. The falcon felt that, as he folded his wings back and sat. Sunchaser blinked his eyes and watched her. To Emma, it was oddly comforting.

"Did Mrs. B upset you?"

"I only wanted a simple answer, and she won't give it to me."

Asset One's stoic face returned. "If you wish to have more time…you and Ryan are welcome to stay on the *Falcon's Claw*…for as long as you wish. If you choose to leave, I will have the ship make landfall…anywhere in the world that you desire."

"Thank you for not forcing me to choose now."

Asset One didn't answer. He turned to one of his men. "Send

for Asset Ninety-five."

The sailor was on the radio.

Fifteen minutes later, Ryan entered the residence. He saw Emma and acted surprised.

"Your friend has had…an upsetting conversation. You should comfort her." Asset One whistled, and Sunchaser flew away from Emma and landed on his gloved arm.

Ryan knelt in front of Emma. "What happened?"

Emma filled Ryan in on what Mrs. B had said. Emma felt her cheeks become wet again. It was hard to talk about the conversation without getting all angry and upset again. Ryan took out a tissue and wiped her cheeks. Then he sat next to her and put his arm around her. Emma appreciated the gesture. She relaxed on his chest and closed her eyes to calm down.

The sailor near Asset One touched his ear piece as a message came through the radio. "Sir—Assets One-three-zero and One-three-one are here. Shall we send them in?"

Asset One cracked a slight grin. "Please do."

Ryan instantly got off the couch and stood away from Emma.

What the hell was that? Emma wondered. *Didn't Ryan like a pretty girl lying on top of him? Especially when she needed him to be close to her?*

The main wooden doors of the residence opened, allowing two red-headed teen girls to enter. They both were dressed in matching leather cat-suits.

Emma couldn't believe how these girls were dressed. Was it Halloween already? They looked ridiculous. Seriously, what rational girl would wear a leather catsuit in public? Then Emma recognized their faces from Mrs. B's briefing. These were the O'Malley twins. The ones Olivia had warned her about.

The two girls strutted inside with the confidence of runway models. They bowed to Asset One.

"Come forward," he said.

The twins did.

"Where have you two been?" Ryan asked. "I've had two messages from you in, like, two months. What's been going on?"

"My apologies, Ninety-five," Asset One said. "The twins have been…in contact…with me during their mission. I neglected to inform you."

Ryan's angry posture subsided. "We are all at your command, of course."

One of the twins—Emma thought it might be Bridget—walked up to Ryan and brushed her torso against him.

"Sorry, handsome. Promise I'll make it up to ya." Bridget planted a large kiss right on Ryan's lips, as if she did it every freaking day.

Anger burned in Emma's stomach. She suppressed the strong urge to slap those red lips right off the girl's face.

Ryan stepped away from the kiss, quite embarrassed. "You lack discipline, Asset One-three-zero. Know your place."

Bridget lifted her chin. "Well, aren't we being a bit formal."

She glanced at Emma. "Oh, swinging' Jesus—is this that girl you've been yearning for all this time?" Bridget walked around Emma like she was a pretty Christmas tree, "So this is my competition, huh?"

Emma fired a look at Ryan.

"She's under the mistaken impression that I'm attracted to her," Ryan said.

Bridget wrapped her arms around his waist. "Oh, I'll break ya down, Ryan my lad. Ya just watch. You'll appreciate me one day."

Her sister Sophia, rolled her eyes. "Bejesus, would ya please spare us all the soap-opera shit?"

"My patience runs thin, girls. Were you successful?" Asset One asked. His tone was serious.

Emma also noticed the falcon was now circling above them all. Was he waiting for a live snack?

Bridget mimicked her boss's seriousness. "The mission was a success. The Gems have been captured unharmed. As per your orders."

"What about the G20 summit?" Ryan asked. His eyes flicked over to Asset One. "Sorry, sir. I was under the mistaken impression that we were going to kidnap the world leaders and hold them for ransom? Wasn't that part of the twins' mission?"

"That mission has been altered. I felt it was the perfect opportunity...to lay a trap."

Ryan's eyes wandered over to Emma, then back to his boss. "I gave Black Opal my word that she would not be harmed."

"And we have honored that word. However, I can-not give the same guarantee...to her friends." Asset One walked around the atrium. "The Authority has been a pain in our side...for quite some time. Decades at least. And we have tolerated them. Like an elephant tolerates a fly buzzing around his trunk. It's time we push back. It's time we hit that fly…with a giant flyswatter. Capturing the Gems was only the beginning."

"What are you going to do with them?" Emma asked.

"I'm afraid they will…not be treated as well as you. They have interfered with our plans…for the last time. I will be honest, Emma. I plan to do…very unpleasant things to them."

"May I please speak with them?"

"For what purpose?"

"What if I could get them to cooperate with you?" Emma asked. "To give you information without resorting to doing— unpleasant things to them?"

"It's not their information that's important. It's the fact that… they are to be made an example of. When you go against Venomous…you suffer the consequences."

Sophia and Bridget flashed sadistic smiles of satisfaction.

"What if I can get them to turn?" Emma asked.

"All three of 'em?" Bridget asked. "I find that hard to believe."

"What do you have to lose? Think of what you could do with four spies inside the Authority. The damage you could do."

"It's worth considering, sir," Ryan said.

"Oh, bejesus, Ryan—you only want to get into her pants."

Asset One's black eyes narrowed. "What was that, Asset One-three-zero?" His tone was sharp and not pleasant.

Bridget immediately straightened and realized her mistake. "It wasn't relevant to the conversation."

Asset One returned his attention to Emma. "I will consult with Asset Twelve. In the meantime, you'll be restricted to your room. Only as a precaution…while your friends are on board." Asset One addressed the twins. "You two will guard Emma. She is to be treated as our guest. Do you understand?"

* * *

Emma went back to her room on board the *Falcon's Claw* with Bridget and Sophia escorting her. Ryan stayed behind with Asset One to "clear up some things." Emma wondered if that included her friends, who were now either on the island or on the ship. So the mission that her friends went on was a trap created by Asset One as the first blow against an offensive against the Authority. So was Asset One using Ryan to trap her as well?

But Asset One said Emma could leave. That she was seen as a guest, not an enemy. If anything, Ryan and Asset One saw her as a powerful ally whom they wanted on their side.

Emma wondered what she was going to do. To be honest, she wasn't feeling loyal to her grandmother right now. Mrs. B had most likely lied to her—or at the very least failed to tell her granddaughter the facts about her parents that would have influenced her decision whether or not to join the Authority.

But Emma still cared about her friends. Asset One wasn't joking around. He was going to do unpleasant things to them, and Emma didn't like the sound of that. Maybe her loyalty to Mrs. B was waning, but Emma felt she was still a Gem.

At least for now.

When they arrived at Emma's room, Bridget took charge. "Stay out here and guard the door," she told Sophia. "I'll be inside with Miss America."

Miss America? Emma wanted to say something but chose not to.

Bridget shut the door.

"So you're staying in here with me?" Emma asked.

"I don't trust ya like Ryan does. Besides, I want to find out what he sees in ya."

Emma held up her chin. "You can search for it on Ooogle. It's called class."

Bridget laughed. "You *are* class, Emma darling. Pure class. And ya got spunk. Ryan likes that in a gal."

Emma ignored her. She glanced around her room and put away some clothes, then straightened up a few things.

Now Emma had nothing to do—but think about what she could do to help her friends.

Emma pulled out a book from her luggage, made herself comfy on one of the chairs, and pretended to read while her mind chewed on the problem.

"My sister likes reading."

Bridget wanted to talk to her now.

How nice.

"Oh—does she?" Emma asked, not paying attention.

"I don't care for reading," Bridget said. "Had enough of that rubbish in school."

Emma nodded. If she had some influence over Asset One, maybe she could convince him to let her friends go. Maybe their freedom could be her price for joining Venomous. That might work.

But she wasn't sold on joining Venomous either. Their methods were brutal. They only focused on money and power, with little regard for people in general. Emma did care about people. Maybe she failed to show it at times—but deep down, she did care. Thanks to her hippie grandmother, Emma saw the world as a beautiful place that needed protection. Maybe her grandmother didn't like how the Authority "protected" the earth, but they still shared the same belief that the world was worth fighting for.

"Ya got a nice bod. I can see why Ryan would be keen on it."

Nice bod? Emma wondered if this girl had any sophistication at all.

"You look nice too," Emma lied. "I love the cat-suit. That's a bold choice for a girl to wear."

Who's not an actual prostitute.

"Ryan fancies it. Can't take his eyes off me when I wear it."

Bridget didn't know Ryan like she did. Of course girls in tight cat-suits would distract him—he was a guy—but Ryan had class too. He saw beyond a young woman's body. He wanted to get to know them. Their thoughts. Their dreams. Their desires. Ryan went beyond his animal instincts and judged a partner on how she made him feel. It was an honest relationship. A mature and loving relationship.

"Did I say something amusing?" Bridget asked.

Emma dropped her smile.

"Ya think you're better than me, Miss America?"

Emma wished Bridget would just go take a nap.

"No, I don't."

"Think a working-class gal from Dublin isn't as sound as some blonde California beach bunny?"

Emma laughed so hard she almost dropped her book. The concept of Emma sitting on a beach in LA with a surf board, beach ball, and large sunglasses felt like a cartoon character. She was more the New York girl wrapped in a heavy coat, enjoying Christmas Eve outside Rockefeller Center.

"What's so funny?" Bridget asked with a sharpness in her voice.

"You wouldn't understand." Emma slipped her concentration back into her book. She had more thinking to do, and this girl was sabotaging that. *Where was she? Okay, yeah. She had to find a way to help her friends. She owed them that. But she also didn't want to join Venomous to earn their freedom—so how the hell was she going to do—?*

Bridget knocked the book clear out of Emma's hands. "Don't talk down to me, ya muppet. What don't I understand?"

"That was unnecessary," Emma said, keeping her cool.

"I'll dance on your face with my boots if ya don't answer my question."

Emma knew she shouldn't, but—

"Okay. For one, you don't understand how to dress. Are you, like, going to San Diego for Comic-Con? You and your sister look ridiculous. How can any grown woman take you seriously wearing a cat-suit in public? You two are embarrassing yourselves."

Bridget opened her mouth but paused. "Sophia thinks we look cool."

"Is Sophia trying to impress Ryan? No, you are. Well, you won't be doing that by looking like Batgirl. Ryan's sophisticated. He's got class. He likes a girl who dresses smart, clean, and stylish. A girl who knows she's sexy, but doesn't resort to advertising herself like a McDonald's combo meal." Emma braced herself for a vocal tirade or a good slap in the face.

But Bridget sat down with her eyebrows scrunched together in thought.

Emma went on. "You and Sophia are beautiful girls. You rock that red hair. But leather cat suits? You can do much better than that. How much is Venomous paying you anyway? Surely you girls can afford to buy the essential items for any decent wardrobe."

"Wardrobe?" Bridget asked as if Emma just spoke Chinese to her.

"Yeah, a decent wardrobe. You know, the essentials. One black dress. One pair of black pumps. A couple pairs of nice jeans. A heavy sweater. A light sweater—yada yada yada—the building blocks to a versatile and practical wardrobe."

Bridget only stared at her.

"Seriously, do you at least have one black dress?"

"I have a yellow one," Bridget said.

"That's okay for Easter Sunday. But what about a night on the town with your gal pals? Yellow would make you look like a little dorky girl. And so far, you don't strike me as a little dorky girl."

Bridget sat back in her chair, her mind busy.

"You just need a little guidance, but you'll get there. You have a lot to work with, so why hide it under poor clothing decisions?"

There was a knock at the door.

"We can talk later," Emma said to Bridget before addressing the door. "Come on in."

The door opened. Ryan and Sophia stepped inside.

"I bring good news," Ryan said. "Asset One will allow you to speak with your friends, if you try to convince them to help us."

CHAPTER 34

Olivia was surrounded by darkness. The three Gems were all in one dark room with no furniture or chairs. For hours or days—Olivia wasn't exactly sure—the three girls were bombarded with flashing lights, screams, air horns, and other unpleasant noises—then greeted with long periods of silence in the dark. Then a new cycle would start. It was horrible. Like some sort of psychological torture. Bombarding their senses with over-stimulation, then suddenly cutting them off.

Another fun thing they would do was lower the temperature inside the room to such a degree that they would have to cling to each other to keep warm. Then the room would heat up to become an oven, making them sweat through their clothes while they coughed on hot air.

Nadia was on the edge. Olivia heard her sobbing during the last period of silence. She hugged her, and Nadia apologized.

"Sorry—I don't know how long I can take this," she said through the tears.

The Authority had trained them on how to deal with interrogations. However, they hadn't covered this level of mental torture.

Miyuki was holding up better than Olivia would have thought. She would close her eyes and focus on doing yoga of all things. Olivia tried to mirror her example, but it was still hard to cut through all the distractions.

Right now the dark room was silent again. But it didn't last.

Projectors came to life and tossed up a series of gross images against the wall of slaughtered animals.

Soon there were screams of animals in pain.

Nadia dived into Olivia, clutching her like a scared little girl as she bawled. All Olivia could do was hold her friend tight.

The darkness came back.

The silence came back.

Nadia sobbed in her arms.

If this kept up, Olivia feared that Nadia would go insane.

A few minutes later—or maybe it was another hour—Olivia still wasn't sure—the main lights inside the room came up. This was the first time they'd been used since they were first brought into the room.

A door slid open and the twins from hell stepped inside.

Miyuki grunted and threw herself forward at the twins in an attempt to escape. But Sophia only had to give Miyuki a gentle shove before the girl fell back to the ground. None of them were in any condition to fight.

Olivia had to squint to even see the twins. The flashes and strobing lights inside the dark room had messed up her eyesight. The big surprise was seeing Emma step inside. Now they had all four of them in a cage.

Two goons followed Emma inside and set up four chairs. Emma sat on one of these as the twins and the two goons formed a perimeter around them.

Olivia helped Nadia to her feet.

"Oh my God," Emma said. "Is she alright?"

"We're all a little freaked out right now." Olivia sat Nadia down on a chair as she took one near her.

Miyuki crawled over to the last chair and pulled herself up to sit. "They tortured us," she told Emma.

"What did they do?"

Olivia explained the darkness, the screams, the lights, and the horrible sounds. The hot and cold room. It was crazy.

"I'll get them to stop that," Emma said.

"How can you do that?" Olivia asked.

"By having you. . .cooperate."

"What do you mean, cooperate? With what?"

Emma flashed a polite smile to Bridget and Sophia before leaning in towards the Gems with her quiet voice. "I'm not saying handing over critical information about Mrs. B or the Authority. But what if—you let them put a recording device on you. Or tipped them off when we were involved in an operation that was focused on Venomous?"

Olivia shook her head. Apparently, she was still groggy because what Emma said made no sense. "What are you saying, love?"

"She wants us to be double agents," Nadia said, regaining her composure.

"You want us to spy for Venomous? Is that what you're asking?" Olivia asked. "I want to hear it from your mouth again."

Emma smiled at the twins again, then turned towards the Gems and dropped it. "It's the only way you're getting out of here alive."

"Okay. We'll go along with whatever you have planned," Miyuki said. "Just get us out of here."

"No—Miyuki—she wants us to flip," Olivia said. "She's turned to the dark side."

"I haven't joined them," Emma said. "We're only dating."

"Dating?"

"That was a bad analogy. Look, Ryan and Asset One want me to join them—but I haven't yet."

"Yet?" Nadia asked. "Does that mean you're thinking about it?"

"There's a lot of unanswered questions I have. Especially when it comes to my parents and the Authority." Emma hesitated. "I don't know if I believe in what we're doing anymore"

"So you're a traitor," Olivia said, her anger rising.

"I haven't told them anything they don't already know. Anyway, that's not important right now. Getting you three out of here is. You're my friends, and I won't let them do this to you anymore."

"If the price of my freedom is to rat out Mrs. B or to betray her trust—then I want no part of this," Olivia said in her loud voice.

Emma tossed another polite smile to the twins before whispering, "Chill out, Joan of Arc. You don't have to mean it, but it will buy me some time to figure out how to get you girls off the ship."

"We're on a ship?" Miyuki asked.

"That dude with a falcon. It's his ship."

So Emma was flirting with the enemy. First Ryan and now Asset One, the head of Venomous himself. Olivia reasoned that Emma had either joined already or was being manipulated by Asset One to confuse and disrupt them.

"You need my help," Emma added. "There are over a hundred armed goons on this ship alone. Plus we're docked next to their secret training island with over a few hundred trained killers on it."

"Correction—we're no longer docked at the island," Bridget

said. "We've been at sea for a few hours."

Olivia noticed an ear-bud resting in Bridget's ear, which meant the room was wired for sound and they were listening to Emma's every whisper.

"I demand a private conversation with my friends," Emma yelled.

"And I demand a cup of vanilla ice cream with chocolate syrup," Bridget said. "That would be grand."

"I fancy some nuts and whipped cream on mine," Sophia added.

"Oh, that is sound, Sophia darling. I'll have that too."

Emma glared at the twins.

"Yeah, nah, we can't give ya privacy," Bridget said. "And ya'd better hurry up. Asset One's waiting on ya."

Emma turned away, her face troubled. Her eyes scanned her friends. "I'm trying to save your lives. Seriously, he wants to kill you. The dude with the falcon? He wants to make an example out of all of you. So if you don't help me save you, this torture room will only be the beginning of what he'll do to you."

Olivia wanted to believe Emma. Wanted to trust her. But the facts didn't add up. The last time the Gems saw Emma, she was conflicted so badly that Mrs. B kept her away from the mission. Now here Emma was, onboard a ship with the godfather of Venomous pleading with them to go against Mrs. B because it would "spare their lives." This was a dog and pony show. A lie. All of this was to convince them that Emma was still on their side. To lure them into trusting her because she was still their friend and looking out for them. Olivia could see right through that illusion now.

"Ryan finally did it, didn't he?" Olivia asked. "He finally convinced you to betray us."

Nadia and Miyuki both glanced at her.

"Hey, I would never betray our friendship. Why do you think I'm freaking here?"

"But are you willing to betray Mrs. B?"

Emma paused.

"That's the answer I was looking for."

"It's more complicated than that."

"No, it's not."

"Don't you ever wonder why we all blindly follow this secret organization that we don't know anything about?" Emma asked. "Who's actually in charge of the Authority? It's not Mrs. B. She answers to the Century Group. And who are they? Do they really care about the world? Or are we only helping a bunch of rich families get even richer?"

The other Gems didn't say anything.

"C'mon, none of you have even seriously thought about it?"

Olivia coughed, then cleared her throat. "I don't see Venomous freeing hundreds of school-girls from terrorists. Or destroying military labs trying to create new weaponed viruses that could kill millions of people. And remember Robert? What government would help him? The Authority has its flaws, but its mandate is quite clear. and I don't question their motives."

"I'm not saying they don't do good things. But maybe we should be questioning their motives. My grandma Bernadette did. She brought up a lot of negatives before I agreed to join. My father even quit the Authority. Humans are not perfect. And neither is the Authority."

"And what about Mrs. B? You don't trust her now? Especially since—" Olivia stopped herself. She couldn't say it in mixed company.

"Since what?" Emma asked. "Since she allegedly gave birth to my mom?" Emma stood up. "I never grew up with her. Mrs. B was never around for me or my dad or even my grandma Bernadette for that matter. To be honest, I can only go by her word that we're even related. She could have lied about that to recruit me. I don't know."

"Don't be daft. Of course she's your grandmother. Mrs. B wouldn't lie about something like that."

"A lie of omission is still a lie," Emma said. "I can't be loyal to someone who refuses to tell me the truth."

"The truth about what? Forget it—they have your mind all twisted up, love," Olivia said. "You're not thinking straight."

"I'm thinking straight enough to know who my friends are." Emma scanned all their faces.

"If the price of your friendship is all of us betraying Mrs. B— you can go to flipping hell."

Suddenly a warning horn bellowed in the hallway outside the open door. The main speakers came on...

General quarters. General quarters. All men to their battle stations. The message repeated as the alarm pulsated throughout the ship. Crewmen scrambled through the hallways. Even the two goons quickly left the room.

"What's going on?" Emma asked. "What does 'general quarters' mean?"

"How would I know?" Bridget asked. "Do I look like a fecking sailor?"

The answer came rushing in as Ryan scanned the room. "Emma, come with me. The ship is under attack."

CHAPTER 35

Emma followed Ryan as he rushed through a myriad of open water-tight metal hatches and busy passageways. Sailors and armed goons were running all over the ship as the alert continued to sound. Finally, they arrived at the ship's main bridge. The large room was surrounded by windows on three sides that overlooked the bow of the ship. A sailor was at the helm as the captain gave him a new course heading.

"I have six targets inbound," a sailor called out.

Emma followed his voice towards banks of radar screens and other types of super-sophisticated equipment crowding the back of the bridge. About ten sailors manned the different stations.

"Heat trail and speed suggest two military fighters."

"And the other four targets?" the captain asked.

"Judging by their speed and altitude—I believe they're helicopters."

"Are they going to attack us?" Ryan asked.

"Don't worry, Ninety-five…" Asset One emerged from the shadows with Sunchaser on his arm. "*The Falcon's Claw* is more than capable…of defending herself."

A speaker came alive with a radio transmission…

This is Lieutenant Commander Henry Simpson—squadron leader of Her Majesty's twelfth attack wing, Royal Navy. We have reason to believe you are harboring a known terrorist wanted by Interpol, the United Kingdom, and the European Union. Your ship is hereby ordered to stop. You will be boarded and searched. Please respond.

The captain went on the radio. "We are a civilian transport traveling through international waters. The Royal Navy has no jurisdiction here."

Falcon's Claw—if you do not stop—you will be fired upon.

"Targets are ten miles and closing," the sailor called out from his radar screen.

The captain turned to Asset One. "What should we do, sir?"

Asset One betrayed no emotion except for a gentle sigh. "They leave us…with no choice. Activate our defenses."

The captain repeated the order to the sailors on the bridge, and Emma could feel a vibration through the floor of the ship. What was that?

Ryan went over to one of the windows. Emma followed. Outside they saw a part of the forward deck rotate to reveal a modern missile battery hidden under it. Emma glanced up at the screens with cameras covering the entire ship. Brand-new missile batteries and heavy machine-gun emplacements were all in view and glistening in the sun.

CHAPTER 36

The Royal Navy F-35 fighter glided through the air like a swan across a pond. The sky was clear. The ocean below was calm. It was a gorgeous day to fly. Lieutenant Commander Henry Simpson was in command of the aircraft. On his wing was Lieutenant Emily Taylor. She was a few years younger than Henry, but still one hell of a pilot.

So far their mission was one of the oddest that Henry had ever experienced in his twelve-year navy career. His two fighters were escorting four Merlin helicopters filled with Royal Marines. Their mission was to stop a cruise ship. Or at least that was how it was explained in the rushed briefing they'd had before they took off from their carrier, *the Prince of Wales*.

Henry assumed that terrorists must have taken over the ship and were holding the passengers hostage. That would be the only reason an entire Royal Navy task force would be diverted from their annual naval exercises with the Americans. Going through all this fuss to hunt down one man was absurd. The demand to search the ship to find an international criminal was only an excuse to put the marines on-board. In fact, those Royal Marines probably knew more details about what was going on than he did. But that wasn't his job. His job was to run a standard air-cover mission for the helicopters as they conducted their operation.

Henry eased his side-stick back, pulling the nose of the F-35 up just a bit. He glanced at his HMDS system, and everything looked normal. The F-35's helmet mounted display system was state of the art. No more constantly checking your forward HUD displays for target locks and other vital information. While his head was turned completely around, Henry could monitor all the information from his flight and defense systems with a simple glance. It took a little getting used to…but overall he liked it.

The HMDS ticked off ten miles to target.

Rabbit Two to Rabbit One.

It was Emily's voice on the radio.

Henry activated his mic. "Go ahead, Rabbit Two."

How would you like to proceed, sir?

"If target ignores our warnings, then a low flyover of their bridge at full thrust should get their attention."

Roger, Rabbit One. I'll follow you in, sir.

"Negative Rabbit Two. Establish a standard air-cover pattern. Flying through my jet wash at such a low altitude is not a good idea. You'll maintain—"

A warning bell sounded as a threat alert flashed on Henry's HMDS system. At first, he thought it was a malfunction. They were flying towards a cruise ship, for heaven's sake. Then his computer identified two missiles coming in hot and fast.

There was no time to waste.

Henry pulled the F-35 into a tight left-hand turn as he pushed the nose down to bleed off altitude.

One missile turned towards him. Four miles.

Henry leveled the F-35 to within five hundred feet of the water and pushed the throttle full.

Two miles. The missile was still on him.

Damn. This wasn't some cheap North Korean missile that couldn't hit the side of a building. Its targeting system was sophisticated. Able to still track him this close to the water and with the F-35's stealthy shape.

Henry deployed his aircraft's counter-measures. A burst of chaff followed by two roman-candle-like fireworks to confuse the missile's targeting system.

One mile.

Henry prepared himself. The next move would be to go full vertical as much as he could get away with and hope for the best.

The missile was veering off course.

Henry kept the F-35 on the deck at full throttle. It was working. The missile dropped off his radar.

Henry took a moment to breathe. *Where in the hell did that missile come from? Surely it couldn't be from that cruise ship. Perhaps another warship had wandered into the area?*

He then remembered Emily.

"Rabbit One to Rabbit Two. What's your situation?"

There was no answer.

Henry made a tight-right turn and put his fighter back on an intercept course. He did a radar sweep that detected the four Merlin helicopters still on an intercept course. But Emily's F-35 was missing.

"Rabbit One to Rabbit Two. Report."

He listened for a moment before repeating the command.

Mongoose Two to Rabbit One. Mongoose Two to Rabbit One. Rabbit Two hit by a missile. We did not see the pilot eject. Over?

Henry closed his eyes for a moment as reality punched him in the gut. His wingman was most likely dead, and he was now in a combat situation. A situation he had trained for every year since he first stepped on board an aircraft carrier. But he never thought it would be like this.

Henry pushed Emily's memory to the side. He was a Royal Navy combat pilot. He now had a job to do. Mongoose Two and the other Merlin helicopters had marines on board. Their safety was the only thing that mattered now.

He activated his mic. "Rabbit One to Mongoose Two, roger. Did you locate the threat? Is there another warship in the area?"

Negative, Rabbit One. Missile launch was detected from our main target.

"Pardon me, Mongoose Two, are you saying our target—the cruise ship—has an air-defense system?"

Roger that, Rabbit One. Mongoose one through four will spread out and continue operation. Can you still assist?

"Roger, Mongoose Two. I'll keep their attention on me. Good luck."

Henry armed all of his weapons, then put his F-35 into another turn. He flew a ten-mile radius around the "cruise ship."

Soon his HMDS alerted him to the ship's targeting radar trying to lock on to his F-35. But so far there wasn't a launch detection.

Henry nudged his side-stick to the right, coaxing the F-35 into a tighter and tighter turn.

He just needed a few more seconds.

Henry got it. He pulled his side-stick to the left, leveling off his aircraft and putting it on an intercept course towards the ship's bow. He shoved the throttle forward as the F-35 broke Mach 1 over the water. Henry dropped back down to five hundred feet as his HMDS display confirmed the target. He opened his weapons bay. The anti-ship missile was armed and ready.

Henry fired.

As soon as the weapon cleared, Henry jerked the side-stick to the right, putting the F-35 into another tight turn. As soon as he was satisfied nothing was coming back at him, Henry leveled off and gained some altitude. Through his HMDS display, he watched the progress of his missile.

It was right on course. Soon the ship would be crippled, and the marines would hopefully have an easier job.

But then Henry's radar clouded up with multiple objects obscuring the target. Heat signatures were detected, causing the F-35's threat alarm bell to sound.

However, Henry knew those weren't missiles. The cruise ship had deployed anti-missile countermeasures.

And his missile had taken the bait. It veered off course and disappeared off the radar.

Damn it, Henry thought. *This ship is a pain in the ass.*

Now what was he going to do?

The answer was quick.

Four anti-aircraft missiles broke through the cloud of objects on Henry's radar.

The threat alarm continued to ring. Three miles. Closing fast.

Henry shoved the F-35 back down to the deck and pulled it into another tight right turn.

Two miles.

Henry's heart beat so fast he was afraid it would crack his ribs, but he kept the aircraft tight in the turn.

One mile.

He caught something flying past his cockpit. His HMDS display showed one of the missiles was moving away from him.

One down. Three to—

His HMDS flashed a threat alert.

Another missile had locked on to his F-35. It was directly in front and closing at two miles.

Henry pulled back hard on the side-stick. The F-35 went almost vertical, like a moon rocket. The multiple g's pushing him against the back of his pressurized flight suit was intense. But Henry hung on.

One mile…

Not yet he told himself. *Wait for it.*

Eight hundred yards…

Five hundred yards…

Henry flipped the F-35 hard to the left while forcing the nose down into a steep dive. He could hear himself breathing fast and loud, almost as if he just ran a marathon.

He activated his countermeasures, then brought the F-35 out of the dive.

The missile that was tracking him veered off.

But Henry didn't see the third missile as it ripped open his right petrol tank, causing the F-35 to explode.

CHAPTER 37

Emma stood on the bridge of the *Falcon's Claw* feeling quite helpless, while Ryan was mesmerized by all the action on the bridge. The sailors calling out targets. Arming missiles. Calling out distances. Firing on targets.

"Splash fighter number two," the sailor stationed at the radar console called out.

But those targets were more than only planes, they were human beings. Two pilots who had families. People who loved and cared about them.

"We have to stop them," Emma whispered to herself.

"What was that?" Ryan asked.

"Those two pilots are dead."

"One of those pilots launched a missile at us."

"Because we were trying to blow them out of the sky."

"Not so loud." Ryan stood in front of her, as if to hide her from everyone's view. "Look, they're all soldiers, Emma. They knew the risk when they joined the military."

"So it's that simple, is it?"

"I think so."

"How many soldiers do you think are on those four helicopters?" Emma asked.

"It's either them or us." Ryan gently held on to both of her shoulders. "Look, I don't like this either, but sometimes bad stuff like this happens. It's life. Those soldiers are only following orders. If you want to blame anyone, blame the people who gave those orders. You can't blame us for trying to defend ourselves."

Ryan released her shoulders and turned back around.

"I can't stand here and do nothing," Emma said.

"If you try anything, Asset One will order me to kill you. And if it's not me, then it will be someone else." Ryan sighed. "When this is over, I'll take you back to your room and you can relax, okay?"

Emma didn't like that answer. She looked around the bridge, wondering what she could do.

But Emma soon realized that she had no clue how anything worked, or how to stop it from working.

"Give me a new status on those helicopters," the captain said.

"Helicopters are closing. They're approaching from four directions," another sailor called out.

"Target and destroy them," Asset One said, matter-of-fact like.

Emma leaned over to Ryan's ear and whispered, "Help me stop this."

Ryan gave her a long look. Was she finally getting through to him?

"Isn't this thrilling?" Bridget asked. The girl had entered the bridge and slipped in between Emma and Ryan. "I've never watched a real naval battle before. How 'bout you, Sophia?"

Her sister stood on the opposite side of Emma, who noted something pressing against her side. She glanced down and saw a knife. Before Emma could protest—

"Ya just stand there and enjoy the show, Miss America. I heard ya gabbing to Ryan about interfering with things." Bridget wrapped her arm around Ryan's torso. "Don't be a hero, Ryan. I fancy ya more than ya know, but I'll hurt ya if ya start misbehaving. Just remember what side you're on, darling."

"Targets locked. Missiles away."

Emma closed her eyes. She could imagine the horror of being on a helicopter burning in the sky. Then Emma saw images of her father's crash. What was probably going through his mind as he knew saving the aircraft was hopeless. As he knew he was about to die.

"Two helicopters destroyed. The other two have evaded our missiles and are skidding near the water's edge. We're having trouble locking on to them."

"The ship's machine-gun batteries can deal with them," the captain said.

"Our satellite has found the enemy carrier's position," a new sailor chimed in. "I have the coordinates entered into the attack computer."

"Excellent." Asset One stood up. "Target that ship. Launch a full spread of anti-ship missiles."

The captain nodded to his crew and they went to work.

"Anti-ship missiles armed and ready."

"Fire anti-ship missiles," the captain said.

"Six missiles fired. All green."

"That should keep our Royal Navy friends busy," Asset One said. "Now we fade away…like the morning fog. Captain, you may dive the ship."

The captain went on the radio. "Attention. Attention. Prepare for dive. I repeat, prepare for dive."

A new and different alarm went out over the ship. Through the windows, Emma watched as the missile batteries rotated back out of sight as if they were never there. Then large metal slats lowered over all the windows. Red lights came on as the bridge itself became darker.

"Dive plane down twenty percent," the captain said. "Make your speed twenty knots."

"Aye sir," the sailor said as he read back the captain's orders.

"Bejesus, I thought this was only a bloody cruise ship?" Sophia asked her sister.

"This is more than just…a mere pleasure craft, young lady," Asset One said, moving towards them. "The *Falcon's Claw* is the ultimate achievement in…naval military design. She can move over the water…or under it with the grace…of a ballerina. I assure you, the Royal Navy won't find us ever again."

CHAPTER 38

Mrs. B leaned on her cane with anticipation as she stood inside the Special Operations room located somewhere inside the Labyrinth at the Authority's California headquarters. Everyone else was seated, but Mrs. B was too wound up to join them. On the giant operations screen was a close-up of the Indian Ocean. A Union Jack icon was plotted on the screen just north of a Venomous icon. The Royal Navy task force had located the *Falcon's Claw* at 1432 hours. That was the last thing Mr. Montgomery of MI6 had passed along before their communications were cut off.

Mrs. B turned away from the screen. "I'm still waiting, Mr. O."

Mr. O was on the phone with his people. "It's a problem with their satellite. We're redirecting the signal."

A monitor flickered on with the image of a man wearing a subdued mustache and tie. "—this is intolerable. Get back in contact with them!"

"We're back with you, Mr. Montgomery. What's happening?" Mrs. B asked.

The man could now see Mrs. B. His face looked grim. "Plenty, I'm afraid. Are you aware that the *Falcon's Claw* is equipped with a modern air-defense system?"

"No, we only knew about the ship's existence the same day as you. We have no intelligence on it."

"The *HMS Prince of Wales* has lost two of her F-35 fighters. The *HMS Lydia* has lost two of her Merlin helicopters with a contingent of Royal Marines on board. We're monitoring the progress of the remaining two—"

A Royal Navy officer came into the picture. "Pardon me, sir. But the task force is under attack."

"Under attack? By whom?"

"From the *Falcon's Claw*, sir."

"What? It's a bloody cruise ship, man."

"The *HMS Eagle* is tracking four inbound ship-to-ship missiles," the Royal Navy officer said. "The *HMS Prince of Wales* is now preparing to launch a concentrated air-strike against the *Falcon's Claw*."

"Mr. Montgomery, I still have people on that ship," Mrs. B said. "Order that captain to literally cool his jets. the *Falcon's Claw* isn't going anywhere that his fighter-bombers can't reach. We have them in a box."

"Two of the Merlins got through, sir," a voice off camera said. "We have a squad of marines on board the ship now."

Mr. Montgomery turned towards the voice. "Do we have a visual?"

"Yes, I do believe so."

"Can you patch us into what you're seeing, Mr. Montgomery?" Mrs. B asked.

Mr. Montgomery hurried off the screen. The image was changed to a body-cam video.

Two Royal Marines were outside and taking positions on the forward deck of the *Falcon's Claw*. An officer motioned them forward as a squad of Royal Marines rushed ahead of the body cam.

A burst of heavy machine gun-fire caused the marines to take cover. The firing continued as they checked in…

Bravo One, we have fire coming from a gun emplacement. Thirty meters to the north of our location.

The firing then stopped.

One marine ran over to a new position and took a look.

Bravo Leader—very curious, sir. Those men firing at us have disappeared from the emplacement.

One marine in the video pointed down. The body cam looked down as sea-water poured over the deck.

Bravo One, I think the ship is damaged. Feels like we're listing to the side or—

The marines retreated across the deck as it disappeared below the water. Soon they were all swimming in the ocean.

Bravo One, the ship is sinking. I repeat, the ship is sinking.

"Mr. Montgomery, I thought you said your aircraft carrier hadn't launched its strike force yet?" Mrs. B asked.

The video switched to Mr. Montgomery at the head of another

situation room table.

"The task force is currently evading a missile attack. They haven't launched yet." Mr. Montgomery paused. "Is it possible your operatives have sabotaged the ship?"

"Of course it's possible. Yet we've heard nothing from them to confirm that."

The Royal Navy officer chimed in. "Charley company is reporting in. They've managed to slip inside the ship, sir."

"Where did they come from?" Mr. Montgomery asked.

"The second Merlin, sir. We're getting a report from them now." The Royal Navy officer paused.

"Well?"

The officer looked surprised. "The ship—is underwater."

"You mean the *Falcon's Claw* has sunk?"

"Not quite, sir. They report—it's now moving underwater."

"You mean like a submarine?" Mr. Montgomery asked.

"Exactly, sir."

"That's brilliant. Any more surprises? Can the bloody thing fly too?"

"We might lose contact with Charlie company if they go underwater. Do their orders still stand?"

"Yes, tell them to find and capture Asset One. If unable to capture, kill him."

CHAPTER 39

Back inside the dark empty room, Olivia, Nadia, and Miyuki sat on the chairs that were brought in before the alarms sounded and everyone ran out of the room like it was on fire. Of course Bridget didn't forget to lock the door before she left, trapping the three girls in their box while whatever was going on in the ship was going on.

Olivia wondered who would be attacking them. It could be a strike force sent by Mrs. B to free them. But she wondered how the woman would know where they were, especially since the twins and their Venomous goons did a superb job searching and finding all their electronic devices.

Maybe it was pirates. Depending on what part of the world they were in, pirates weren't loyal to anything but money, and a rich-looking cruise ship like this one would definitely interest them.

Gunfire could be heard outside the walls. The fighting was getting close.

"We might have to hide," Olivia said, rising from her chair.

"Where can we hide in here?" Nadia asked.

"We're sitting ducks," Miyuki said. "Maybe they are the good guys."

"They could be pirates," Olivia warned. "Becoming the prisoners of pirates is not an upgrade."

Suddenly the door lock exploded, causing the Gems to hit the floor. The door was then kicked in as a soldier swept the room with his rifle.

Olivia held up both hands in surrender. "Hold up. We're civilians." She then recognized the familiar uniform of the British Royal Marines, her father's old unit. "Hold on, love. We're citizens of the UK. We're being held as prisoners."

The marine lowered his weapon as his eyes took in how they looked the part. "All right then—stay here until I tell you to come out."

Gunfire erupted behind him. The marine dived behind the door-way as bullets sprayed into the room, ripping up one of the chairs as the Gems hit the floor again.

The marine fired back into the hallway, then paused for a moment before storming out of the room to take a new position in the hallway.

After about ten minutes, the gunfire faded as the fight drifted into another part of the ship.

Olivia noted that their door was still wide open. "Let's get out of here."

"The soldier told us to stay," Miyuki said.

"That marine might not be back. We have to go now while we still can. Is everyone up for it?"

Miyuki and Nadia both nodded.

"If we can get out on the deck and find a boat, we can get off this ship."

Olivia tip-toed out of the room with Nadia and Miyuki behind her. As the three Gems headed down the passageway and climbed up some stairs, echoes of gunfire drifted in from all around them. It was hard to tell what was going on or who was winning.

Suddenly, Miyuki pulled Olivia and Nadia around a corner and out of sight as an armed squad of Venomous goons ran through the passageway in a big hurry.

"Thanks," Olivia told Miyuki.

The three Gems continued through more passageways. Up more stairs. And climbed through a few open hatches before reaching a door to an outside deck.

Olivia tried the door, but it was locked tight. "Why the flipping hell is it locked?"

Curious, Miyuki went up on her toes and peeked through the thick glass window in the door. A school of yellow fish passed by, making their way over the upper deck of the ship, which was underwater.

"Are we sinking?" Miyuki asked.

Nadia went up on her toes too and looked. "I don't think so. We've submerged underwater."

"Are you putting me on, love?"

Nadia invited Olivia to take a look and she did. "This ship can run underwater."

"Oh, that's brilliant. Well, that snuffs out my plan. What the hell do we do now? Can't even jump off the stupid boat."

"We need to somehow surface the ship," Nadia said.

"Right, and how do we do that?"

"Take over the bridge!" Miyuki said, excited.

"Are you daft? With only the three of us?" Olivia sighed and thought about it. "Nads, is there some kind of system you can hack into—you know, do some of your computer magic?"

"I'd have to look over their system and see what I could do," she said. "I would need access to one of their main computers."

"And where could we find one of those?"

Nadia sighed. "Most likely on the main bridge."

"That's not very helpful."

Miyuki clapped her hands and got very excited. "I know! I know!"

"You know what?"

"The Hunt for Red October," she blurted out.

Olivia had no idea what Miyuki was talking about. According to Nadia's puzzled glance, neither did she.

"Didn't you see the movie?" Miyuki asked them.

"Oh—you're talking about a movie?"

"I know how we can get them off the bridge," Miyuki said. "In the movie, Sean Connery was a Russian captain who had to get his sailors off the submarine without suspecting he was turning it over to the Americans. So he triggered a false radiation alarm. Why can't we do something like that?"

Olivia checked with Nadia.

She thought about it. "I don't think this ship has a nuclear reactor. If so, we would have seen radiation-warning symbols next to the fire-alert ones that are located over the open hatches. Plus the ship was burning coal. I could tell from the smoke escaping from one of their stacks that night our helicopter circled in for a landing."

"Guess we'll have to nix that idea too."

"No, wait. Miyuki has the right idea," Nadia said. "However, we don't need them to abandon ship. We only need to convince them to leave a small part of it."

Olivia now saw where she was going with that.

"I'll go find some matches, love."

CHAPTER 40

The windows on the bridge of the *Falcon's Claw* were still shut tight, but the darkness lifted as the red lights were switched off and replaced by the normal illumination. The crisis was over.

"Excellent." Asset One stood up. "The Royal Navy will be searching…the entire Indian Ocean…while we slip away to Africa. Well done."

Emma felt the pressure on her side ease as Sophia stepped away and put up her knife. Emma moved over to Ryan, who protectively put his arm around her, causing Bridget to frown.

Asset One petted Sunchaser. "I'll be in my quarters…contact me when we reach—"

"We have intruders," a sailor reported. "Royal Marines are on decks six and seven. Moving forward from the stern."

"How many?" the captain asked.

"Security reports at least a squad, sir."

"One of the helicopters must have dropped them in before we submerged," Ryan said, reasserting his loyalties.

"Put the ship back on alert," the captain said. "Repel all boarders."

"They're on deck six?" Asset One asked, allowing himself to look a little worried. He drifted over to one of the sailors manning a position. "Bring up the cameras inside the interrogation box."

The sailor made a few mouse clicks. The image of the square room came up on the main viewer. Only four chairs and an open door were left.

"What happened to the prisoners?" the captain yelled.

"They were no doubt freed by our…unwelcome visitors." Asset One faced the twins. "One-three-zero and One-three-one."

"Yes, Asset One," Bridget said.

"Go find them. Do whatever you must, but—bring them back

to me."

"I'll go with them," Ryan said, turning to Emma. "You'll be safe here."

"The twins won't need your help, Ninety-five. I need you to stay here...with Emma. Her friends might try to rescue her."

Emma wondered if they would. But after her conversation with Olivia, Emma thought the chances were slim. Still, she hoped that the marines would somehow take her friends off the ship to help ease her guilty conscience.

"Do you smell smoke?" Ryan asked Emma.

She took in a deep breath, and her nose did detect a burning smell like someone overcooked the microwave popcorn. "Yeah, what is that?"

A bell rang as the fire icons over the hatchway doors flashed.

"What is it now?" Asset One asked, still in a calm, yet tired voice.

"Fire alarm," a sailor called out. "It's for this deck, sir."

"Smoke is coming in from the back door," Ryan said, pointing.

The captain went over to look. "Son of a bitch. Henderson, put the ship on auto-cruise. Same heading. Salamanca, order a fire team to the bridge. Until they can declare this area safe, we'll have to evacuate."

Asset One was already on his way out through another door.

"Let's go, everyone out," the captain ordered.

Ryan and Emma followed Asset One out through the same door. The bridge crew followed, and the captain brought up the rear as they made their way downstairs to a lower deck. There they waited for the fire team to do their work.

After fifteen minutes, the captain's portable radio came alive...

The marines are all dead. The ship is now secure, sir. The fire team is reporting now. Stand by.

"Excellent," Asset One said. "Your crew is most efficient, Captain."

The radio came on again...

The fire is out. The fire team reports it was only a rag that was lit and left in the main corridor to the bridge.

The captain traded a puzzled glance with Asset One before responding. "Are you saying that someone lit that fire on purpose?"

"Why would someone from the crew do that?" Ryan asked.

"No one on my crew would do that," the captain said. "And the Royal Marines have been neutralized."

Asset One stared at Emma.

She looked away.

"Go back to the bridge immediately," Asset One said, his voice still calm.

The bridge crew raced back up the stairs to the upper deck, well ahead of the captain and the rest, who followed at their own pace. When Emma and the rest of them reached the hatchway to the bridge, it was shut. Crew members struggled with the door.

"It's locked, sir," a sailor said.

Asset One sighed.

"Check all the hatchways," the captain ordered.

Other sailors scattered to all the different hatchways. Soon the picture became much clearer on the radio. . .

Port hatch is locked.

Bow hatch is locked.

Stern is locked as well.

"And we're at the starboard one," the captain said. "We're cut off. But why?"

"The fire was a trick." Ryan peered into Emma's eyes. She couldn't stop herself from smiling. "To clear us from the bridge."

Asset One wasn't smiling. "I should have let the twins...kill your friends in the warehouse."

CHAPTER 41

Olivia couldn't believe it worked. She made herself a promise that as soon as they were safely back home again, she would watch *The Hunt for Red October* with Miyuki and Nadia. It wasn't a typical choice for girls' movie night, but sometimes it was good to shake things up. Besides, how many times can you watch *Clueless*?

As soon as the crew evacuated, Olivia and Miyuki slipped on to the bridge first to punish any stragglers who were still left. Thankfully, they were all gone. Then Nadia came in and jumped on a computer to do her magic. She studied the security protocols and soon found the ones for the bridge. Nadia activated one that locked all the hatchway doors.

"Brilliant," Olivia said. "That should keep them away."

"A slight problem," Nadia said. "I don't see any navigation or helm controls at any of these work-stations."

Miyuki wandered over to the large wheel in the front of the bridge. She glanced down at the controls. She selected something and turned the wheel. As she did, Olivia felt the entire ship lean to the right. She quickly grabbed on to a monitoring station to maintain her balance. But Nadia found herself rolling across the floor in her chair. Olivia reached out and grabbed her before she rolled into the bulkhead.

"What are you doing over there, love?"

Miyuki realized and pulled the wheel the other way. Soon Olivia felt the floor level out again, so she let Nadia go.

"I think she found the helm controls," Nadia said, testing the floor before getting up from the chair.

Miyuki laughed. "I turned off the auto-cruise. The controls are so sensitive. Where do you want to go?"

"We need to surface the ship," Olivia said.

Miyuki pulled up gently on the wheel. Olivia could feel the bow of the ship slowly lifting. "Oh—" Miyuki said, looking down at her controls. "We're five hundred meters under the sea. Is that deep?"

"Yes," Nadia said. "That's very deep. It could take us some time to surface."

"How long do you think?" Olivia asked.

Someone pounded on one of the hatchway doors, but couldn't get it opened.

"The crew still can't open the doors, right?" Olivia asked.

"At the moment, no."

Olivia tilted her head towards Nadia. She could sense a but in that hesitation.

"Their network allows these security protocols to be accessible from other secure stations on board the ship. Since the bridge crew knows the command codes, they can reset the system. When they realize that—"

"They can reboot the system and override the locks?"

"We should hurry," Nadia said.

"What about the compressed air tanks?" Miyuki asked.

"The compressed—?" Olivia shot Nadia a look. "What is she talking about?"

"Blow the water tanks with compressed air for emergency surface," Miyuki said. "They did it in the movie—"

"*The Hunt for Red October*?" Olivia asked.

"Yes!"

"Thought I'd take a stab at that one," Olivia said. "All right, love. Since you're our naval expert, I'll let you find the—flipping hell!"

An intense force pushed Olivia to the floor—as if all the gravity on the ship had doubled in an instant. This left all three Gems stuck to the floor.

"What did you do?" Nadia screamed.

"I hit the button!" Miyuki yelled.

"Was it marked—don't push this button under any circumstances?" Olivia asked.

"This is amazing." Miyuki squealed with glee. "I can feel the blood leaving my head."

"And I can feel my soul leaving my body," Nadia yelled.

Miyuki laughed. "You two are funny."

Soon the force pushing them down eased enough that Olivia was able to stand back up. Nadia used the monitoring station to pull herself back to her feet.

Miyuki poked her head up and jumped back up to take the wheel.

"Don't do anything else!" both girls said at the same time. Olivia and Nadia then glanced at each other and smiled.

Miyuki did her happy clapping. "We're surfacing now!"

"Can we lift these blinds back up?" Olivia asked.

Nadia grabbed her chair and rolled it back to the workstation. She went through a couple of menus, and soon the blinds rolled up, revealing daylight coming through the windows. The bow of the *Falcon's Claw* weaved on top of the blue ocean again.

"That's a brilliant sight," Olivia said. "Now we can get off."

"I'm putting the ship back to surface mode," Miyuki said. "I hope that means it's a ship again."

"How do we get off?" Nadia asked. "If we use a boat, won't they chase us down and capture us again?"

"Not if we fly off in that old Huey helicopter they brought us here with, love." Olivia pointed at a security camera screen, which showed two helicopters inside a large indoor hangar. "If we can get up to the heliport deck, I can fly us out of here."

"What about Emma?" Miyuki asked. "We can't leave without her."

"Yes, we can. She's one of them now."

"She's only confused. Maybe we can convince her to come with us."

"There's no time for that. Once we break out of here, the whole ship will be after us. We have to head straight for that heliport deck. It's our only chance. Emma got herself into this mess, so she can get herself out of it."

Miyuki crossed her arms. She wasn't happy at all.

"Look, you're coming with us. That's an order," Olivia said, arching her back, wanting people to respect her.

"Emma's grandmother would never forgive us if we didn't try to save her," Miyuki said.

Olivia paused. She wasn't thinking about that. She liked Emma's grandmother, and a part of Olivia felt a loyalty to her as well.

"That's true," Nadia said. "However, we can't save Emma if they capture us again. We should escape, check back with Mrs. B, and then see how we can help Emma get out of this mess."

Instead of arguing, Miyuki thought about it. "Okay. I'll go. But please stop saying bad things about Emma."

"All right, love." Olivia said, relaxing. "We need all our wits to get off this ship, anyway. Let's get started."

Nadia returned to the computer. "I'll flip the locks open."

"Hang on a minute." Olivia walked over to the monitoring station and flipped through the security cameras at all four hatchway exits.

Camera one: Six armed Venomous goons hanging out.

Camera two: Four armed goons and a sea of bridge crew members behind them, crowding the passageway.

Camera three: Another armed squad of goons ready to rush in.

Camera four: One gigantic Venomous goon who took up most of the camera angle. Most likely there were others like him hiding just out of view.

A sea of dread washed over Olivia. "We have a slight flaw in our plan."

Miyuki came over and saw the cameras. "Oh—how do we get out?"

"Hey, Nads. Can you trigger another false fire alarm?"

"I can, but the chances of that fooling them a second time are —"

"You're right. Flipping hell. All right—let's think about this— how can we get out of here?" Olivia cleared her mind and focused.

Nadia did the same.

Olivia wondered if they could somehow break one of the windows on the bridge and climb down. She went over to a window and tried to calculate the drop. It was fifty meters at least. Too far to jump without injuring themselves. They would have to use ropes to rappel down. That was if they had climbing equipment —which they didn't.

Olivia turned around in defeat, then noticed Miyuki wandering around the bridge with her eyes staring up at the ceiling. Olivia shook her head. Sometimes Miyuki was utterly useless. Didn't she realize how serious a jam they were in? They had accidentally created their own prison, and soon the guards would be coming in to nab them.

Miyuki stopped. Her head tilted to the side as a grin spread out across her face. The girl showed off her gymnastic skills by jumping up and hanging from a metal handle in the ceiling. She used her other hand to pop open some kind of hatch that allowed Miyuki to climb up into the ceiling.

Olivia rushed over to her.

Miyuki popped upside down from the ceiling. Her glasses were barely clinging to her forehead. "Lookie what I found!"

Miyuki had discovered a maintenance crawl space that went over the bridge. It was tight, but Miyuki went far enough inside it to make sure the crawl space went to a quiet and unoccupied passageway.

Miyuki hung upside down again, this time holding her glasses in place. "We ready to roll."

"C'mon, Nads. We're getting out of here," Olivia said.

Nadia was glued to the computer. "Just a moment." Her fingers danced on the keyboard. "I'm disabling the ship's air-defense systems. That way they can't blow us out of the sky when we leave."

When she was done, Nadia ran over to the hatch in the ceiling, where Olivia helped her up through it. Using Nadia's chair, Olivia stood up and grabbed one of the handles beside the hatch. She then lifted herself and kicked the chair out of the way before Miyuki helped her up into the crawl space. Miyuki shut the hatch.

Inside the crawl space, it was tight. The three Gems were basically on top of each other.

"I believe we all need a bath," Nadia said.

"I vote for a spa treatment," Miyuki added.

"A spa sounds brilliant to me," Olivia said. "Mark that on our social calendar for when we get back to civilization." Olivia peered down the dark and narrow crawl space. "Is this as big as it gets?"

"Yup," Miyuki said. "One person at a time."

Olivia hated closed-in spaces. She wasn't terrified of them like Emma was with flying. But Olivia was still nervous about it. However, it was either this or getting put back into that room from hell to be tortured again. Olivia sucked up her courage and crawled forward into the darkness.

CHAPTER 42

Inside the crowded passageway, Emma peeked over Ryan's shoulder as one of the hatches to the bridge opened with a loud clunk as a voice on a radio announced…

Security override completed.

Armed with pistols, sailors from the bridge crew opened the hatch wide and rushed on to the bridge. Soon the captain and a couple of security goons followed the sailors in.

Asset One waited with Ryan and Emma.

"Bridge is clear, sir." the captain announced.

Asset One looked troubled as he went through the hatchway and emerged on to the bridge. "What do you mean…clear? Where are those girls?"

"I'm not sure."

Ryan stepped through the hatchway and offered Emma his hand. She took it and stepped inside too.

"Did we not have…all their exits blocked? If so…why are they not here?"

The bridge crew went back to their various workstations.

"Give me a ship status, quickly," the captain ordered.

"I'm waiting for an answer," Asset One said, betraying zero emotion.

One sailor cleared his throat loudly. "They could have used the maintenance crawl space." The young man pointed up at the ceiling.

The captain sighed and closed his eyes.

Asset One rotated slowly towards the young sailor. "There's a crawl space…above this bridge?"

"Yes, sir. There are two. One above and one below. They're narrow and tight. You have to be pretty small to fit into one of them."

Ryan glanced at Emma. She didn't hide her smile. Her friends were still alive.

"Teenage girls are rather small," Asset One said.

"We might have overlooked—"

"I don't like failure, Captain…it makes me sad." Asset One's steel cold eyes slowly rested on his subordinate. "My sadness often leads to madness. I tend to make very…rash decisions when I'm sad. How will you relieve me of this…burden, Captain?"

The captain took a step away from Asset One, his face now dead serious as he addressed the bridge. "Order every man to search for those teen girls. Search every inch of the *Falcon's Claw* and don't stop until you find them."

"We should submerge the ship…as soon as possible," Asset One said.

"Agreed," the captain said. "Prepare to dive."

"Water tanks are empty. We're filling them up now," a sailor called out.

"Acknowledged. Do it quickly."

An alarm went off on the bridge.

"Radar—I have two targets moving inbound and closing," a sailor reported.

"Identify targets."

The sailor paused. "Judging by their speed and heat signature, I would say ship-to-ship missiles. Impact in four minutes."

"Four minutes?" the captain asked. "Why didn't we get a warning sooner?"

"The radar system was powered off. I have it operating now."

"Ah, another gift…from the Royal Navy," Asset One said, his voice only slightly elevated in emotion. "They tracked us the moment we surfaced."

"Can we dive?" the captain asked.

"Tanks are still filling up with water. I estimate five minutes."

"Activate defenses. Prepare to intercept missiles." The captain waited for the confirmation, but no one replied. He marched over to the weapons station. "Activate defenses," he repeated.

The sailor at that station shook his head. "I can't activate them. There's something wrong with my weapons computer."

The captain pushed the sailor away from the computer and tried to access it himself. "Damn it. Someone has locked out the controls. Reboot the weapons system immediately."

"Yes, sir."

"Three minutes to impact."

"How long…will that procedure take?" Asset One asked.

The captain glanced over at the weapons station.

"Two to three minutes," the sailor said. His screen was blank as the system reset itself.

Ryan took Emma's hand. "I have a bad feeling about this."

Emma hoped he was wrong. She squeezed his hand and flashed him a positive smile. Somehow—someway—this would all work out. Emma just had to believe it.

"Status report on the tanks. When can we dive?" the captain asked.

"Three minutes, I would say."

"Two minutes to impact."

While everyone on the bridge focused on the incoming missile attack, Emma noticed Asset One slipping unobserved through an open hatchway in the back. Where was he going?

"Status on the defense system?" the captain called out, his voice tense.

"Still loading, sir."

"One minute to impact."

Ryan suddenly pulled Emma close and kissed her. The kiss was so deep and loving that Emma fell away from reality as if drifting away on a cloud.

The anxious voices. The blaring alarms. The ship.

It all fell away.

Her hands gripped his torso. She wanted to feel him. The boy who was brave enough to think about her and offer his heart at the very last moment of his life.

Emma was so happy. At least she would die knowing someone loved her. But Ryan didn't know for sure. She never told him the words. And she needed to tell him now because he deserved to hear them. Because Emma loved him too.

"Impact in five…four…three…two…"

But before the words left her lips—

The lights on the bridge went out as the world exploded.

CHAPTER 43

Using the crawl space, it took Olivia and the other two Gems about five minutes to reach the other ceiling hatch. Miyuki went upside down first to check the passageway before dropping down. Nadia and Olivia did the same. They jogged down the empty passageway and stopped at a junction to clear the next passageway. Soon they found stairs and hurried up a couple of flights.

"What floor is the heliport deck on?" Nadia asked, breathing hard.

"A couple more decks up," Olivia said, pausing for a breath.

"Oh my—is this what a step class feels like?" Nadia asked, still climbing the stairs at a steady pace.

"A step class from hell."

"How many decks are there on this ship?" Miyuki said, still climbing as well.

"We can't think about that, love. Push on. We keep pushing on until we get there. You can rest on the helicopter once we're clear."

After what seemed like the tenth set of stairs, a sign with two welcome words greeted their eyes.

Heliport Deck.

"Push on! We're almost there." Olivia dug deep inside and pushed her tired legs forward as she followed the sign's arrow to another junction.

She took a peek around it. Two Venomous goons were guarding the door to the heliport deck itself.

"Of course they have guards," Olivia said to herself.

Miyuki looked. "Monkey balls! Why can't we catch a break?"

Nadia peeked and let out a long sigh. She retreated and slid down the wall until she ended up on the floor. "Those stairs wore me out. Can we sit here for a few minutes?"

"I'm pooped too," Miyuki said. "But we must keep moving."

Olivia knew Miyuki was right. Time was something they didn't have much of. Even though her legs were screaming, Olivia knew her body well enough to know she could push it further if she had to.

"Right, let's run right at them," Olivia said. "Do it with everything you've got left in the petrol tank, and we'll beat the flipping crap out of 'em."

"My petrol tank is low," Nadia said. "I'm so tired."

"Three on two is better than even odds. We need you, Nads."

Nadia took a deep breath, closed her eyes, then nodded. She lifted herself off the floor and prepared herself.

"I won't let you down," she said.

Olivia gave her a confident smile, then checked with Miyuki. She gave her a thumbs-up. "Let's roll!"

But before they could move—a long alert whistle sounded throughout all the passageways.

Now hear this. Now hear this. By order of the captain, all crew members are ordered to search the ship for three teenage girls. Ages sixteen to seventeen.

The announcement went on to describe each Gem's physical appearance before ending with...

These girls are extremely dangerous. Approach with caution and detain. Report any sightings to the bridge.

"Well, that's not bloody helpful," Olivia said.

Nadia shushed her. "Let's see what they do."

After the order was repeated a second time, the tall Venomous goon chuckled to himself before he turned to the shorter one. "Surprised the captain doesn't mean those two red-headed girls."

The short goon smiled.

"Yesterday the bossy one told me I had to ask for her permission before I can go have a smoke on deck. Do you believe that? I'm a middle-aged man and this little girl is telling me when I can take a break? Christ, she hasn't even graduated high school yet."

"The twins are ranked," the short one said. "We have to take their orders."

The tall one brushed off his comment. "I don't care if they're teens. Those two girls need a proper belt to the rear end. Like my dad did to me. If those kids are the future, then we're f—"

"You'd better cut it out," the short goon warned.

"I know. I know." The tall goon sighed before glancing towards the door of the heliport deck.

"Should we go have a look?" the short one asked.

The tall goon slung his rifle over his shoulder. "Which way?"

Olivia tensed up. He meant which way down the hall. If the goons came this way, they would have to attack them.

"Fifty-fifty, you pick."

The tall goon glanced down one end of the passageway, then down the other. He set off in the opposite direction with his short partner following.

The knot in Olivia's stomach relaxed as the goons disappeared around a corner.

"I think we just caught a break," Nadia said.

Miyuki did a silent happy clap.

"Right—up on your feet, you two," Olivia said. "We're getting out of here."

The Gems rushed on to the heliport deck. There, sitting on an elevated landing pad, was the old Huey helicopter they flew in on. The landing pad itself was enclosed inside some type of indoor hangar, but Olivia could see two large doors in the ceiling that looked like they retracted to allow the landing pad to lift the helicopter out on the deck. The controls to the landing pad were right over to her left.

Olivia allowed herself to relax.

They made it.

"Hey, Nads—go over there and figure out the landing pad controls while I go prep the helicopter for takeoff."

"Before ya do all that—" a girl's voice called out.

"Ya muppets should check with us first," a second girl answered.

Bridget and Sophia emerged from the opposite corner of the heliport, with knives in both hands.

CHAPTER 44

Olivia was pissed off. She was sick of these girls. All they wanted to do was get off the bloody ship. They already had Emma. Wasn't that enough? Didn't it hurt the Gems enough that Emma had turned against them? Now these girls wanted to put them back in that room? That psychotic prison that only a madman like Asset One would dream up?

No—Olivia wasn't going to let Venomous have any more of her team. Even if that meant she had to hurt these girls.

Sophia moved forward towards them, licking her lips with anticipation as she gripped her knives.

"Hold that thought, Sophia, darling," Bridget said. "Ya forget that Olivia and I were room-mates once. I owe her a fair play."

Sophia frowned but took a step back.

"Tell ya what. If ya muppets surrender, I promise no harm will come to ya," Bridget said. "Straight up. I'll even make afternoon tea for ya. Biscuits and everything. Because that's the type of girl I am."

"Bloody tea and biscuits?" Sophia asked.

Bridget shot her a look to shut up. Sophia did.

"That's a lovely offer, Bridget," Olivia said. "But you know where you can shove your biscuits."

Miyuki covered her mouth as she laughed.

Nadia was too focused as she poised herself into a fighting stance.

Bridget dropped her smile. "Don't say I wasn't fair to ya. Tell ya what, when we cut ya up like sausages, I promise to bring ya tea at the hospital."

"Do ya want us to spare your faces?" Sophia said, moving in again.

"They do have lovely faces. Very grand. We'll only stab them below the neck," Bridget said. "That's fair play."

"Get on with it, then," Olivia said.

Sophia licked her lips again, then attacked Miyuki with a thrust that was knocked away. Sophia countered with a spin kick that almost clocked Miyuki in the head.

That was when Bridget threw one of her knives. The projectile sailed toward Nadia, and she jerked away within inches of the blade missing her arm. As Olivia watched that near miss, she felt something sharp rake the side of her torso.

Bridget was already on her, holding on to the second knife that just ripped her green Heart the E T-shirt. A sharp, stinging pain from the shallow wound distracted Olivia, but she ignored it as she launched her palm against Bridget's face—but she missed her.

Bridget followed up with a knee in Olivia's stomach, which caused all the air to escape from her lungs.

Olivia stumbled away, coughing. Trying to breathe before someone shoved her to the ground.

Turning on her back, Olivia noticed Bridget attacking Nadia with a series of knife thrusts and quick kicks. Nadia was holding her own, but it was difficult without a knife.

Sophia tumbled across the floor thanks to a strong kick by Miyuki, who now turned her attention to helping Nadia. But then Miyuki fell. She grimaced in pain as she rolled to the side to see a knife lodged in the back of her knee.

On the floor, Sophia wore a huge grin, pleased with her knife-throwing skills.

Olivia got mad.

She scrambled from the floor and launched herself at Sophia, throwing a series of palm strikes and kicks at the girl.

Sophia countered every move as she grunted. She threw a quick kick that spun Olivia back, then followed up with a round-house kick that sent Olivia across the floor.

Olivia stopped for a moment. She could still feel the stinging pain from the knife wound. Her stomach was tender. And Sophia's kick was still ringing in her ears.

But Olivia pushed herself to get back up.

Pushed herself to ignore everything that hurt.

Pushed herself to help her friends.

Nadia faked Bridget out and caught her on the chin with a palm strike that knocked the girl on her butt. Nadia stomped on the girl's hand and kicked the knife away—right in between Sophia's feet.

She picked up the knife and was ready to throw it at Nadia—when Olivia knocked Sophia hard to the floor, causing them both to go down.

Bridget was back on her feet. She faced down Nadia, who was waiting for her.

The two girls paused.

Each of them trying to read the other.

Finally, when Bridget made her move—

The lights in the heliport deck went dark as the world exploded.

CHAPTER 45

The ringing of multiple alarms. The acrid smell of smoke. The coldness of the floor. It all came rushing at Emma when she regained consciousness. She also heard something else.

What was that?

Was that her name?

Emma opened her eyes to find Ryan hovering over her and yelling into her face.

"Emma!"

She tried to respond, but her head felt light, woozy.

"Can you hear me?" Ryan asked.

Emma managed a nod.

"Are you hurt?"

Emma tried to shake off the wooziness. "I can't—I don't know."

Ryan scooped her off the floor and put her in a chair.

Emma examined the bridge. It was a mess. The work stations were destroyed, and a large hole was in the starboard side of the bridge where the explosion had managed to penetrate through the bulkhead. The bodies of sailors littered the rubble. At that point, Emma had to look away.

Ryan brushed the hair away from her eyes. "Are you hurt anywhere?"

Emma swallowed. "I don't think so. I must have been thrown to the floor in the explosion." Emma noticed a cut across Ryan's forehead and touched it with her fingers. "What about you?"

"Something grazed my forehead, but it doesn't hurt. Come with me. We need to get out of here."

"I've ordered the crew to abandon ship," the captain's voice said.

Emma now noticed the captain standing alone at the helm. His once white uniform was now stained with blood. His right hand nursed a large gash in the side of his torso that was bleeding. His face also had multiple gashes and cuts. His right eye was injured too.

"Asset One has evacuated too. I suggest you two do the same. The fire on board has now cut the bridge and upper decks off from the back. There are two escape pods still at the bow. If you can get to them."

"Thank you, Captain." Ryan paused. "It's been a pleasure to be on board your ship, sir."

The captain glanced at him for a long moment before nodding. "Tell Asset One—that I never abandoned my post." The captain straightened his back with much strain and effort. It looked painful. "Together, our venom strikes as one," he shouted.

"And the one serves the many," Ryan said.

"So say we all."

"So say we all," Ryan repeated.

The captain returned his attention to the windows and the blue sea beyond it.

Ryan pulled Emma to her feet. She then fell back on him. "You're not okay."

"My head is still kinda—soft," Emma said. "If you hold my hand, I think I can—"

Ryan scooped her up in his arms. "Relax, I'll save you."

"Save me? But I—" Emma stopped complaining as Ryan carried her through the port hatch and down one of the passageways towards the bow of the ship. A part of her liked the prince-saving-the-princess scenario going on right now. It was an act of love and protection, which a girl should expect from her guy, right? However, the wooziness was fading, and the part of Emma's brain that was raised by her grandmother was waking up and not liking this one bit. Grandma Bernadette's words came echoing back. "Never let a man carry you around like a pet. You're a woman. Not a cat."

"Ryan, I'm feeling better now. Can you put me down?" Emma asked.

Ryan slowed down. "Are you sure? We have to get off this ship."

"We can move faster without you carrying me."

Ryan agreed and put Emma back down. "The escape pod

should be around the next corner."

Her mind was fully awake now. And it realized something.

"Where are the other Gems? Did they make it off the ship?" Emma asked.

"I have no idea. But we can't waste time looking for them." Ryan grabbed her hand.

Emma shook it off. "No, I'm not leaving without them."

Ryan suddenly forced her over to the wall. "Reality check, Emma. This ship was hit by two missiles. It's on fire and sinking. The decks are smashed up. We're not going to find them. If anything, we'll get trapped on this ship and die."

Emma was shocked by Ryan's intensity toward her. But she matched it. "I have to know if they're safe. I promised them."

Ryan tried to scoop her up in his arms again—but Emma pushed him away.

"No, Ryan. The princess must go save her loyal friends from certain death. And the prince should be helping the princess, not treating her like she was a cat."

Ryan shot her a puzzled look.

"What?" she asked.

"Treating you like a cat?" he asked.

"Yes."

"What the hell are you even talking about?"

They were wasting too much time arguing about it.

"Whatever," Emma said, as she headed back. "Go save yourself, then."

Ryan grunted. He was getting pissed at her.

Emma didn't care. Maybe the princess didn't need help from her prince anyway.

She rushed around the next corner and could smell smoke up ahead.

"Damn it, Emma." Ryan jogged up to her. "Okay, fine. If you're determined to get us both killed—I know this ship better than you. Since the missiles hit the starboard side, let's keep close to port. It should be more accessible." Ryan paused. "That smile of yours won't work on me right now. C'mon—before I change my mind." Ryan offered his hand.

The wise prince had returned.

Emma took his hand and followed him through a maze of passageways that took them deeper inside the burning ship.

CHAPTER 46

Olivia opened her eyes when the emergency lights on the heliport deck flashed on. She could taste the smoke in the air and hear the fire alarms blaring in the distant passageways of the ship. A part of the indoor hangar had collapsed. The large ceiling doors had dropped on top of the landing pad, crushing the Huey helicopter into useless pieces. Half of the hangar was now open to the blue sky. Or what sky she could see through the smoke and the flames just outside the hangar.

Olivia wondered what had happened. *Did someone set off a bomb? Did Asset One blow up his own ship so he could get rid of the Gems once and for all?*

She then remembered her team, and her sense of duty pushed Olivia to her feet. She looked around. There was rubble everywhere. Sophia was passed out on the floor with a fresh gash across her forehead.

Olivia kept moving. She saw Miyuki sitting up, but tilted to the side. "Are you alright, love?"

Miyuki shook her head and pointed to the knife still lodged in the back of her leg.

"Do you want me to take it out?"

"Yes," Miyuki answered, her voice quiet, her eyes in pain.

Olivia hesitated, then pulled out the knife. Miyuki grunted and slapped the floor with her hands as the pain shot up her leg.

Olivia examined her wound. "You're not losing much blood. I don't think it went in that deep. Can you stand?"

"I'll try," Miyuki said.

"Help!" a voice cried out. "Help!"

Olivia recognized Nadia's voice. She stood up. "Where are you, Nads?"

"Over here," Nadia yelled.

233

"Keep talking, love." Olivia followed her voice until she found her.

Nadia's leg was trapped under a piece of the ceiling. Her cheeks glistened with tears. "I think my leg is gone."

"How do you know that?"

"I can't feel it at all."

Olivia was worried. Was Nadia's leg crushed? Would she have to saw her leg off to save her? Olivia wiped away those awful thoughts. She didn't know how injured her friend was. All she could do was to keep Nadia's spirits up and hope they could move her.

"You silly cow, the reason you can't feel your leg is because you have a big piece of concrete on it. Don't worry, I'll get that off."

Miyuki managed to hobble over and hold Nadia's hand as Olivia took off the piece of concrete. Nadia cried out in pain.

"I'm so sorry, love. But that's a good sign. At least you know your leg is still there. Most likely it's probably broken though," Olivia said. "We need to get you to a doctor."

"What about you?" Miyuki pointed.

Olivia noted the gash across her torso was still bleeding. And her stomach had a nice large bruise as well.

"Right—we all need a week at the spa, love," Olivia said. "Let's get off this flipping ship so we can schedule it."

"What about the twins?" Miyuki asked.

Bridget was on the floor, moaning. Sophia was still out cold.

"We have our own problems," Olivia said. "Can you handle the pain for now?"

"I'll try," Nadia said.

Olivia helped Nadia put weight on her good leg. The girl grimaced, but nodded as she used Olivia as a crutch.

"Can you walk?" Olivia asked Miyuki.

"It hurts, but I can walk." Miyuki glanced over at Bridget. "Are we going to leave them like that?"

"They almost dropped you out of a helicopter, love. I say it's just deserts."

"She's right," Nadia said. "We should at least try to help them."

"Well, I don't want to," Olivia said.

"I don't hate those girls," Miyuki said. "I pity them. Dr. Yes used them, turned them into instruments that could be manipulated for his purposes. No one has shown them a different path. Venomous has only shown them the dark side of humanity."

"Then we would be just like them," Nadia added.

"What?"

"If we left them to die…we would be acting like the twins."

"If they were girls who went to our school, " Miyuki said, "would we leave them like this?"

Olivia scoffed. Miyuki was making sense and it was pissing her off.

"Ease me into that chair over there, please," Nadia said. "You and Miyuki should go help them."

Miyuki smiled and hobbled her way over to Bridget.

Olivia gave up. She carefully placed Nadia down on a chair.

Miyuki took a knee before flopping down on the ground. Her teeth clenched from the pain in her leg. Once that subsided, Miyuki pulled some red hair out of Bridget's eyes. "Can you hear me?"

Bridget's mouth cracked open. "Yeah."

"Are you hurt?"

Bridget's eyes drifted open. She took in the image of the girl talking to her.

Then grabbed her throat.

Miyuki gasped. Bridget's grip tightened and Miyuki began choking.

"Oy—stop that, you stupid cow!" Olivia dropped to her knees and grabbed Bridget's arm.

But the girl wouldn't let go.

So Olivia bit her.

Bridget yelped and let go of Miyuki's throat. The poor girl leaned away and gasped for fresh air.

"Flipping hell," Olivia said. "You and your sister are quite a pair. Total bloody lunatics."

Bridget's dark eyes eased over to Olivia. A smile lifted her cheeks. "Hello, roommate. What's going on?"

"We don't know. Something on the ship exploded. Whatever it was damaged the hangar deck. Your sister is unconscious—"

"Sophia?" Bridget's smile was gone. "What's wrong with her?"

Before Olivia could answer, Bridget pushed her away and tried to get to her feet. But she was so woozy Bridget fell over into Olivia's arms.

"Easy. Give it a moment."

Bridget slowly nodded. Her eyes found Sophia on the floor

among some debris. Miyuki was now with her.

"She has a gash on her head," Miyuki said.

Bridget stood up straight. Nodded to Olivia, who let her go. Bridget walked over to Sophia and knelt.

"Sophia…get up, ya muppet. Stop playing around," Bridget said in a loud voice.

Her sister didn't react.

Bridget held her hand over Sophia's mouth. "She's breathing."

"Yes," Miyuki said. "I feel a good pulse too. I think she's just knocked out."

"What if she has a concussion?" Bridget asked. "She needs a doctor."

"That's your problem, love," Olivia said. "You look well enough to carry her to one."

Olivia went back over to Nadia. "Let's get out of here."

"Where are you going?" Bridget asked.

"We're getting off this stupid ship." Olivia let Nadia use her shoulder to get back up and lean on her. "Don't try to stop us."

Miyuki got to her feet. "I'm sorry about your sister. I hope she'll be okay." Miyuki hobbled over to Olivia and Nadia.

"Wait a fecking minute," Bridget said. "We're coming with ya."

"Piss off," Olivia said.

Miyuki and Nadia shot her a look.

Olivia scoffed. "Seriously?"

Her friends nodded.

"Alright—but if that girl chokes you again, I'm not doing a flipping thing about it."

Miyuki grinned.

Bridget went to her knee and noticed one of her sister's knives on the floor. While Olivia and Miyuki were looking away, Bridget picked up the blade and slipped it into one of her empty sheaths.

She picked up her sister. "*Bejesus*—ya need to lose a few pounds, girl."

"Do you need help?" Miyuki asked.

Bridget took a few steps forward with effort. "I'll manage it."

"You'd better not try anything," Olivia said. "My patience is completely gone."

"I only care about my sister right now," Bridget said. "Let's make a truce. Then it's game on. Agree?"

"Go on."

"We bury the hatchet. For now. My sister needs a doctor. And so do your friends. So we find one together."

"Even if it means getting off the ship?" Olivia asked.

Bridget nodded.

"Straight up?"

Bridget smiled. "Straight up. Avondale girl promise."

"All right," Olivia said.

The four girls made their way back into the passageway and did their best descending one flight of stairs to the next deck. Nadia was a good sport, but Olivia could tell she was suffering, and that worried her, especially if they had to go down more stairs.

This particular deck was crowded as sailors and Venomous goons rushed through the passageways. At first, Olivia was worried. The Gems were in no condition to fight. If Bridget gave the order, she could have them all re-captured and thrown back into their box of horrors. But one goon elbowed Bridget to the side, making her crash into the passageway wall with Sophia in her arms.

"Watch it, ya gobshite," Bridget yelled back at him.

The goon kept on moving without hesitation. That made it clear to Olivia that no one on the ship cared about finding them. It was every man for himself now.

"Shouldn't we follow them?" Olivia said. "Maybe they know where some boats are."

"No," Bridget said. "The ship doctor's cabin is four more decks down."

"Four more decks?" Olivia knew Nadia couldn't take that much constant pain. "If we have a chance to get off the ship, we should take it. Let's follow the crew."

Another group of sailors crowded the girls to the side of the passageway as they all fled in the same direction.

"Do what ya want, then," Bridget said. "I'm going to the doctor."

"How do you know the doctor will be there?" Miyuki asked.

"Don't be daft," Olivia said. "Can't you smell the smoke and hear the bloody fire alarms? This ship is doomed. You have to get off."

Bridget glared at Olivia, but then looked down at her unconscious sister. Her glare faded into a nod.

The five girls made their way slowly through the passageways, moving in the direction the other sailors had gone.

Soon they came upon an outdoor deck that looked undamaged. There were nine empty launch slots where escape pods had been housed. Olivia knew this because the tenth escape pod was still in its slot and packed with people.

"Lookie!" Miyuki pointed.

"Stop them!" Bridget yelled. "Get over there before they—"

A loud hiss of steam escaped from the launcher as it kicked the escape pod into the water. The craft floated and bobbed above the surface as it floated away from the ship.

"Flipping hell," Olivia yelled. The frustration of it all was getting to her.

"Are there any—" Nadia paused as she absorbed some pain "—boats stored on this deck?"

Miyuki hobbled around and searched the outdoor deck. Bridget went over it as well. Neither of them saw anything that looked like a boat.

"Aren't they supposed to carry small boats for emergencies?" Olivia asked.

"This ship is equipped with escape pods," Nadia said. "They're more advanced, able to survive in the open water, and keep their passengers protected from the elements twice as long as a conventional escape boat."

"How do you know about that?" Olivia asked.

"Leonardo DiCaprio."

"What, sorry?"

"*Titanic*. The movie. I had a crush on Leonardo for the longest time. I'm over him now." Nadia paused to allow some pain to pass. "But I was also fascinated by the disaster itself. There have been many advances in maritime safety since the *Titanic* sank." Nadia stopped herself. "I'm talking too much, aren't I?"

"Yes…you are," Bridget said.

An explosion made the four girls grab on to the railing as flames burst from some windows on their side of the ship.

"We need to quickly find more of these escape pod things," Olivia said.

"What a brilliant observation," Bridget said.

Miyuki hopped over to another door. When she tried to open it, Miyuki jerked her hand back.

"What's wrong?" Olivia asked.

"The lever is hot."

"Don't open it," Nadia said. "That means there's a fire on the other side."

"Then we'll have to go the way we came in," Miyuki said.

"What if these are the only escape pods we have access to?" Olivia peeked over the railing at the water below. It was a decent drop, but they could make it. Then Olivia remembered they were on the ocean. Trying to stay afloat without life jackets would be extremely hard. For Nadia and her broken leg, the task would be almost impossible. And what about Sophia? There was no way her sister would leave her.

Olivia closed her eyes. Heading back inside a burning ship where things were exploding was the only logical choice…in a world that had gone totally mad.

CHAPTER 47

Emma and Ryan searched all over the deserted fourth deck. There was no sign of her friends. The fire alarms had stopped working in this part of the ship, and the smell of smoke lingered everywhere. The deck lights flickered off and on.

"If the fire gets to the engine room, we'll lose all the lights," Ryan said. "That's if the ship doesn't blow up first."

"You don't have to rub it in," Emma said. "You didn't have to help me."

"Yes, I did and you know it." Ryan reached an intersection of two passageways and stopped. "Wait—doesn't one of your friends know how to fly a helicopter?"

"Yeah, she can fly anything."

"We should check the heliport deck. If the helicopter is gone, will that satisfy you that they got off the ship? Because there's no other way off besides jumping overboard or taking an escape pod."

Emma hesitated as the lights flickered again.

"It'll be hard to find our way back when the lights go out," Ryan said. "Just saying."

"Okay, if they're not there—we'll get off the ship."

Ryan led Emma down another passageway, then up a flight of stairs. They reached a sign pointing them towards the Heliport Deck. They followed it and saw one of the entrance doors to the deck had been blown off. Ryan slipped through the open doorway, and Emma was right behind him. She took in all the damage.

"The helicopters are destroyed. Sorry, Emma, I don't think they made it up here."

Emma was now worried. Where were her friends? Were they trapped? Did the fire already get them?

Ryan squeezed her hand. "I'm sorry, but we have to go now."

She hated to say it but, "Yeah, you're right."

Ryan guided her out of the heliport deck and raced down two flights of stairs, coughing most of the way. The ship's ventilation system was overwhelmed with smoke. Ryan led the way back to the escape pods on the bow, guiding Emma through all the smoky decks and passageways. She felt confident Ryan could get them out.

Five minutes later, Ryan and Emma cleared a flight of stairs and were now on the same deck as the escape pods. Emma now knew where she was. She picked up her pace and flew around the next corner...

Right into someone.

"Flipping hell!" that person yelled.

Emma jumped back and couldn't believe what she saw. Olivia had a knife wound in the side of her body that was still bleeding. Her mop-like hair was damp and sweaty. And she was propping up Nadia, who was favoring one of her legs.

"Olivia! Nadia!" Emma shouted. She was so excited to see them.

Her friends were less enthusiastic.

"Oh—it's you."

Before Emma could figure out that response—Miyuki hobbled over and gave Emma a big hug. "We're so happy to see you!"

Emma noticed a wound in the back of Miyuki's right knee. "What happened to your leg?"

"Think my sister threw a knife in it," Bridget said with a smirk.

Emma noticed Bridget carrying Sophia in her arms. The girl was out cold.

Ryan went over to her. "What happened?"

Bridget's eyes softened. "Something from the ceiling knocked her out, but she's still alive."

"Miyuki, get away from her," Olivia said.

At first, Emma thought she was talking about Bridget. But Olivia's glare was centered on her.

"Wait. We're here to help," Emma said.

"Get away from us, you traitor."

"What? I'm not a traitor."

"We don't believe you, Emma," Nadia said.

Why didn't they believe her?

Emma then realized Ryan was with her.

Didn't Mrs. B say that the Gems wouldn't know about her mission? That they would think Emma had turned against them.

Yes…but her mission was a mess.

Emma had told off Mrs. B and basically flipped the Authority the bird. Her refusal to join Venomous had also cost the Authority an opportunity to gain valuable intel on one of their most ruthless enemies on the planet. Most likely her days of being a Gem were numbered.

Well, if she wasn't going to be a Gem anymore, at least Emma could still be a friend.

"Please believe me when I say…the only reason I'm still on this ship is because I wanted to make sure you're safe. You girls might hate me, but I—" A wave of emotion hit Emma out of nowhere. "I—I still love all of you. We're sisters. We stick by each other. And I wasn't going to let my sisters die on some dumb boat."

Emma felt the tears running down her cheeks. She didn't mean for it to come out that mushy. But it was how she really felt.

Bridget rolled her eyes. "Swingin' Jesus, ya make me want to cut off my own ears."

Miyuki wiped off her cheeks. "I love you too! We sisters. No matter what."

"Oh God, please stop," Bridget said.

Miyuki faced Olivia. "I trust her."

"Well, I don't," Olivia said.

"Maybe—" Nadia sighed. "I don't quite trust her either. However, what choice do we have?"

"Seriously," Emma said. "If you don't come with us now, you'll die on this ship."

Olivia hesitated.

"Can we go now?" Ryan said.

Bridget walked past all of them, carrying Sophia.

Miyuki went next.

Olivia scoffed before helping Nadia continue.

Ryan squeezed Emma's hand again before they followed the group down the passageway.

The seven teens finally emerged on to the outdoor deck. There was one escape pod left, and it was empty. Emma was relieved.

Miyuki clapped her hands with delight.

"What's her problem?" Bridget asked.

Emma ignored her. She looked over the railing and noticed the bow of the ship was underwater. The ocean itself was only two feet lower than the deck they were standing on. "The ship is sinking!"

Olivia peeked over the railing with Nadia.

"I love the movie," Nadia said. "But I never wanted to be *in* the movie."

"That makes two of us," Olivia said.

"What movie?" Emma asked.

"Never mind," Olivia said. She took Nadia and helped her climb inside the escape pod.

Ryan laid Sophia out. Bridget placed Sophia's head on her lap to cushion it. Miyuki was the last one inside. She sat next to Emma.

Once everyone was on board, Ryan shut the hatch and pulled the cord. A loud hiss of steam was released as the launcher kicked in.

Emma felt the pod jerk as it was launched over the water. When it hit, the pod bounced up and down as it got used to rolling on top of the ocean. Emma peeked out a clear plastic viewing window. They were drifting away from the doomed ship. Half of the *Falcon's Claw* was now underwater as fire consumed what was left above the water. Emma followed the smoke as it rose above the ship. She then noticed a bird in the air.

No—it was a falcon. A black falcon. It was circling the sky above the ship.

Was Sunchaser looking for his master?

Or was he chasing the sun—for one last time?

* * *

The sun had disappeared over the horizon, painting the sky a distinct tangerine. Emma didn't know how long they had been at sea. Had it been only an hour? Or was it three? She wasn't quite sure.

Emma heard the ocean waves pushing their craft along with the current because everyone inside the pod was quiet. Bridget tended to her sister, who was still unconscious. Nadia had fallen asleep on Olivia's shoulder. Emma hoped her leg was only broken. Broken legs could be fixed.

Ryan found a first aid kit and used it to clean up and bandage Miyuki's knife wound.

"Do you want me to treat that?" Ryan pointed at the gash on Olivia's torso.

She glared. "No."

"It looks infected."

Miyuki tilted her bandaged leg towards Olivia. "He does a good job."

Olivia examined her wound. Even at this distance, Emma could tell it was looking yucky, and that wasn't good.

"Let him treat you," Emma said. "Please?"

Olivia closed her eyes. "I hate this. All of it." She opened her eyes and sighed. "Right, go ahead."

"It'll be easier if we could take this off." Ryan referenced the dirty and ripped Heart The E T-shirt Olivia was wearing.

Olivia reluctantly took off the T-shirt. She only had a sports bra under it.

Emma noticed how large the bruise on her stomach was.

Ryan knelt in front of Olivia and applied some antiseptic cream to her wound, causing Olivia to grimace and jerk at the pain.

"Bloody flipping hell—that burns," she said.

"That's what it's supposed to do," Ryan said as he continued to rub it across the entire wound.

"Oy—eyes off my bra!"

Ryan stopped and looked in another direction before continuing, using only his fingers to guide him. Soon he managed to cover most of Olivia's wound.

"What an egg," Bridget said. "Come over here, Ryan. Ya can rub sunscreen on my back without a fuss."

Emma restrained herself.

Ryan finished up by putting bandages over Olivia's wound before calling it quits.

"How is your sister?" Miyuki asked.

Bridget flashed her a look as if she thought Miyuki was joking. Then Bridget's face relaxed. "She's still breathing and has a strong pulse."

"That's good. I'm glad."

Bridget pulled a strand of hair away from Sophia's face. "I suppose ya want me to thank you for saving her life on the helicopter."

"That is not necessary," Miyuki said.

"Why didn't ya?"

"Sorry—why didn't I what?"

"Why didn't ya let her die? If the roles were reversed, Sophia wouldn't have helped ya. She would've let you die."

"That isn't the point," Miyuki said. "I couldn't have lived with myself if I didn't try to help her."

Bridget nodded. "That's decent of ya. Not many people I know would do that for someone else."

"Perhaps you should spend your time with better people."

Emma smiled to herself. She was happy Miyuki was in her life. She *was* better people. Emma turned around to look out through the clear plastic viewing window. The endless ocean rolled on and on, the white crests of the waves appearing and disappearing. A ship's bow cutting through the waves…

A ship?

Emma wiped away the condensation on the plastic for a better look.

It was a fishing boat cutting through the waves. And it was on a course towards them.

Fifteen minutes later, a fishing boat out of Mombasa, Kenya, brought the escape craft aboard. Since Ryan was the only man in the group, the captain told him in his limited English that he was responding to the automated distress call the *Falcon's Claw* had made over the emergency radio channel. When the captain of the fishing boat asked what happened, Ryan told him that the small cruise ship and its skeleton crew were on their way to Cape Town for repairs when something exploded.

"We were lucky not to be carrying passengers at the time," Ryan said.

The captain agreed. After sending off a radio message to the other rescue ships about picking up badly injured survivors, he ordered his fishing boat back to Mombasa as quickly as possible.

At the dock, an ambulance was waiting for the fishing boat. A boarding ramp was lowered, and the fishing boat's crew carried Sophia and Nadia on litters to the ambulance. Its red and blue lights flashed as the ambulance sped off to the nearest hospital.

The city lights of Mombasa were popping on as night was quickly approaching. They would need somewhere to sleep. Emma dug in her pocket and could feel her slender wallet still there. That was good. Hopefully, her gold card still worked in Africa. Now they could find the best hotel in town, order up room service, and pamper themselves.

"The captain told me the hospital is only a few blocks away from the port," Ryan said to Bridget. "We could walk there if you want."

"Yeah, nah. I'll visit her later." Bridget pulled her knife out from its sheath. "We need to take care of business first. Game's back on, ya muppets."

"Seriously?" Emma asked. "After all this—shit—you want to keep fighting? Your sister's in the hospital. Go see her."

"We have our orders. We'll tie ya up and call our people here to help us. Don't forget, you're still Asset One's prisoners."

"Let them go, Bridget," Ryan said. "I promised Emma that her friends could leave unharmed."

"And Miss America believed ya because she's thick in the head. That's her problem. Ya don't have to pretend ya love her anymore."

Emma couldn't believe it. She didn't want to believe it. No, he wouldn't do that to her. Not now. Not after all this time. Ryan was not playing her. He wasn't like everyone else.

Bridget pointed the blade toward Olivia and Miyuki. "Ya gonna make this difficult? Or do we need to call another ambulance?"

Olivia and Miyuki thought about it. Emma knew they wouldn't surrender. They would fight. Again.

Sometimes Emma was sick of the fighting.

"Put the knife away, Bridget," Ryan said.

"Don't be an egg. I'll take care of these two if ya wanna wrestle your girlfriend."

"Put the knife away. That's an order, Asset One-three-zero."

Hearing her codename, Bridget paused. "This isn't what Asset One would want."

"Asset One isn't standing here. But I am. And I outrank you."

Bridget turned toward Ryan, still gripping the knife. "Letting them go would be a mistake."

A coldness returned to Ryan's face. "Asset One-three-zero—I don't have to explain my orders to you. All that's required is your obedience."

Emma recognized that tone. It wasn't Ryan talking now. It was that thug who assaulted one of his men to a bloody mess after that man admitted to using electric shocks during her interrogation. A thug who could unleash a torrent of violence in a short amount of time. That thug was capable of anything.

Bridget's eyes wandered over to Olivia and Miyuki, then slowly came back to Ryan. "With respect—we can't—"

Ryan raised his right arm to smack Bridget across the face—but Emma grabbed it.

"No!"

Ryan's fury turned on her. "Release my hand."

"Hitting a girl to get your point across is barbaric. It's below you, Ryan."

"You don't understand. You're not one of us. Discipline must be maintained. It's our way."

"It's not your way. Don't make Venomous change the core of who you are."

"Too late for that, love," Olivia said. "He's turned like last week's milk."

"Let go of his hand," Bridget said.

She faced Ryan. "It's not like I haven't been hit by a man before." Bridget didn't smile as she lifted her chin. "Go ahead, Asset Ninety-five. Smack me in the mouth. Punch me. Do your worst. I deserve it. I questioned ya, so I won't fight ya on that."

Emma reluctantly let go of Ryan's arm. The boy's face melted a bit, as if a part of him questioned what he was doing.

Bridget shut her eyes, preparing herself for whatever Ryan would unleash.

Emma moved to where Ryan could see her. Their eyes met. Her boy had returned. The wave of anger had passed and he seemed calmer.

"Will you obey my orders?" Ryan asked.

Bridget opened her eyes. "Together—our venom strikes as one."

"And the one serves the many," Ryan said.

Bridget lowered her chin. "So say we all."

"So say we all." Ryan flicked his eyes over to Olivia and Miyuki. "Get the hell out of here. We're done. Until next time."

Olivia grabbed Miyuki's hand and pulled her away.

"Wait, isn't Emma coming with us?" Miyuki asked.

Emma checked with Ryan. He gave her no clue. Did he still

want her? Did he still need her? Was he playing her like Bridget said?

Stopping Ryan from hitting Bridget was a sign that he did need her. Ryan needed someone to help him keep control of himself. Emma was willing to do that for him. If they could be alone together, maybe they could work things out and finally be free of everyone who was trying to complicate their lives.

"Can you tell my grandmother that I'm okay?" Emma asked Miyuki. "I don't want her to worry."

"Which one?" Miyuki asked.

Emma smiled to herself. "Both."

"Please come with us, Emma. You belong with us. Not them."

Miyuki was so loyal. It was nice to have a friend who always believed in you.

Emma glanced at Ryan again. "Do you want me to stay?"

"Maybe it's better if you left," he said. "I'm in enough trouble as it is."

"Are you sure?"

Ryan's face softened. "Yes. I'm sure."

Emma hesitated but walked over to Miyuki and Olivia before taking another look back.

Bridget was already walking away from the pier. But Ryan was still there. Watching her.

Emma waved goodbye. Maybe under the circumstances it was kinda stupid. But she felt like doing it anyway.

To her surprise, Ryan waved goodbye too before following Bridget off the pier.

CHAPTER 48

A week later, the Gems were back home in California. It was the weekend, and Emma was looking forward to doing normal things. Kayla had wanted her to go to the football game tonight against Central Oakland High. Not that Kayla loved football, but she did love watching Ian Montana, West Berkeley's star quarterback, run around the field like a wild hen as other boys in helmets chased him around. Emma passed but promised she would take Kayla to the mall tomorrow. On Monday, Emma would have to do extra school-work to play catch up in all her classes, so her personal time would be non-existent. That was why tonight she only wanted to relax inside her grandma Bernadette's house and read.

Nadia came into the living room on her crutches. Her broken leg was in a new cast. Olivia followed her in, carrying two drinks, and waited for Nadia to sit down on the couch before putting her drink down. When Olivia joined her on the couch, a flash of pain made her face tighten.

"Is that bruise still bothering you?"

Olivia gave Emma a dirty look and didn't answer.

Emma turned back to her book.

Something touched her arm. Emma noticed Miyuki looking sad, but trying to smile. As if she were saying...*don't let her bother you.*

Emma flashed her a smile so she wouldn't worry.

Her grandmother closed her book on East Asian architecture in the fourteenth century and scanned the room like she did during her college lectures. "Okay. I'll bite. What's going on with you girls? You've been quiet and lifeless since you came back. I know I'm not supposed to ask about how you all got injured. Yet I'm feeling some unresolved hostility simmering between you all. Can you fill me in on that at least?"

All four Gems traded looks.

Olivia stared at Emma. "It's classified."

Miyuki touched Emma's arm again.

"Is this how it'll be during dinner?" Emma's grandmother asked.

An uncomfortable silence settled inside the living room.

Snoopy waddled downstairs. He checked on each human in the room before getting bored and moving on.

"Well then," Emma's grandmother said. "Guess I'll be discussing my art book with the dog."

The doorbell rang.

Emma's grandmother stood up. "Are we expecting anyone?"

None of the girls answered.

She went to the door and opened it.

Mrs. B and Aardvark were there. The daylight behind them was fading.

"May we come in?" Mrs. B asked.

"Normally I would be underwhelmed to see you, Laura. Yet tonight might be the exception." Grandma Bernadette stepped to the side.

Mrs. B and Aardvark entered the house.

"Making vegetable soup for dinner. Simmering now but should be ready in a half hour. Are you staying that long?"

"Is that an invitation?" Mrs. B asked.

"It's whatever you want it to be."

"Thank you."

"Something's wrong with these girls. They won't talk to me, so I guess they need to talk it out with you since it's—classified." Grandma Bernadette made air quotes with her fingers. "Yet—you already knew that because why else would you be here without an invitation?"

"Your powers of observation as well as your understanding of subtext is a credit to your academic prowess, Professor."

"You can quit buttering my toast, Laura. Do you want me to take a walk around the neighborhood for a while?"

"That won't be necessary. May I use your backyard?" Mrs. B asked.

Ten minutes later, all four Gems followed Mrs. B out into the backyard of Grandma Bernadette's house. Aardvark lit up the fire-pit and the orange flicker of its flames lit up the entire backyard as night came on full. They sat around the fire-pit as Aardvark walked around the fence with his cell phone out. Emma wasn't too sure why he was doing that. Most likely he wasn't checking on his social media.

"How's your leg, Nadia?" Mrs. B asked.

"I saw the doctor yesterday, and she said it was a clean break. It should heal with time."

"What about you two?"

"My leg is feeling better, thank you. I will see the doctor on Monday," Miyuki said.

"We're on the mend, ma'am," Olivia said. "We'll tell the kids at school we were in a car crash. I've already written up a cover story and plan to have Miyuki and Nadia memorize it so they can recite it back later if anyone asks."

"Good thinking," Mrs. B said.

"What about me?" Emma asked. "Was I in this car crash? Because I don't have any injuries."

"You weren't in the car with us, love. You were too busy sleeping with the enemy."

"Oh my God. I didn't sleep with him."

"Emma, you and Ryan were inseparable," Nadia said. "And there are no marks on you whatsoever. You were treated like a guest. So you must have slept with him."

"Why do I have to keep repeating myself?" Emma asked. "Ryan isn't that type of guy. He never was. Okay, I might have kissed him a little."

Olivia and Nadia glared.

"Okay, fine. I kissed him a lot. But we never went the full way. He's still a gentleman. In fact, I think Ryan's still a virgin."

Olivia and Nadia both laughed.

"What? He is."

"He's a bloke, Emma. They can't control themselves. I bet he and Bridget have done it."

Emma then remembered how affectionate Bridget had been towards Ryan on Asset One's ship. She scrubbed that memory out of her head. "Hey, you're making that up. You don't know that for sure."

"We should not make assumptions about each other," Miyuki said. "It isn't helpful."

"Why are you still defending her?" Nadia asked Miyuki. "Emma left you in that torture chamber too while she was off doing—whatever she was doing with Ryan. Emma abandoned us."

"I didn't even know you were on the ship until later. And I demanded that you were let out."

"You're lying," Olivia said. "I think Ryan finally succeeded in recruiting you for Venomous. I don't think we can trust you anymore."

"I'll have to stop you all right there," Mrs. B said. "I kept something from you all. I secretly gave Emma a different mission. Because of her relationship with Ryan, I ordered her to become a double agent. I thought if Emma could get close enough, we could tap into the inner workings of Venomous and use the information to destroy their operations. However—after reading your report, Olivia, it appears that I've made a grave error in judgment. One that almost led to your deaths. The failure of the mission rests on the shoulders of the woman who ordered it. I put all of you in difficult positions, and I apologize for that."

All four of the Gems took in her words for a moment.

Nadia's face softened. "Emma, you're a wonderful actress. I actually thought you were a traitor. I'm sorry."

"I always knew that she would never turn against her friends," Miyuki said with pride.

Olivia was quiet.

Emma crossed her legs as she waited.

It took a stern look from Mrs. B before Olivia shifted in her chair.

"Right—sorry about accusing you of sleeping with him, love. It was all—frustrating, you know? Day to day we didn't know what the hell was going on—sorry for cussing, ma'am."

Mrs. B nodded. "I smell that lovely vegetable soup Emma's grandmother is cooking. Why don't you three girls go check on her progress while I have a private word with Emma."

Olivia and Miyuki helped Nadia up on her crutches before all three of them disappeared into the house. This made Snoopy come out of the house as he waddled his way to the fire-pit. He gave out one bark to let everyone know he was there. Mrs. B bent down and picked Snoopy up. When she put him on her lap, Snoopy's tail wagged its approval.

"Thank you for telling them," Emma said. "I wasn't sure whether or not you wanted me to bring up—"

"Have you turned on us, Emma?" Mrs. B asked. Her eyes were deadly serious.

"What? No, I didn't betray anyone."

"I didn't use that word. However, it's interesting that you did." Mrs. B brushed her fingers against Snoopy's fur. His tail wagged again. "What happened with Ryan? I have yet to receive a report from you."

"I love to read words—but I hate writing them. Essays and book reports—yuck—I hate doing them. But I promise to write that report sometime this week."

"Tell me now. I need to know."

"Everything?"

"Please."

"We might miss dinner."

"Despite your grandmother's fondness towards nature and the environment—she still owns a microwave, does she not?"

Emma uncrossed her legs and pressed them together. They suddenly felt cold, so she rubbed her hands over them. "Where should I start?"

"Montreal, if you please."

Emma nodded. She told Mrs. B about meeting Ryan there. About eating bagels. About the sightseeing. About the Venomous goons who forced them in a car and interrogated them. Emma told her about the training island run by Asset Twelve. About her talks on the beach with Ryan. About Asset One and his ship.

"What did Asset One offer you?" Mrs. B asked. "In exchange for betraying us?"

"Seriously, I turned him down. I didn't want to join."

"Was I not clear? Didn't I want you to flip sides?"

"Well, but you also said that if I wanted to flip Ryan, now was the time. I thought grooming him to become an asset was what you wanted me to do."

"Emma, you had the opportunity to do both. Becoming a trusted ally of Asset One would've meant a treasure trove of information. Plus if you had flipped Ryan, you could have fed us the intel while Ryan would be there to support you. It was a wasted opportunity."

Emma lifted her eyes to the sky. "I did the best I could. It wasn't easy."

"Continue. How did Asset One react to your refusal?"

Emma told her about how Asset One was cool about it. She even asked him if it was okay if she still hung out with Ryan. Emma then expressed her wishes not to join anyone.

"I even told him that I was thinking of quitting the Authority," Emma said.

"So your phone call to me was an act? A way to convince Asset One that you were serious about leaving?"

Emma hesitated.

Mrs. B fired off a look.

"Yeah, I was acting," Emma said. "It was all an act."

Mrs. B's jaw tightened. Her hand that was petting Snoopy now firmly gripped the dog's neck. "I remember the day this little dog came into your life. How you accidentally hit him with your car. And then you rushed him to the animal hospital and saved his life." She rubbed the top of the dog's head with one of her fingers, but kept the other hand firmly around his neck. "And he's given you so much love. So much companionship. He's been a lovely dog, hasn't he?"

Emma leaned forward.

Mrs. B leaned back with Snoopy. "You would do anything for him, wouldn't you, Emma? You love him just as much as you do your grandmother. Would that be a fair statement?"

Emma's heart raced. She didn't like where this was going.

"Yes. Why are you holding him like—"

"Would you swear on Snoopy's life that you are telling me the truth?"

Emma hesitated again.

"This poor thing has been through enough in his life. Do you want him to feel more pain?"

Emma tried to get up, but someone held her in place. It was Aardvark. He was frowning, as if he didn't want to do this. But Mrs. B was giving the orders.

"I demand your complete cooperation. You will tell me the truth. Here and now. Was our phone conversation an act?"

Aardvark's grip on Emma's shoulders was solid. As if a building were leaning on them.

Emma gave in. "I wasn't acting. I was pissed at you. I don't—I seriously don't know if I want to work for the Authority anymore."

Mrs. B didn't say anything.

Emma continued. "I mean—I get that we're going after bad

people. But what are the motives of the people who give us the orders?" Emma looked up at Mrs. B. "I don't mean you. I mean the people who support the Authority—you know, the Century Group—what are their motives? Did my father find something about them that he didn't like? Is that why he left? Was it really only about my mom's death?"

"Did Asset One bring up these questions?" Mrs. B asked.

"Not all of them. But he has a point. We're acting like the good guys, but—I don't know if we are. Venomous doesn't hide who they are. They're pretty upfront about what they do and what to expect when you join them." Emma hesitated. "Because of my father's estate, I have plenty of choices when I turn twenty-five. I have the luxury to do whatever I want to in life. Right now, I'm not sure if this is it."

Mrs. B's hand was petting Snoopy again. His tail wagged as if nothing was wrong.

"I have questions that I need answered," Emma said. "Otherwise, I might have to walk away like my father did."

Mrs B absorbed what she was saying. "Thank you for not lying to me." She glanced up at Aardvark, and he walked away.

"Can I meet the Century Group?" Emma asked.

Mrs. B held back a smile. "That is quite impossible."

"Why?"

"As a group, they only meet once every two years. Always in person. No one below control level can even request an audience. Even I must put in a request."

Emma softened, her voice turning upbeat. "I'm your granddaughter. Can't you put in a request for me? Please?"

Mrs. B lifted her chin. "You're my granddaughter by blood. However, you're also one of my operatives, and I can't give special treatment to any of my operatives. It's not the way I run my ship."

"So you won't lift a finger to help me?"

"I can't, Emma."

"Then since I'm going to quit—you'll have to relocate me and Grandma Bernadette. Or do you plan on killing us?"

Mrs. B gripped the handle of her cane. She glanced away from Emma, her mind working things out.

Emma wondered if she should have said that part about killing them.

"When you first joined, didn't you read everything I gave you about the organization? About how the Century Group was formed? Why they felt the need to stand up for humanity? Our goals and our mission?"

"Yes, but I want to hear that from them. I want to hear it from their own mouths. And only the Century Group can tell me why my father left since— 'that's not how you run your ship.'"

"Watch your tone."

"Or what? You'll strangle a little dog to get your point across? That's supposed to convince me that we're the good guys? To be honest, the only people I've trusted since becoming a Gem are those three girls inside there." Emma pointed at the house. "Maybe Aardvark too—but tonight I'm not so sure."

Aardvark's eyes fell to the ground.

"I've wanted to believe you for so long. I've wanted you to be honest with me about my mom and dad from day one. But you know—Grandma Bernadette was right. I can't trust you. And that makes me sad."

Emma felt the waterworks coming, and she brushed the tears off her cheeks.

Mrs. B was silent.

Emma wondered if the woman had any more feelings left inside her old body.

Mrs. B watched the fire for a couple of minutes.

Emma thought about going inside and leaving her out here.

"Take some time to think about this," Mrs. B said. "Give yourself a few weeks to work things out in your mind."

"I don't need a few weeks."

"What if I told you about your mother? How she died. Would you then give me those weeks?"

Emma sat up. "Yes. I would."

"Excellent. Come to my office on Friday and I'll tell you."

"You're not going to tell me now?"

"Not here. In my office."

Emma wasn't too sure about this compromise.

"Give me a week and I'll see what I can do about your request." Mrs. B used her cane to stand up. "Suddenly I'm becoming quite peckish. Are you hungry? I'm sure your Grandma Bernadette's soup is done by now."

Emma didn't feel like eating, or talking with anyone while she was not eating.

"I want to be alone for a while."

"Of course," Mrs. B said. "Aardvark?"

The large man nodded and followed Mrs. B back into Grandma Bernadette's house.

Emma relaxed on a long chair as she watched the flames dance inside the pit. Snoopy jumped up and licked her nose. Emma kissed him and cuddled him with both arms. Knowing a good thing when he saw it, Snoopy plopped himself down, snuggled up to her, and yawned.

The warmth of the fire cradled Emma like a baby. She was so emotionally spent right now that one nod off would be enough to put her to sleep for hours.

But she only slept fifteen minutes before Snoopy's barking woke her up.

"What is it?" Emma moaned.

His barking continued.

Emma noticed Snoopy had moved off her lap. He now stood on the grass. His body was rigid. His tail not wagging. His head focused on the sky.

She looked up and saw a black falcon circling above them.

Emma shook herself awake for a better look. Yes, it was a falcon. A familiar falcon.

Sunchaser dive-bombed Snoopy, causing the dog to move away from Emma—before the falcon allowed himself a soft landing on the table next to her. The bird blinked and tilted its head in her direction.

Emma checked the house. No one had come outside to investigate Snoopy's barking.

She turned to Sunchaser. "What are you doing here?"

The falcon squawked, then picked at its leg. Emma saw a small pouch tied to it.

"Is that for me?"

The falcon tilted its head again and waited.

Emma carefully untied the pouch around his leg. Inside it was a computer thumb drive and a small message. She unraveled the message and read it...

I hope this message finds you well, Emma. As you can see, Sunchaser and I are well despite losing our beautiful home. Don't worry, I don't hold you responsible. I wish we had more time to discuss your future. Perhaps we can have another delightful conversation over dinner. However, before we have that dinner, I feel obligated to inform you that Mrs. B will never tell you the truth about your mother. Why? Because she was the one who ordered your mother's death. The proof is on this thumb drive. Plug this into any Authority computer and you can read the report for yourself. Regards, Asset One.

THANK YOU FOR READING!

Dear Awesome Reader,

I hope you enjoyed *Man With The Golden Falcons*. This book had a lot going on. Since Asset One and Ryan wanted to recruit Emma, that part of the book was already set. However, I wasn't so sure about the other Gems. I didn't want them to be stuck at school. So I created Cody, Gabi, and the Heart the E story line and folded that back into Asset One's overall plan against the Gems. The cherry on top of that sundae was adding Bridget and Sophia from *Dr. Yes*. Since Bridget and Olivia were room mates in that prequel, using Olivia as the viewpoint character in this story became obvious. I think it all came together nicely in the end. The only crumb left was Emma's story. The truth about her parents and the Authority could push Emma over the edge. But we'll explore that in the next novel.

Book reviews are so **important** to help spread the word about books. If you have time, I would love a review of this book on the website of your bookseller of choice. Love it or hate it. Doesn't matter. I would just enjoy the feedback

What did you think about the novel? What kind of stories would you like to see in future Gems novels? I'd love to hear from you! Please feel free to write me at doug@dougsolter.com, or send me a tweet, or visit www.dougsolter.com for more options to stay connected.

Thank you again for reading **Man With The Golden Falcons!**

All the best,

Doug Solter

ACKNOWLEDGMENTS

Another large shout-out to Laura Benedict for doing a beta read through my awful draft. Her honest feedback always makes these books so much better.

Travis Miles, for yet another wonderful book cover. He's amazing and I'm so lucky to have found him way back in 2012.

Pauline Nolet, for her eagle-eye editing skills. I'm lucky to have found her as well. She's always been amazing.

Max Adams, for her support and her amazing screenwriting classes.

For their constant support: Jeff Benedict, Jerry Bennett, Lela Fox, Joe Kinkade, Trevor and Talon Lane, Valarie Lawson, Erin and Tatum McHenry, Brenda Maier, Ginny Myers, Anna Myers, Ann Whitmire, Helen Newton, Sherry Spurrier, and Angela Townsend. The Oklahoma chapter of SCBWI. My filmmaker comrades through Max Adams' AFW program. I love you all!

A big thank you to all my friends and family.

Finally, a giant thank you to my dad.

ABOUT THE AUTHOR

Doug Solter began writing screenplays in 1998, then made the switch to writing young adult fiction in 2008. His first novel *Skid* was a screenplay before it was adapted into a book. Doug has worked in television for over twenty years. He has directed rap music videos and short films. Doug respects cats, loves the mountains, and one time walked the streets of Barcelona with a smile. Doug is an active member of the Society of Children's Book Writers and Illustrators.

Connect with Doug through his website...

www.dougsolter.com

ALSO BY DOUG SOLTER

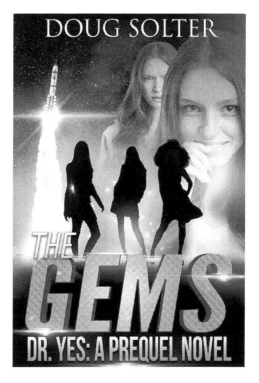

Before Emma. Before California. The three Gems met the
O'Malley twins. Things didn't go well.

Keep reading for a sample chapter from the book!

DR.YES
SAMPLE

Olivia stepped into the enormous dinning hall filled with girls wearing their full dress uniforms. It was noisy as everyone was visiting across one giant table which ran the length of the room. It reminded Olivia of those long tables at Hogwarts in those *Harry Potter* movies.

Her dress flats clapped against the stone floor as Olivia followed Bridget O'Malley down the long table. Many of the girls turned and waved at Bridget who flashed them an acknowledging smile. A few of the girls even threw out compliments about her hair.

Nadia and Miyuki sat near each other, but not together. They watched Olivia pass by and didn't smile.

Close to the head of the table, Bridget reached three empty places. She tucked the bottom of her skirt under her and sat before offering Olivia the spot next to her. Olivia tucked in her skirt and took a seat.

It was a half past six when Dr. Glenn Joyce and all the school's instructors emerged into the hall wearing their best dress clothes. There was a smaller dinning table that faced perpendicular to the student table to form a large T. The instructors took their places at this table while Dr. Joyce stood in the middle.

"May I have your attention?" Dr. Joyce asked.

The girls continued their loud conversations.

Dr. Joyce tapped his knife against a water glass. The clanging noise simulated a bell as the girls become quiet.

"Thank you," he continued. "Welcome to Avondale's ninth school dinner of the semester. This is a time for us to be together as one. For fellowship. For encouragement. And for community. We are a family. Those aren't just words. It's a reality. As far as I'm concerned, you are all daughters of this school. We want to bring out the best in each and every one of you. Every young woman here has a dream. Something that calls to you and only you. The faculty and I want you to succeed beyond your wildest expectations. We want you to be stoked about the future. And if not, we'll do whatever needs to be done to help you achieve your dreams." Dr. Joyce's smile was infectious. "I also want to challenge you all to support and help each other. Remember that when you lift up another student, you lift up the class. We all rise together. A strong tide that lifts all boats."

Dr. Joyce's attention shifted to Olivia. "Before we begin our dinner together, I'd like to introduce a new student. Lisa, would you please stand?"

Olivia hesitated. She had no idea Dr. Joyce was going to do this.

"Oh, don't worry. We won't bite ya," Bridget said.

The girls laughed.

Olivia stood up.

"This is Lisa and she comes to us from Portsmouth, England. Please make her feel welcome," Dr. Joyce said.

Soon the entire room said in unison…

"Welcome to Avondale, Lisa."

The greeting was warm. Most of the girls had smiles and seemed to mean what they were saying. Olivia thought it was a nice gesture.

Drinks were served first. Then baskets of fresh baked bread that smelled delicious and made Olivia hungry. Bridget showed her a local jam that was on the table. Olivia tried it on her bread and the local fruit tasted delicious.

"It's from a farm only a few kilometers from here," Bridget said. "I'm an addict for their jams. They're absolutely class."

"It's quite lovely, thank you," Olivia said.

Finally the garden salads come out. The vegetables were crisp and fresh. The vinaigrette tasted homemade.

Olivia had eaten about half her salad when another girl with red hair came running into the dining hall.

Dr. Joyce wiped his mouth with a napkin before clearing this throat. "You're pretty late, Sophia."

Everyone stopped eating to gawk at this girl who rushed past the student table and dropped herself into the third empty seat next to Olivia.

The girl named Sophia threw back her long fiery-red hair. "Sorry…won't happen again."

Olivia had to blink twice. This new girl had a striking

resemblance to Bridget.

No, it was her twin.

Olivia's eyes bounced to Bridget who displayed the most satisfied smile. She was enjoying this.

"Who the hell is this?" Bridget's twin asked.

Bridget didn't hesitate. "She's my new roommate. Her name's Lisa and she's from the UK. So far she's been grand."

Bridget's twin Sophia examined Olivia like a new car. Her eyes judging every square millimeter.

"She has nice brown skin. Her hair's nice as well." Sophia leaned in way too close as she checked Olivia's eyes. "And she doesn't have crazy eyes like that *Eegit* Molly had."

"We'll see how she is tonight," Bridget says. "I hope she doesn't snore like a plow horse."

Flipping hell. Olivia wanted to run away. These girls were having an entire conversation about her...while she was literally right in front of them.

Sophia backed away, but not by much. "You don't snore do you? My sister hates girls who snore."

"I don't think I snore," Olivia said.

"You're not a lesbian are ya?"

"Bejesus, Sophia!" Bridget said. "You can't ask her that. It's none of our fecking business."

Sophia blew off her sister and kept her focus on Olivia. "Only asking because my sister prefers men. However, if ya want me to introduce you to some girls ya fancy, I don't mind."

Olivia was overwhelmed by the girl's aggressiveness. She didn't hold anything back. "Right, I appreciate the offer, but I'm not a—"

"You can stay in the closet if you want. My sister and I won't tell anyone," Sophia added.

Olivia froze. A part of her wanted to slap the crap out of this girl for not even trying to listen to her.

"I'm not in the closet," Olivia blurted out. "I'm not even gay."

"It's all grand, ya don't have to come out of the closet."

"Not that there's anything wrong with ya being gay," Bridget said.

Olivia sighed. "Of course not. It's lovely. But not for me."

Bridget nodded and ate some more of her salad.

Sophia sat back, still fascinated with Olivia. "What's it like to be black?"

The main entrees were brought out to the student's table. "Oh look," Olivia said. "We're having fish tonight!"

After dinner, Olivia headed into the dorm and went upstairs to her room. She changed out of her uniform into some shorts and a T-shirt before putting away the rest of her things. Olivia sat on her soft bed and checked her phone. No word yet from either Nadia or Miyuki. Mongoose advised the two girls not to contact Olivia until they found a secure place to meet.

Olivia wanted to go downstairs and see if either one of them were there. However, she talked herself out of it. It was better to wait for their signal. She didn't want to screw up another mission because of her impatience.

Olivia scanned her new dorm room. Well, it was more Bridget's than hers right now. The girl's belongings had taken up most of the room. Olivia did have a small closet to herself. A small desk and wooden chair. And a bed. For some reason, it all made her sad. Maybe it was the strangeness of the place. Maybe it was because she was halfway around the world in a country that spoke English, but still had a foreign landscape that she was still getting use to.

Another reason was her mom and dad. Olivia hadn't seen them for quite a while. Maybe a year. She should have contacted them before she left England. It would have been nice to hear her mum's voice again.

A fatigue fell over Olivia. The stress of traveling to Avondale, meeting new people, and understanding new surroundings had taken their toll on her body.

Olivia went to bed early, hoping things would become easier as the week went on.

Dr. Yes: A Prequel Novel is not available in stores.

To get your free eBook copy go to
www.dougsolter.com

Tap on Subscribe and join his email list.

Also by Doug Solter

Thunderdog

Tomorrow Always Lies

Spies Like Me

Dr. Yes

Skid Racing Series

Printed in Great Britain
by Amazon